P9-EEQ-969

# Gunman's Moon

# OTHER FIVE STAR WESTERN TITLES BY LAURAN PAINE:

*Tears of the Heart* (1995)
*Lockwood* (1996)
*The White Bird* (1997)
*The Grand Ones of San Ildefonso* (1997)
*Cache Cañon* (1998)
*The Killer Gun* (1998)
*The Mustangers* (1999)
*The Running Iron* (2000)
*The Dark Trail* (2001)
*Guns in the Desert* (2002)
*Gathering Storm* (2003)
*Night of the Comancheros* (2003)
*Rain Valley* (2004)
*Guns in Oregon* (2004)
*Holding the Ace Card* (2005)
*Feud on the Mesa* (2005)
*Gunman* (2006)
*The Plains of Laramie* (2006)
*Halfmoon Ranch* (2007)
*Man from Durango* (2007)
*The Quiet Gun* (2008)
*Patterson* (2008)
*Hurd's Crossing* (2008)
*Rangers of El Paso* (2009)
*Sheriff of Hangtown* (2009)

# Gunman's Moon

## A Western Duo

## Lauran Paine

**FIVE STAR**
*A part of Gale, Cengage Learning*

GALE
CENGAGE Learning™

Detroit • New York • San Francisco • New Haven, Conn • Waterville, Maine • London

Set in 11 pt. Plantin.
Printed on permanent paper.

**LIBRARY OF CONGRESS CATALOGING-IN-PUBLICATION DATA**

Paine, Lauran.
Gunman's moon : a western duo / by Lauran Paine. — 1st ed.
p. cm.
ISBN-13: 978-1-59414-805-7 (alk. paper)
ISBN-10: 1-59414-805-8 (alk. paper)
I. Title.
PS3566.A34G8475 2009
813′.54—dc22 2009027503

First Edition. First Printing: November 2009.
Published in 2009 in conjunction with Golden West Literary Agency.

Printed in the United States of America
1 2 3 4 5 6 7 13 12 11 10 09

# CONTENTS

★ ★ ★ ★ ★

# Odd Partnership

★ ★ ★ ★ ★

# I

It had been snowing for three days, and, although that first day it had been a heavy, wet snow, the kind that encouraged people to believe it would shortly turn to rain, this had not happened, and now the gunman was three days into strange country with a heavy, continuing snowfall all around him. That would have been bad enough, but the countryside gradually had turned hilly and rolling, and by the time his laboring horse reached the last ridge and halted in two feet of snow, lungs pumping, hide stained by snow and sweat, the gunman realized that he had just about reached the end of this journey whether he liked that idea or not. A horse could plow through three-foot drifts and two-foot stands of snow for just so many miles, with a sixty-pound saddle and a hundred-and-seventy-pound man on his back.

He did not let the horse halt for long atop that snowy ridge, although the animal wanted to, in order to catch his breath. That was how a man foundered a horse, letting him stand atop a ridge like that sucking down big lungfuls of icy air. The gunman felt bad about doing it, but he nudged the horse on over and down into the fringe of yonder trees, explaining the necessity as he rode along.

Fortunately, going downhill in two feet of snow was no particular chore; the horse only floundered once, just before reaching the trees, and that was where a shallow erosion gully lay hidden beneath the snow. But even that was cause for little more than a lurch and a grunt on the horse's part, then they reached the trees. The beast was breathing easier, and, while the overhead treetops were ominously weighted down with snow, underfoot there were visible layers of matted pine needles, with only an occasional skiff of light snow here and there. Finally they could halt.

The gunman dismounted a little stiffly, although he was not that old, and, as he stamped circulation back into his feet and swung his arms, the horse dropped his head to go dragging the reins in search of a few blades of grass. One thing was clear. Unless they found something for the horse to eat soon, the man was going to have to walk beside his animal, through those drifts.

Turning back was out of the question for two reasons. The foremost reason was that they knew all the land behind them. There was no grass back there, either—in fact, there was nothing at all back there but miles of empty, rough country—and they'd never be able to get back out of the hilly snow country before the horse collapsed. The second reason was because somewhere, up ahead, there were people. Not that the gunman particularly wanted to find people, but he knew for a fact they were up there, somewhere, and, where a man found people, he usually found a settlement, which meant horses—and hay. The trouble was, he had nothing but a sketchy idea of how far he had still to travel, and as the gaunted-up, but valiant horse kept struggling, he steadily grew more tucked-up and weaker. And the snow was still falling, only now the flakes were half as large as a spur rowel and feather-light, which meant that the snow stuck when it reached the ground; it did not melt. It became, in fact, an endless, beautiful, white death trap for the animal, and maybe even for the man, although he was not thinking much about himself. He had survived for almost forty years; he had an unshakable conviction in his ability to go on surviving based upon the plain fact that no man, and no animal, and very few situations in his lifetime had ever been able to beat him.

He was not a particularly impressive man in appearance. He was no more, and no less, than average height. He was compactly, powerfully put together, and his features were even without being either thin or coarse. The two most noticeable aspects of his face were rock-hard, steady gray eyes that faced life head on, and a line-lipped mouth set flat above a square-jawed chin. The impression he gave at first sighting was of confidence, strength, and near indestructibility. At second sighting he did not quite look like a range rider; maybe the ivory-handled six-gun helped give that impression, and the illusive quality of his face that suggested personal discipline and fearlessness. He was probably in his late thirties, although with any man whose life has been spent mostly out-of-doors that could have been incorrect. He looked weathered, and even standing there in the snow his face was tanned.

He rolled and lit a cigarette, stood and studied the lay of the land, with smoke trickling upward, and decided that he should never have left the stage road ten miles back. But he had left it, and with his own good reasons for doing so, and right now retrospect wasn't worth a damn. In fact, it could be fatal, so he traced out the lift and fall of the onward country, decided that a couple of miles distant, across the far swale that showed no higher swales beyond it, the land leveled out. Maybe the settlement was over that low hill.

He looked at the horse, which was still searching for grass and finding none, and decided that if there was nothing beyond that next swale, he was finished. Before he'd let the animal go on from there, dying on his feet, he would shoot him, hang his outfit in a tree, and go on afoot until he, too, gave out. He dropped the cigarette, watched it die in the snow, burning its passage several inches through, then he went over to the horse, wordlessly climbed astraddle, and started down through the good footing in among the trees to that formidable layer of heavy snow on ahead. The horse hung in the bit, which he had been doing since yesterday, and the gunman did not have the heart to use his spurs to force the animal out of the shelter, so he talked to the horse, and perhaps less because the horse was influenced by the tone of his rider's voice than because he fatalistically accepted the need for it, he floundered on out into the snow and pantingly worked his way along, head down, legs growing heavier after each step, and, eventually, his lungs pumping again.

The sky was not gray and low as it usually was during a snowstorm; it was pale and opaque and seemed to begin underfoot, seemed to be part of the silent immense world of virgin snow. It was not actually very cold. It was below freezing, of course, otherwise this would have been rain not snow, but a world enveloped in this kind of white fall furnished its own unique insulation. The temperature was probably hovering right around thirty degrees above zero, which was not cold when a man was dressed for it, and when a horse was exercising as hard as the gunman's sorrel gelding was.

Midway across the level land between the forested slope at their back and the less-forested swale up ahead, they got a surprise, and halted to watch as a big wolf dog came up out of his snow bed, every hair erect, to stare unbelievingly at them. There was red on his vest and around his jaws. He had caught a snowshoe rabbit, had eaten most of it, and had been lying near his kill, resting, when he'd picked up the oncoming sounds of the horse and rider.

They stared steadily at one another for a full minute, before the man called out, then the wolf dog turned and fled, leaping high, sinking deeply, then leaping high again. He would have been an easy target if the gunman had been inclined to shoot.

He wasn't. He and the horse stood another minute or two, until the vanishing wolf had plowed his way part way up the yonder swale, then disappeared very abruptly near the base of a tree, and, as the man lifted his reins, the horse started on again, a little stronger after this brief rest.

They finally reached the foot of the swale, and turned off on an angle to begin the ascent. Here, the gunman left the saddle, patted the horse's neck roughly with a gloved hand, and started up, breaking trail for the animal. That way he was sure the horse could make it to the top. The other way, with his weight on the horse's back, he wasn't sure at all. The snowfall continued steadily. It limited visibility and viewed from a window with a fire at a man's back, it would have been something magnificent to behold. Hiking through it, with its moisture seeping through past his boot tops, it was still beautiful, but it was also subtly deadly.

They halted thirty feet from the rim's top to blow a little. This time, the horse was breathing easily and the man was sucking air. He grinned at the horse, dumped a weighty load of snow from his hat, then turned and hiked onward.

There were four trees atop the low ridge. They were about a hundred yards apart, like spaced-out sentries. The gunman headed for the nearest one from habit, not because a single tree on a ridge top was beneficial to either of them in a snowstorm. He was a Southwesterner. Where he had lived his formative years, trees had been rare, and valued. Of course, above Raton Pass into southern Colorado it was a different story; there were more trees than people could possibly use, or even possibly count, except right up along that low top out.

Ten feet from the skyline he slowly removed one glove, reached to tug loose the tie down thong holding his ivory-stock six-gun, then he plodded the last ten feet without putting the glove back on. When a man, or a faithful animal, struck out for the Sand Hills, he should start his journey from atop a rim, and beneath a friendly tree. There were no other kinds of trees, not in the world the gunman and his horse knew.

A little ground-swell breeze came up from the yonder side of the broad, low little hill, lifting snow and whirling it around man and animal, then it hurried on down the south side of the hill to begin covering the tracks, back there out across the level ground. The man raised his head slowly, to be sure the wind-driven snow was gone, and covered the last few yards to the protection of the tree, his horse, with white on its whiskers, its eyelashes, and upon the thick hair of its ears, moving up that last little distance almost beside the man.

Another gust of roiled wind came upward. They had to stand humped, heads lowered, until that passed along, too, then they cautiously looked outward and downward. There was a dark, skinny spiral of smoke rising from a stovepipe down there where a snow-camouflaged log house, log barn, and spidery network of working livestock corrals stood, in another stretch of level land like the stretch they had crossed to reach the rim top, only out where that ranch headquarters lay the entire broad flow of land ran for miles with only gentle swales far out, and only hills so far away that the gunman could not even guess where they were in this country of hills and mountains.

He looked a long time. So did the horse. Maybe understanding for the horse was minimal, but the man knew it was there. Some things all animals shared, and one of them was an instinctive feeling for the closeness of death—and their sudden deliverance from it. The man raised a hand roughly to pat his sorrel's neck, then, without waiting or without speaking, he turned down the gentle side hill, and this time neither one of them felt the least tired as they plowed dead ahead in the direction of that big log barn through the drifts of cloying, cold snow.

# II

There was a strong set of tracks deep in the snow that led from the log house to the barn, then back to the log house again. The gunman, who led his animal into barn shelter from out back, read those signs correctly; someone had come out not long before to pitch down feed to the stalled saddle stock from the barn loft, then he had plowed back to the crackling fire of his house.

The gunman went back to his horse, tied the beast, off-saddled and off-bridled, then picked up handfuls of hay and rubbed vigorously, until the horse was almost entirely dry and until the gunman was perspiring beneath his jacket and shirt, and long-john underwear. Then he stalled the animal, climbed aloft, forked down a big bait into the manger, and afterward stood in the loft for a while, gazing out a crack where he had opened the loft door.

By God, there was a town yonder. More like a settlement, actually, not as large as most towns, but big enough to have a series of business establishments on both sides of its east-west main roadway, and around it were clustered houses, mostly of log but some of clapboard and stone. Nearly every chimney had smoke rising straight up into the snowfall, too, and most of the windows showed lights. The town did not appear to be more than a half mile distant, but it was only visible as a bunch of peaked snow lines from the ground, while from the loft door it showed up clearly, half hidden by snow, but clearly enough.

He climbed back down to the drafty interior of the barn, stood a while listening to his sorrel eating, which was a mighty fine sound to any stockman, especially under these circumstances, then he strolled elsewhere and looked in other stalls. There were three horses; two of them were big pudding-footed team beasts, and the third one was a fine-boned, tall but lightly built blooded bay gelding, as pretty, the gunman told himself, as a painting he'd once seen over a backbar down at Socorro in New Mexico Territory. He stood longest looking at the blooded bay. The animal was shod; the harness horses were barefooted. There was a good Porter saddle on the rigging pole, with braided reins and romal, along with a Santa Barbara spade bit worked over into a half-breed, draped from the saddle horn. Out back, where the corrals were in a curving manner that took them along the north side where the barn wall could be utilized as one segment of a corral, there was a round, breaking corral with a cedar snubbing post almost as thick through as a man, planted deep down in the center, and a series of other working corrals that all opened into a particularly stout, high-walled log corral where the working chute was. Two branding irons partially obscured by snow hung from two spikes on the side wall of the chute, and there was a heading plank, reinforced with steel, and made operational by a length of lariat rope at the front end of the chute.

The gunman made a smoke, stood easy in the rear barn opening looking out approvingly at all this, and at the wise way it had all been put there, and decided that his unknowing host was a horseman, not a cattleman. A man never built his central working corral with walls that high, nor made his chute as high or as massive just for cattle. Also, in a storm like this, there would have been humpbacked old cows standing out a discreet distance bawling their heads off to be fed, if this had been a cow outfit. Not that it mattered; what mattered was that the place had been here, with a dry stall for the sorrel, with hay in the loft, and with a dry place for the gunman to bed down. That was everything a man could have asked for, when he had been only a couple of minutes away from shooting his mount and otherwise plowing ahead himself until he could no longer place one foot ahead of the other foot.

He finished his smoke, went to the saddle, hoisted it to the pole, draped the bridle, flung the blanket over both, and the last thing he did was dig out the only remaining tin of sardines he had left from his flat saddlebags, then ambled up to the front barn opening while he opened the can and slowly ate, and drained off the fish oil, too. It was a lot short of roast prairie chicken, but it sure beat a snowbank.

He studied the house, where the smoke still rose, admired the orange glow from a window where lamplight shone out upon the white world, wondered if the horseman in there had a family, wondered what the man's reaction would be to having someone ride in upon him at the height of a storm, decided not to put any of it to the test, and went up into the loft to burrow into the hay and sleep, although it was not quite evening yet, was, in fact, little more than mid-afternoon. But a man required rest as a result of exhaustion, and the little spidery hands of a pocket watch did not have anything to do with it. He slept soundly, too, totally warm in the hay, still bundled in his coat and gloves, subconsciously enormously relieved that he and the sorrel were still alive, still able to make it for a while longer.

When he awakened, it was pitch dark in the loft, and down below where the snow had stopped falling, the barn's interior was ghostly from white reflection coming inside, from out front and out back.

A man's deep, gruff voice had awakened him. Its first rumbling words were lost, but as the gunman eased up into a sitting position, he heard the second sentence.

"There's a strange horse in this stall over here."

The gunman leaned to hear more as a second voice, not as gruff, spoke up. "What d' you mean, a strange horse? Damn it, he's got eight or nine head."

"Yeah," grumbled the gruff voice, "but this here one's been ridden today, and look yonder, Jase, there's another saddle on the rack. Listen, Jase, maybe he's got a friend in there, maybe the two of 'ems lyin' out yonder, just waiting."

For a while there was no more talking, but the gunman heard two men moving down below, which did not sit too well with him. He only had that one saddle and outfit, and he had no desire to lose them to a pair of night skulkers.

He eased over very gently, placed both hands upon the hay loft floor, and eased upright to his full height in the darkness. He was in his stocking feet, which was probably just as well since boots made noise. The square hole where the loft ladder came up showed as a ghostly pale opening. He crossed to it, one step at a time, then leaned to see what was down there, but visibility was not that good despite the eerie brightness being reflected inside from the snow, so he had to get down on all fours and ease his head through for a better look.

They were up near the front opening peering off in the direction of the house now, and they both had carbines, which struck the gunman as odd; thieves did not ordinarily carry saddle guns along when they went foraging at night. He reached back, palmed his ivory-stocked Colt, got down still lower, shoved his gun hand through, and softly called to the men whose backs were to him: "Don't move!"

But they did, probably inspired to it by panicky astonishment when that voice hit them in the back, from above them; they both emitted a squawk and sprang out of the barn into the snow, and vanished from the gunman's sight before he could have shot, if he'd intended to shoot, which he hadn't.

He pulled back, holstered the Colt, scratched his head, and stood perfectly motionless for a full ten minutes, speculating about those two skulkers, then decided he'd go down and look around. Not because he felt they had been able to make off with anything—as nearly as he could see neither of them had had anything in his hands but a carbine—but because he wanted to be reassured by tracks in the snow that they hadn't slipped around the barn, perhaps out back, to try and come inside again, which, now that they knew he was in the barn, could make their next meeting painful for someone. He went back for his boots, sat down to pull them on, then returned to the loft ladder, looked carefully all around first, then descended.

Out front, the tracks in the deep snow were a good eighteen inches apart. He also smiled. Whoever they were, he had startled them so badly they'd jumped out there like a pair of snowshoe rabbits. The tracks went around the barn on the south side heading for the rear, exactly as the gunman had expected they might, but instead of turning in, out back, the tracks skirted wide of the back wall, skirted just as wide over by the corrals, and headed arrow straight toward that distant settlement.

He did not try to track them very far, just until he was satisfied they were neither one of them slowing down in their floundering charge, then he returned to the barn, looked in on his sorrel, and the drowsing animal cocked one eye at him a trifle disgustedly, so he went over upon the opposite side where those other stalls were and looked in on the three animals over there. Like his sorrel, the team horses and the breedy blood bay, were more annoyed at being awakened than concerned with what had happened, so he trooped up to the front of the barn and peered off in the direction of the house.

It was as dark as a tomb, and he could no longer tell whether smoke was rising from the stovepipe. He sighed, swore under his breath, looked long at the diaphanous veil of tattered storm clouds overhead, picked out a few watery-looking stars that were weakly showing through, decided that the storm was over, and climbed back to his loft. But he did not bed down immediately. He walked to the loft door, opened it, and leaned there, looking across at the town, which was almost totally dark now, except for three or four windows still showing lamplight, and he tried to guess what time of night it was. There was no moon and the horizon was a blur of white and dirty gray that could have been a mile away or a hundred miles away. The time could have been anywhere between 10:00 and 2:00. He did not own a watch. Once, he'd owned one, but he'd kept forgetting to wind it, so it was never reliable, and the last time he saw it, a red-headed, red-faced cowboy was admiring it as part of his winnings in a poker game down at Tucson.

He went back to the hay, shed his boots, placed the Colt where his fingers lay lightly atop it as he slept, lay back, and burrowed in again. This time, though, he did not drop right off. He did not expect those skulkers to return; their kind behaved like coyotes; once they were flushed, they didn't stop running or even look back until they were again holed up in their own den. But he could not sleep anyway, even without worrying about the skulkers. His mind wandered without restraint, passing from event to interlude to event again, back and forth over the years as though time were something interchangeable. A lot he remembered from fifteen years back, seemed as fresh in thought as though it had happened only yesterday, and some much more recent things, which his mind perhaps did not especially want to recall, occurred to him as blurry, distant things.

He sighed, concentrated on relaxing fully, and finally was able to sleep. But it was only seemingly for moments; down below someone was moving with heavy steps, crunching his way through the yonder snow from the direction of the house.

The gunman blinked, sat up with a groan and a solid effort, brushed off hay and chaff, dumped the hat upon the back of his head, and reached to pull on his boots. Outside, the heaving tread halted out front, and the gunman, arising to brush off more hay, knew that the man out there had come upon three fresh sets of tracks, his, and the tracks of the two skulkers. The horseman was standing quietly out there for a long while, evidently trying to read some sense into that sign.

The gunman went to the ladder, poked his head out first, then turned and crawled downward hand over hand. He reached the earth floor just as the horseman out front stepped over into the front opening.

They stared at one another. The horseman was graying, massively thick, no taller than the gunman, but half again as wide, and he had a three-days' growth of grizzly whiskers that made him look forbidding. That look was enhanced by his bleak, unsmiling expression.

The gunman nodded. " 'Morning. My horse and I used your barn last night. I'll pay for the hay I forked him. And we're obliged to you. It was pretty bad, riding through that storm yesterday."

The burly man moved in, looked left and right, then said: "Are you alone?"

The gunman understood the purpose for that and replied accordingly: "Yeah. But last night . . . I don't know what time it was . . . a couple of skulkers slipped in here. They wakened me, talking down below, and I poked my head through the crawl hole. They ran off like rabbits, heading down in the direction of that settlement northeast of here."

The burly man scratched his face, looked at the gunman's boots, then he said: "I'll be damned." Then he studied the gunman more closely, and finally he said: "Well, let's fork down some feed, then head for the house. I got some flapjack batter rising on the stove." He smiled.

# III

His name was Andrew Tully, he explained to the gunman, and he was obliged to the gunman for scaring off the skulkers, but if they were horse thieves, which Tully seemed to think they probably had been, they had been almighty bold to go right up into a man's barn to steal horses.

The gunman said: "Mister Tully, they were carrying carbines."

The unshaven man turned from his work at the stove, pointed to a cupboard, and said: "Plates and cups and tools in there, if you'd care to set the table." Then he gazed steadily at the gunman. "You didn't say what your name was."

The gunman was moving toward the cupboard when he answered. "Lewis Morgan. Folks call me Lew. And, Mister Tully, maybe you're right, but I've never heard of horse thieves packing Winchesters when six-guns would be plenty good." He returned to the table to set out the dishware and utensils. Andrew Tully said no more about the skulkers, so Lew Morgan let the subject lie. There was more to be said, but if the burly man didn't think it was worthwhile, that was all right with the gunman.

When they sat down to eat, Tully was reaching for the butter as he said: "Folks call me Andy." He smiled briefly, then concentrated upon his meal until the gunman asked about the nearby town. Then Tully responded almost indifferently: "Used to be a way station for freighters and stages southbound down into New Mexico from up north as far as Fort Collins and the Springs . . . Colorado Springs, below Denver. Then it just sort of grew. First there was a trading corral, then a harness and buggy works, then a church and some houses, and so on. When the railroad got as far as Denver, they took a lot of the freight business away, and even the stages cut down considerably. Now, we don't get a coach but once a day, if we're lucky, and about the only freight outfits that still pull through got deliveries to make up and down the road to towns and cow outfits. Nothing very big or important any more. So the town sort of shrunk until now it's no bigger than you see."

"No telegraph?" asked the gunman.

Andrew Tully wagged his head. "Nope. Never had one. I remember years back there was some talk, but it died out. The town's called Forrest . . . with two Rs . . . not for the trees round here, but for some old gent who was a Confederate cavalry general, or something like that." Tully raised bemused eyes. "I don't know exactly how it got named for a Secesh general, out here in Colorado where folks hardly even knew there was a Civil War, back in those days, but one name's about as good as another."

Lew Morgan smiled. Some of the names where he came from in the lower Southwest were just as inappropriate, and a lot harder to pronounce or make any sense of—like the mud-wattle, ugly town he had wintered in last year, whose name was Sangre de Cristo, meaning the blood of Christ. "You make mighty fine flapjacks," he told the burly man, and Andrew Tully put a thoughtful gaze across the table.

"Depends on how long it was since you last ate," he said.

Lew Morgan laughed. There was a lot of truth in that. "Day before yesterday. It was windy and cold. I shot a rabbit west of here, made a dry camp in some broken hills, and had a hell of a time finding enough twigs to make a fire with, then I had a time keeping the fire alive until the meat was cooked."

Andrew Tully reached for his coffee cup. The west country from around Forrest was solidly wooded for a hundred miles. Southward, though, the country was broken and practically all treeless grassland. "Didn't you see the storm coming?" Andy asked, and the gunman's reply was plausible. "Yeah. I saw there was a change coming, Mister Tully, but I didn't figure it was going to blow up into a blizzard."

"You heading any particular place, up north?" asked Andrew Tully, then emptied his cup as he listened to the gunman's answer.

"Not exactly, but some fellers I met three, four days ago told me there was a settlement up in here somewhere." Lew Morgan smiled as Andy arose to go after the coffee pot. "I thought maybe I'd lie over a day or two, then push on upcountry. After all, this here is springtime. It's not supposed to blizzard in springtime."

Andy filled the gunman's cup, then his own cup, and put the pot back upon the stove. "Mister Morgan, springtime in Colorado, even down here in the southern part, can fool the hell out of a man. Just when you think it's time to shed your long johns, it'll do something like this . . . blow up one big, final snowstorm." He resumed his seat and fished forth a tobacco sack. "Care for a smoke?"

"I've got my own, thanks."

"Well," stated the burly man, rolling his cigarette with meticulous care, "two days of sunshine and you'll never know we had a couple of feet of snow." He lit up, studying the taller, leaner man. "All the same, you started upcountry a little early in the season. But I'd guess you probably wanted to be one of the first riders to apply for work along the way, eh?"

Lew Morgan withheld his answer until he, too, had lighted up, then he leaned upon the table to be comfortable. "I never was real good at cowboying, Mister Tully. I was a lot better at breaking and reining horses."

Tully said: "It don't pay as much, Mister Morgan. I know, because I used to have the same problem. I worked the cow outfits from Montana to Mexico, and, when I'd make a cast, the blasted critter'd either run right through my loop, or duck his head and the lariat'd slide across his back. But I was a fair hand with horses. Trouble was, I kept getting leaner an' leaner. Horse-handling jobs are blessed few and far between." Andy Tully inhaled, looked out his kitchen window, then exhaled. "Well, it's not snowing. I've got to head over to town. You're welcome to come along if you'd like." Tully arose. "Just don't expect too much." He went to a wall rack where a gun and shell belt hung with several jackets and two hats. He swung the gun belt around his middle first, then picked off one of the hats, and the last thing he took down was a thick, tan-cloth coat. He put it on while facing away from Lew Morgan, who was packing their plates and cups to the wash pan, but as he buttoned the coat he turned casually to say: "You can't travel for a few days anyway, Mister Morgan, and, if the snow starts up again, you'll be house bound for maybe a week."

Lew turned to speak—and froze. On the right side of the tan coat was a deputy U.S. marshal's badge.

Tully waited, watching Morgan's face, then he moved with a shrug toward the door, settling the coat better across the shoulders with that shrug, and not looking at his guest until he had his hand on the latch. Then he turned. "Might as well come along, Mister Morgan. Nothing to do here, and your animal's snug and cared for."

Lew retrieved his hat, his jacket, and followed the heavier man outside, where the cold air was beginning to seem slightly warmer, and where there was a scent of wood smoke to make a man feel right. The sky was still leaden and low-hanging, but there was no snow falling, and the morning brightness seemed to be increasing a little as time passed. Maybe the storm was over.

Tully did not head for the barn, as Morgan expected. He struck out through the deep snow swinging his arms and breathing deeply. Lew followed, without any arm swinging, and gulping air because, the farther they got from the log barn, the harder it was to plow through. Then they came upon those tracks from last night, only this far out there was only one set of large imprints, and one set of smaller imprints, because Lew Morgan had not pursued the skulkers this far.

Andrew Tully paused, shoved big hands into his jacket, and stood a long while studying the sign. Lew Morgan also examined it, but there was nothing much to be read from snow tracks under the best of conditions, and, when they were this old, and made in such deep snow that almost every track had been partially filled by crumbling snow, there was nothing special to be deduced. Still, Marshal Tully stood like an oaken statue until Morgan began stamping his feet to keep the circulation moving, then Tully sighed, shook his head, turned, and, without a word, trudged onward.

When they finally stepped up on to the ice-slick plank walk Morgan looked back. It wasn't much of a distance, but he felt as though he had just taken the longest and most grueling hike of his lifetime. When he looked around, Andy was grinning at him through his disreputable beard stubble.

"Not like the desert country, is it?" he said, and turned onward without awaiting a reply.

Lew said nothing. It certainly wasn't like the desert country, but he had a small suspicion that Tully hadn't asked the question that way because he was seeking for a contrast to a couple of feet of cold snow. Lew thought the lawman had asked it that way to confirm a suspicion in his own mind that Morgan had indeed come up from the south country—not the west country. The biggest mistake a man could make was to underestimate other men. Especially lawmen. Not that it mattered. At least, at this stage it did not matter, and, if Forrest had no telegraph office, along with a couple of feet of snow on the roadways, it wasn't likely to matter for a week.

They walked carefully as far as the log jailhouse, and there Lew said he'd look the town over and return. Andy was entirely agreeable. He put a sardonic little smile upon Morgan. "But there's no saloon," he said, and at the look he got over that announcement he offered an explanation. "When the town got big enough, a couple of fellers, one named Crawford and one named Kincaid, owned most of it. They were both hallelujah-shouting, Bible-banging Methodists. Well, Kincaid died two years ago, and old Crawford died six or seven years before that. But still, folks decided they didn't really need a saloon." Marshal Tully raised a thick arm. "See that place yonder with the red horse painted on the window? That's the pool hall." He dropped his arm but kept gazing across the roadway, northerly, at that red horse painted on the window up there. "A schoolma'am passed through a few years back and told some folks that out in San Francisco they call 'em billiard parlors, so now some of the people call it that . . . but to me it's a pool hall. Anyway, you can get a drink over there. There's a little bar and the old buck who owns the place makes beer and ale out in a horse shed." Tully's blue eyes turned slowly back to Lew Morgan, a hint of irony in their pleasant depths. "The whiskey's god-awful, the beer is terrible, but the pool games they get worked up over there, sometimes, are real interesting."

Marshal Tully walked into his jailhouse office, closed the door, and Lew Morgan pushed back his hat, hooked thumbs in his shell belt, and very slowly turned his head from left to right.

Forrest did not really resemble most of the cow towns the gunman had been in, but the similarity was close enough. There was a trading barn at the lower end of town, with some cribbed public corrals and a stone trough out front. There were a number of big trees that in summertime no doubt made the town look very cool and pleasant, but which, right now, were bowed with loads of snow, and their limbs were bare. Smoke rose up from stovepipes atop most of the business establishments, and where the harness shop was, beside it stood a gunsmith's establishment. Both were small structures. In fact, except for the general store, and that pool hall or whatever it was with the big red horse on the window, the entire settlement looked as though it had been scaled from town size to village size.

# IV

Morgan did not go over to the pool hall. Not right then, at any rate. He strolled up as far as the harness works, entered, and two older men, one wearing a beeswax-stiffened old canvas apron, who was behind the low counter at a cutting table, and the other man who was drinking black coffee, on the customer's side of the low counter, both turned candidly to stare. Strangers in villages were always a novelty. Lew Morgan did not object to the staring, or to the obvious thoughts, judgments, and assessments the harness maker and his cowman customer were mulling privately. He nodded, said—" 'Morning, gents."—and went over to plant his cold legs wide with his back to the wood stove that was crackling with a fresh load of knotty wood. "Fine weather for sleighing."

The cowman with his thick white cup half raised replied to that: "Yeah. For sleighing, mister, and also for the rheumatics . . . if you happen to have 'em."

The cowman looked old, perhaps as old as sixty or more, but he was lean and wiry, weathered to a perpetual red ruddiness, with lines in his face that crossed through other lines. He did not seem to be wearing a gun, although it was hard to tell because his old soiled buckskin coat reached to the knees and flapped loosely.

The harness maker, busy laying out a template for a California-style saddle skirt, turned, spat into a box of sand, shifted his chewing cud, and peered over the tops of his steel-rimmed eyeglasses at Morgan. "Hell of a time of year to be traveling," he said bluntly, and kept his light blue eyes steadily upon the gunman.

Lew agreed, with a little smile. "Sure is. Unless a man has in mind getting ahead of all the other seasonal range men who'll be heading north looking for riding jobs."

The harness maker was satisfied, evidently, because he went

back to his work on the cutting table.

The shop smelled the way a saddle and harness works should have smelled. Of heat and new leather, beeswax and leather dye. In a settlement that had a pool hall instead of a decent saloon, men would probably congregate in a shop like this, or maybe down at the trading barn. Perhaps some of them would sit around the stove in the gunsmith's shop. It was Lew Morgan's guess that, especially today with all that cold and snow outside, men would be in the harness shop. At least he'd decided to try it first, and, since he was not going anywhere, a little wasted time wouldn't make a bit of difference.

The cowman finished his coffee, dunked the thick white cup in a bucket of water, then hung the cup from a whittled peg on the south wall. He said: 'Walt, favor yourself a mite and put those heated stones in your bed like I told you, and the rheumatism'll get better." He then nodded to Lew Morgan and walked out into the cold roadway.

For a while, until he was amply warm, the gunman remained motionless and silent in front of the stove, watching the old harness maker roll his half circular, razor-sharp cutting tool along the edge of the template. He waited until the skirt had been cut out, then he asked: "Was that feller from one of the local ranches?"

The harness maker looked up. 'Yep. Name's Hal Blue. His wife's a Kincaid. Hal's got about the best land anywhere hereabouts, most of it coming to him with Anita, from her paw, at their hitching years back." The pale blue eyes rose over the tilted-down eyeglasses again. "Why? You looking for a riding job?"

Lew said: "Might be."

"Too early," replied the saddle maker, holding aloft his cut-out to inspect the cut closely. "Too early by maybe a full month." He put down the California skirt. "Wouldn't know the saddle and harness trade by any chance, would you?"

Lew's eyes twinkled. "Mister, I can't even draw a straight line."

The older man studied Morgan for a moment, then smiled a little. "Well, being honest sure never hurt no one. Too bad, though. This damned rheumatism's making it harder for me to do the work every blasted winter. And that damned ice out there, hiding beneath the snow. You know, mister, when a man gets my age, his enemies ain't no longer people or horses, they're things he never figured could possibly harm him. But you fall out there on that damned ice and bust a leg or a hip, and they might as well put you out of your misery. I'm going to close up shop and go south where there's no snow and cold, and no damned ice at all."

The harness maker tossed his skirt down upon the cutting table, perched upon the edge of it, and began carefully honing his semi-circular cutting tool.

Lew fished out the makings. "Mind if a man smokes in here?" he asked, and the older man shook his head without looking up.

"Nope. Just don't allow no chewing and spitting in here is all. Didn't used to mind that, except that half the fellers who chew, when they spit, couldn't hit the broad side of a barn from the inside. It stained up my wall and floor something fierce, so I took out the sand box and put up a sign against chewing." The old man looked up again. "My name's Walt Kenyon. Yours?"

The gunman almost laughed. "Lew Morgan," he said.

The old man saw the hard twinkle and half smiled back. "Tell you something else, Lew. When a man gets as old as I am, he don't have to observe all the rules. He can up and ask a man his name straight out. Who's going to roll up a fist or draw a gun or cuss out an old man? No one, so you don't have to be as mannerly about personal questions as you was forty years back. How'd you happen to walk in here this morning, Lew?"

The dark man's black eyes slowly kindled, but he said nothing. Those pool-shooters fifteen feet away went right on with their game, suspecting nothing, talking briskly back and forth. The half-breed, or whatever he was, stood and glared and did not part his lips. Lew sighed, dug out the silver coin, placed it atop the bar, and, as the other man reached, Lew said: "Leave it lie, friend. I'm not through yet. I may want to stack another dime or two on top of it."

The other man eyed Morgan narrowly, his expression altering subtly. He drew back his hand, then reached for the bottle, poured the glass full, and set the bottle aside. Lew smiled at him.

"That's better. You rolled out on the wrong side of your bunk this morning. Well, we all do that now and then. Care to join me . . . fetch another glass if you do."

The black-eyed man turned on his heel, walked back over to the window, and flipped out the old newspaper to begin reading it again, wearing a black scowl of concentration. Just once, while Lew was leaning to put his second silver coin atop the first one, with his attention diverted from the hawk-faced man, did the half-breed raise his eyes just a trifle above the edge of his newspaper and study the man standing over along the bar. He saw the ivory-stocked six-gun, the flesh-out holster, and the general appearance of the gunman. Expressionlessly the half-breed then dropped his head a little and went back to concentrating very hard on reading his newspaper.

## V

Marshal Tully laughed, his entire round face creasing from the exertion. "His name is Pete Moss, and I'd guess he's maybe a third or a half Indian, but he's just that way . . . some days he'd bite your head off, other days you couldn't ask for a nicer feller." Tully eyed the gunman. "Weather like this, you've got to





This time Morgan did laugh. Walt Kenyon was right. An old man could ask blunt, personal questions, and younger men couldn't do any more than stamp away or growl under their breath. Age evidently had its advantages, even though sometimes it was accompanied with rheumatism. "There's no saloon," he told the harness maker. "Where else would a man go, except to the livery barn or the saddle shop?"

"You might try the pool hall," said old Walt Kenyon. "They'll have more answers down there than I'm likely to have." The pale blue eyes never wavered in their contemplation of the gunman. "That's it, isn't it, Lew? You got a question or two that needs answering?"

Morgan did not smile this time as he returned the old man's look. "Just one question, Mister Kenyon."

"Mister my butt," stated the old man, holding aloft the razor-like cutting tool to examine its honed edge in reflected window light from the white snow. "Mister is for men who got wives and families. I never had neither. I'm just Walt." He lowered the tool, gently put it into a leather scabbard nailed to the wall above the cutting table, and raised his face. "What's the one question?"

"How many men do you know around here with the first name of Jase?"

Old Walt straightened up off his perch upon the table and went to an old chair where he eased down very gingerly, favoring one side over the other side of his body. "How many do I know named Jase?" he muttered, removing his glasses and rubbing his eyes with a scarred, stained old knotty fist. "Well, just two fellers. That man who was visiting in here a while back, Hal Blue, has a son named Jason. He's range boss for his paw. Hardworking, tough-minded young buck. The other feller's the blacksmith. He's got his shop down next to the public corrals." Walt glanced up shrewdly. "Why d' you have to know that?"

"Just curiosity," replied the gunman truthfully.

Old Walt sat thoughtfully studying the man by the stove for a long time, then he sighed. "When I was your age, I was up along Wind River with a band of Crows after buffalo. Those were sure good years. Used to stack dead limbs outside my hide house, keep the fire burnin' low day and night in the center of the lodge, and do nothing but eat meat and tell big lies, and now and then rumple a husky squaw in the bear hides. I feel sorry for fellers your age nowadays."

Lew eyed the old man. He had heard that story before, from other old men, and it hadn't varied very much, as long as the old men were lamenting their lost good years, but when they were recalling those days as they actually were, it was different. Horses froze to death tied to trees, Sioux and Cheyenne and Blackfeet raided Crow camps—for some reason none of the other north country tribesmen had ever liked Crows—and those husky squaws fought like catamounts, and as for all that good cooked meat, Lew had talked to many an old-timer who said when he'd come out of hibernation in springtime, every damned tooth in his head was loose.

Walt saw Lew's expression, shifted slightly in the chair, and introduced a new subject. "Which Jase you want?"

"Maybe neither," replied Lew, and straightened up to depart. He turned to glance out the window. It was snowing again!

"Damnation!" he exclaimed.

Old Walt was not very perturbed. "Well, I told you it was a month early, didn't I?"

Outside, the gunman turned up the collar of his jacket, glared balefully out at the big falling snowflakes, and went carefully down the slick plank walk in the direction of the pool hall.

Down there, two men were having a game at a battered pool table, but the other three tables were empty, and except for a black-haired man looking like a half-breed who was reading a





newspaper with great concentration and not much sı room was empty. The black-haired man lowered his unsmilingly gazed at the gunman. He had a hair-fine over one eye, a beaked nose, and eyes as black as tw holes in a blanket. To Lew, the dark man looked exac picture of an old-time pirate he had once seen in a boo that this man had no gold ring in his ear and his hair clubbed in back.

Lew went to the small, impoverished bar, and, as t proprietor walked over, tucking the newspaper bene arm, he said: "Whiskey, beer, or talk?"

Lew gazed into the hard, scarred face and did not sr recollection of Marshal Tully's recommendation, he "Whiskey."—and remembered something else the marsh said about the old buck who owned the place. Normally someone an old buck simply meant they were not esp young, and they were seasoned, but it also meant a man be part buck Indian. Lew decided this latter thought had in Marshal Tully's mind when he had made his remark watched the hawk-faced man fish for a bottle under his decided the man must be about a fourth Indian, then dismi these thoughts as he reached for the bottle and poured hin a glassful with the stony-faced man unsmilingly watching. W Lew pushed away the bottle, the hawk-faced man said: "Th be a dime, mister. Ten cents a shot."

Lew, his shot glass half lifted, looked steadily at the kni scarred man. They were about the same age and build. Th Lew deliberately raised the glass, dropped his straight sh down, gently put aside the glass, and leaned, making no attem to fish in a pocket for the little silver coin.

"You know," he said quietly, "having to look at you is ba enough, but having you badger a man before he even smells the glass is worse."

remember that folks get cabin fever. You can't do a hell of a lot but look at one another's faces, and it's the same faces you've already looked at enough." Tully eased back in his chair at the desk, and made a gesture in the direction of his popping little pot-bellied wood stove. "Have a cup of coffee," he said, then laughed again at the sober expression upon Lew Morgan's face. "You'll get used to it."

Lew said: "Like hell. I'm heading out of here."

The marshal twisted his oaken body and glanced from his office out the window to the roadway. "You looked out there lately? You'll be here for at least another couple of days, and, if this snowfall don't let up, you could be here for a full week."

Lew crossed to the stove, filled a cup, and returned to the wall bench over beside the front door. The marshal's office was snug and warm, and very pleasant. Across the room, in the west wall, there was a bolt-studded massive wooden door with strap hinges that reached a foot from the wall. There were cells beyond that door, more like steel cages. A former lawman had brought them down from Denver in two wagons, in sections. Jase Buell, the local blacksmith, had riveted the sections together. Each cell resembled a large birdcage. The last time anyone had been confined in the cell room had been the previous summer when a Blue range man had pulled his boot knife on a freighter at the pool hall. His mistake was not to look behind him first. Andrew Tully had knocked him senseless with a pistol barrel from behind.

Now, Andy worked leisurely at cleaning his weapons. He had a fair arsenal for a place no larger than Forrest was, but of course deputy U.S. peace officers were not confined to towns; their territory included the entire west, from the Missouri River on the east to the Pacific Ocean in the west, although as a rule they were assigned to specific areas, and, as in Andrew Tully's case, sometimes they were permitted to patrol a particular locality for a number of years. Tully actually was assigned out of the U.S. Marshal's Office in Denver, but he had not been up there in three years. As he cleaned his weapons, littering the desk with oily rags, and drank coffee, and from time to time stepped to a barred front window to glance out, he told Lew Morgan some of the things he'd been obliged to do over the years, and, although he seemed either to remember only amusing incidents, or made a point of making even the dangerous ones sound amusing, Morgan drank coffee, smoked, and watched the burly man, thinking to himself that Andrew Tully was a man who laughed because he wanted life to be worth laughing about, but that even though this might be part of his character Tully would be a bad man to have for an enemy. He did not look dangerous, but then, in Morgan's experience, the really dangerous critters rarely looked dangerous at all. A sleeping bear, for instance, looked big and amiable and furry, while a cougar sunning himself upon a tree limb was a picture of grace and beauty.

Finally Lew left the bench for the window nearby and leaned there, empty cup in hand, studying the size of the snowflakes. "Big as a half dollar," said the marshal, squinting down a shiny carbine barrel. "That usually means it won't keep up."

Lew looked back. "Usually damned near got me and my horse killed, Marshal."

Tully put down the carbine and picked up its companion. "It was close, maybe, but not as close as you thought it was, Lew. My place was out there, and the settlement was over here. You just didn't know it, was all. Still, it don't seem to me you did a very good thing, starting out when you did, with a closed sky above you."

Lew leaned and watched the burly man, trying to make up his mind whether Marshal Tully was making conversation, or whether he was probing. Lew had had this thought before. He hadn't been able to arrive at a conclusion then, and he also failed to reach one now. Probably, if he knew the lawman better, he'd know what Tully thought. But he didn't know him better. "How about the country north of here?" he asked.

Andy answered while again squinting down a glistening gun barrel. "Be worse, the farther north you go. We actually don't get very many storms as bad as this one in the south parts. Maybe once every four or five years. But up north, the farther you go the deeper the snow is, and the colder it gets." He put down the last clean weapon, dried his hands upon a rag, and fished forth his tobacco sack and papers. "I've got plenty of room, plenty of feed, a dry barn, and an empty house." He looked around genially. "Glad for the company in fact." He lit up and took the weapons back to the wall rack. "Only thing I worry about is that some damned fool will come busting in here yelling his horses have been raided, someone's rustled some of his cows, or maybe there's been a damned gunfight ten miles away, among the cow camps. Next to riding out in weather like this, Lew, there's only one thing I like worse, and that's having to stay out in it, in some soggy cow camp." He returned the last two weapons to his rack. They were scatter-guns, shotguns that had had their barrels sawn off until they were only two feet long. As he strung the chain through each trigger-guard and snapped the lock into place at the far end of the rack, he turned toward the stove for coffee.

Lew went across to rinse his cup and put it aside. "No one'd steal cattle in two feet of snow, and he'd have to be pretty hard up to try and make off with a horse." He looked up and saw the lawman watching him. "How about those two fellers in your barn last night?"

Tully dropped his head, filled the cup, then went back to his desk to sit down before answering. "Well, for one thing they weren't after horses, were they?"

Lew dried his hands, held them extended to stove heat, and

shook his head. "Not carrying carbines, they weren't."

"Maybe saddle or harness thieves, then?"

Lew shook his head again. "I just told you, Marshal . . . not packing carbines."

"Then what were they after?"

Lew turned. "You . . . and, when they stood up there in the front of the barn, Marshal, holding their damned guns, looking toward the house, I couldn't hear what they said, but I'd be willing to bet a spanking new silver dollar they were figuring some way to get you to come busting out of the house so's they could burst your skull like a rotten melon."

Andrew Tully punched out his cigarette and smiled at the man over by the stove. "Funny you should figure it that way, Lew, because that's just about the way I've got it figured. Only I can't imagine why."

Lew was sardonic. "Can't you? Andy, how long you been behind that badge?"

"Eleven years."

"Even in a place like this, Andy, a feller behind a badge has rounded up his share of worthless bastards, and maybe sent some of them off for a long time. Men like that remember, and they think a lot about it in prison, and, when they come out, the first thing they want. . . ."

"Oh, hell," scoffed the marshal, rubbing a hand across his bristly jaw. "If it was someone like that, why wait until dark and come to my barn? Why not just lie on a roof top over across the road, and, when I step out of here, let fly?"

Lew had no answer, but he had an objection. "All right, then tell me this . . . why those damned carbines?"

Marshal Tully hitched up massive shoulders, and dropped them. "Who knows? The hell with it. Let's amble up to the café and get some grub. The food in this town is like the liquor . . . if you've been without a long while, it's not bad at all." He arose, eyes twinkling, picked off his hat and coat, and put them on. He was still smiling when he opened the door and stepped out—and the gunshot came.

Lew was still in the middle of the room. When the ripped-out, flat explosion came through the snow, Lew reacted with a draw that was so fast that if there had been watchers they would not have seen the gun leave leather. Then, staring out through the open doorway, he let go with a fierce curse and jumped through.

Marshal Tully was lying half on, half off, the icy plank walk, his hat had rolled out into the dirty snow near the hitch rack. He was lying on his side, as big-looking as a bear, without moving. From somewhere below the throat of his tan-cloth coat a trickle of dark blood ran downward into the snow. Up the road someone yelled, or called, and, as Lew Morgan flattened along the front of the jailhouse, he swung slightly, twisted from the waist actually, in the direction of that call. A man was standing up there pointing rigidly and yelling. Lew swung back, ducked down, and peered upward. He did not catch much of a glimpse, just a shadowy shape of blurry movement through the thickly falling snow, but he saw the carbine, saw how stealthily the man up there on the roof top was moving, and he fired without aiming. The man on the roof top dropped.

Up the road, that pointing man started yelling again, but this time he was exulting, and Lew did not pay any attention as he stepped ahead, gun up and ready in case there was another one, and sank down to flip the lawman onto his back, then powerfully haul that solid dead weight back upon the duckboards.

Two men called from across the road, over in front of the general store. One of them left the walkway and ran across through the snowfall. Lew waited until the man was close, then said: "Take him back inside, and, if you got a doctor, fetch him." Then he passed the man in a dart toward the opposite side of the road.

The storekeeper was inside, looking ashen. He had heard the first gunshot and had seen the marshal fall, from his front window. He was still stunned when the gunman snarled at him. "Where's the stairs to your roof top, mister?"

The storekeeper turned, wordlessly pointed to a door, then sagged against his shelves as Lew moved on across the room.

The stairway was evidently rarely used. It smelled musty and had an accumulation of dust on each step. He was halfway up toward an overhead trap door, secured in place by two lengths of chain, when he heard men shouting from out in the roadway. He assumed it was more people running down toward the jail-house, now that the first astonishment had passed.

The trap door was heavy, and, as nearly as Morgan could tell in the gloom up there, it had not been opened recently. He lifted it, felt cold air in his face, felt stinging snowflakes against his cheeks, and peered all around. If there was anyone up there, he had to be behind the trap door.

With one powerful shove Morgan flung the door all the way back, until the restraining lengths of chain halted it from falling all the way back, then he waited, listening, trying to arrive in his own mind at some kind of conclusion, and finally he crawled out upon the roof top, bent low and turning steadily in a complete circle. All he saw was snowflakes, half as big as a man's hand, it seemed, coming down thicker than ever now, and dead ahead about fifty feet a lumpy form lying darkly with the snowfall steadily whitening it.

He stepped to the carbine first, picked it up, slid back the lever, saw the shiny glitter of brass, gently eased the lever fully back into place, leaned the gun against the roof's roadside wall, and went back to toe the downed man over onto his back. If he hoped the man might only be wounded, so that he might have forced him to explain why he had shot the marshal, it was a vain hope. Morgan's bullet had caught the bushwhacker just in front of his left arm, low, and, because Morgan had fired on an upsweeping angle, the slug had torn upward, too. The man had been dead before he'd settled into the snow upon the roof top.

Morgan holstered his Colt, leaned, sifted through the assassin's pockets, stuffed everything he found into his own jacket pockets, then he studied the dead man's face. He had been young, perhaps in his late twenties, but no older, dark-eyed and dark-haired. He looked as though he had been a range rider.

Over in the trap door opening that part Indian proprietor of the pool hall had his head and shoulders sticking through. He was clutching a shotgun in both hands as he yelled across through the snowfall. "Who is he?"

Lew did not answer. How in the hell would he know who the dead man was? He'd only arrived in this country the night before.

The hawk-faced man yelled again. "Is he dead?"

This time the gunman looked around. "Yeah, he's dead. Come take a look. Maybe you'll know him."

# VI

It required four men to lower the corpse through the trap door, then go down those steep stairs with it. Lew Morgan remained behind upon the roof top, leaning upon the waist-high false front, gazing through snowfall over in the direction of the jailhouse, where men came and went, crowding in as the town, which had been so quiet earlier, came alive with excitement and shock.

The snowfall continued, but it did not actually seem very cold to the gunman, and the big flakes did not melt the moment they touched down, so he had an accumulation of them across his shoulders when he finally turned and saw the half-breed, Pete Moss, examining the bushwhacker's carbine.

Moss looked up, saw Morgan's stare, and gave his head a little exasperated wag. "It's got an ivory bead on the front sight. I don't see how a man could be accurate using an ivory bead in a snowstorm."

Morgan wasn't interested in the gun. Moss had not recognized the assassin. Neither had any of the other men who'd climbed to the roof top to take the corpse away. Hell, he and the marshal had just finished mentioning someone taking a shot at him from a roof top. It was almost as though some kind of eerie second sight had arrived moments before the lawman had stepped out into the roadway.

Moss held out the Winchester and Morgan took it, then he went toward the trap door, almost reached it when Pete Moss said: "Hey, there's a fire ladder down the back of the building. If that bastard didn't come up through the store, then he had to climb that ladder. There should be some sign over there in the snow."

Morgan turned back and followed the half-breed. They did not have to go all the way to the rear wall of the building. Pete pointed to very faint boot-mark indentations in the freshly fallen snow. Then he backtracked to the wooden ladder nailed to the rear-alley wall and stopped. "That's how he did it. Climbed up from the alley." Pete turned. "Why?"

Morgan's reply was terse: "To shoot Tully."

"Yeah. But why did he want to shoot Andy?"

"How in the hell would I know?" snapped Morgan, and turned back in the direction of the trap door.

Downstairs, the storekeeper was in earnest conversation with a number of men, and, out front, more men stood and talked. When the gunman and the half-breed appeared, men turned to stare without speaking.

Out in the roadway Walt Kenyon, still attired in his dirty canvas apron, stopped Lew Morgan with a question. "How'd he get up there . . . by the fire ladder? Well, then, his horse's got to be out back somewhere, don't he?" The gunman looked at Pete Moss and without a word the half-breed turned away to go search the alleyway. Old Kenyon then said: "That his rifle?"

Morgan glanced at the gun in his hand. "Yeah."

"Take it up to Art Lane."

Lew studied old Kenyon. "Who's Art Lane?"

"The gunsmith. I forgot, you don't know the country. His shop is next to mine. If a man can tell you anything from that man's gun, it'll be Art."

Lew handed the carbine to the harness maker. "You take it up there, Walt. I'll be along directly. I want to see what shape Tully's in."

"Not very good shape," stated the old man, taking the Winchester. "The slug caught him square through the lights." Kenyon turned and walked away.

Across the road, with newly fallen snow beginning to form a floury crown atop the older, dirtier, snow, four men, one of them from a cow outfit from the looks of his attire, stopped speaking as Lew Morgan plowed through and reached the plank walk, then pressed past and entered the jailhouse, which was full of people.

Marshal Tully was conscious. Someone had dragged one of the narrow cots from a cell and put it by the stove in the little log-walled office. A grizzled-haired man with rolled-up sleeves and a pursed set of lips was gravely studying Tully as he gently pulled up an old Army blanket to cover the wounded man's bare, bandaged upper body. When Tully saw Morgan come up and look down, he spoke in a fading voice.

"You got to look after the horses."

Morgan answered shortly. "Don't worry about that, or anything else," then, when a man bumped him, crowding up close to stare, the gunman turned. "Clear out," he growled at the stranger. When the man lifted a hostile look, Morgan reached, caught the man's coat, and pushed hard. Then he raised his voice. "Clear out, all of you, and close that damned door!"

They went, mostly in sullen resentment, but they departed. All but the man with the wiry, grizzled gray hair, and he completely ignored the gunman until he had made Tully as comfortable as he could. Then he looked up and spoke. "That was good shooting, mister. You down there in front of the jail-house, him up there on the roof, and a heavy snowfall betwixt the pair of you."

Morgan recognized the man now. He had been standing up the road calling, and pointing. "Everyone's entitled to one accidental good shot," he replied. "Is the slug still in him?" The gray-haired man pointed to a basin with pinkish water in it. On the bottom lay a misshapen slug of lead. Morgan was impressed. "How'd you get it out so fast?"

The older man reached for a rag to dry his hands upon as he replied. "Wasn't much of a chore. When I got his shirt and underwear peeled down, and rolled him over, there it was, a little black shadow, like a lump, right under the hide in back. I just cut through the hide and picked it out." The man looked steadily at Morgan for a moment before also saying: "Nobody makes that kind of accidental shot, mister." Then he reached for a sheep-pelt coat and shrugged into it as he looked down at Andrew Tully. "You're lucky, you know that, Andy? Of course this is bad weather. You could catch pneumonia or lung fever, or something like that, if you get chilled. Otherwise, you ought to make it." He buttoned the coat, solemn as a judge, picked up an old hat and crushed it down over his mop of thick, wiry hair, and rummaged in a capacious side pocket until he found what he sought, and pulled forth a pony of brandy that he regarded for a moment, then leaned, and put it beside the marshal on the cot. "It probably won't really commence to hurt until maybe tomorrow, but when it does, nip a little on that firewater." He turned toward the door without facing Lew Morgan again, and left the office. Just before closing the door, with his head and shoulders still visible, he said: "We'll put that bushwhacker in the icehouse." Then he was gone and the gunman shook out of his soggy jacket, draped it upon the back of a chair near the stove, tossed down his hat, and stood a moment with his cold hands stretched toward the stove. He did not look at Andy Tully, and the wounded man, while watching the gunman, made no attempt to speak, or even to move. He had lost color, and he was as weak as a kitten. There was actually very little pain except in his back and shoulders, but where the bullet had passed through, there was only a sensation of mild breathlessness. He felt slightly sick to his stomach, and shock had made every limb as heavy as lead. He was perfectly content just to lie there.

Morgan turned, finally, when the warmth had abetted the passing of shock, sighed, and pulled up a chair to sit down. "What was it we were saying about someone being on a roof top?"

Tully's wide mouth lifted slightly at the corners, but he did not answer.

"The gun he used is being looked at by your local gunsmith. No one knew him, Marshal. Pete Moss and a dozen other fellers saw him, and not a one of them recognized the feller. I got a feeling you'd know him, though. Later, maybe we can get them to haul his carcass up for you to look at." Morgan reached in a shirt pocket for the makings. "There's something I didn't tell you last night. I heard one of them call the other one Jase. They did that while they were still in the barn, before they went out front. I asked around a little this morning. Seems there's a cowman with a son named Jason, and a blacksmith called Jase, too." Morgan lit up, settled back in the pleasant warmth, and gazed pensively at the impassively relaxed face of the man on the old cot. "They were out to kill you, like I figured. If there was a way to prove it, I'd guess that gun he used this morning was out there last night in your barn. Maybe, when we find the other one, we'll be able to prove it. But there's a stumbling block, Andy. How in hell are we going to find that other son-of-a-bitch?" Morgan leaned forward. "I figure it this way. They know why they want to kill you, and you know. I sure as hell don't know, and I'd guess no one else around town knows, either. Therefore, unless you can help me find that other one, you're still going to get killed, only now it'll be a heap easier because you're a sitting duck, lying strung out in here as helpless as a foal. Andy . . . ?"

Tully weakly rocked his head from side to side without attempting to speak. He groped feebly for the pony of brandy, and Morgan helped him pull the cork and hoist it until he could take a couple of swallows. The reaction to that fiery liquor came almost at once. While Morgan sat there, holding the little bottle and watching, Tully's color began improving, his eyes brightened noticeably, and, when his tongue darted over his lips, it moved swiftly and surely.

"I told you," the marshal said, "I've got no idea."

"Who threatened to come back and square things when you sent them to prison?" asked Morgan.

Tully sighed. "No one. I don't recollect anyone making that threat, not in eleven years. But. . . ."

"But what?"

"It could be anyone. In my time I've shot men. They wouldn't come back, Lew, but they'd have kin. . . ."

Morgan pondered that, and the longer he dwelt upon it the larger it kept getting, the more hopeless the task began to look to him. Hell, the people who might want a lawman killed could be motivated by anything the lawman had done in his eleven years of upholding the law. A vengeful bushwhacker did not have to be kin to anyone Marshal Tully had shot; he could be anyone at all who imagined himself to be justified in killing a lawman.

Morgan arose, went to the stove to open the door, and pitch in his cigarette, then, because the fire was dying a little, he also tossed in two pieces of wood from the box in the corner, then he went back to the chair, and sat down.

Tully's eyes were closed. His color was still good and his breathing, although shallow and fluttery, seemed to be maintaining a kind of cadence, which Morgan thought probably was favorable. He sat a long time, until someone opened the door and jarred him out of a reverie. It was Pete Moss. Morgan put a finger to his lips, grabbed his hat and jacket, and went outside to talk to the pool hall proprietor. It was still snowing, and again the sidewalks were empty. No doubt the excitement remained high throughout the village, only now folks were discussing it around their stoves, indoors.

Moss said: "How is he? Jeb told me he got the slug out."

Morgan answered curtly: "He don't look dead. Who is Jeb?"

"Nearest thing we got to a doctor or veterinarian in these parts. He runs that apothecary shop up the road from here. Jeb Hazelton. About the horse . . . there wasn't one."

"He walked, then," said Lew Morgan, but Moss scowled that away. "Nope, there *was* a horse. There was two horses, both shod. Someone came on one of them and untied the horse tied out back of the store, and led him away. The tracks are just about covered with snow now, but you can still make out the faint indentations where this feller led that tied horse up the alleyway. I'd guess as soon as he heard the commotion around here in front, he guessed what had happened, and took away his partner's animal."

Morgan stared steadily at the knife-scarred, hawk-faced man.

"That was running a risk," he said. "Maybe someone saw him. You could ask around."

Moss was willing. "Yeah. But it sticks in my craw that, if I was with a feller who tried to kill someone, then got killed himself, I'd only take that kind of a chance if that tied horse might be a danger to me. Maybe by his brand, or what was in his saddle pockets, or something like that."

Morgan reached to tip down his hat brim to keep snowflakes out of his face. Maybe Pete Moss had an unpredictable temperament—hell, most half-breeds did have, for that matter—but he was no one's fool. "I'll be over to your place as soon as I can get someone to sit with the marshal," he said, then stood and watched the hawk-faced man go trudging back across the road, northward, thinking that if anyone in this village was going to be able to help him find the remaining bushwhacker, it probably was the half-breed.

He opened the jailhouse door, felt heat come out, saw that Tully was still sleeping, and eased the door closed very gently before striking out in the direction of the apothecary's shop through the falling snow.

Out in the roadway, because there had been no traffic to speak of all morning, there was a beautiful carpet of pure white, from one plank walk to the opposite plank walk. Hell, even if he got lucky, he wasn't going to be able to get out of this village for a week! It was one thing to need a little seclusion and privacy for a while, but it was something else having so much of it shoved down a man's throat, along with a ton of snow.

# VII

It had not occurred to Morgan, at the jailhouse when the apothecary had put that pony of brandy near Tully's cot, to wonder why a man would be carrying such a thing in his coat pocket, but even if it had occurred to him, he wouldn't have thought much of it. In this kind of weather men would carry cast-iron wood stoves, if they could, and brandy was the next best thing, when a man needed to keep warm by stimulating his circulatory system, but he hadn't been in the small, dingy druggist's store ten minutes when he began to suspect there was another reason for Jeb Hazelton to be carrying brandy around with him. The man was a drunkard. If not a chronic drunkard, then he certainly drank more than most folks drank. It was early afternoon when Morgan walked in up there, and loosened his jacket because the little building was unnecessarily hot, and was greeted by Hazelton whose breath would have made the eyes of a buffalo water.

Morgan looked around. There were bottles of patent medicine on shelves, but there were also other shelves, behind an immaculate, shiny wooden counter, that held less flamboyant bottles with names Morgan could not pronounce, and beyond was a small area evidently used for making up special medicines. Hazelton watched Morgan's head slowly turn, and crookedly smiled as he said: "There's an old widow woman lives out back of town, to the north, who swears up and down I concoct spells."

Morgan turned back slowly to the man himself. He had not paid much attention to the apothecary at the jailhouse. Now, he studied the man as he said: "We need someone who can sit with Tully. I can't be there all the time. We need someone who can maybe shoot a shotgun."

Hazelton's bushy brows climbed. "Shoot a shotgun, Mister Morgan?"

"In case that roof top son-of-a-bitch had a friend."

"Do you think he had one, Mister Morgan?"

Lew finished his assessment of the druggist. Drunkard or not, he was all the village had evidently in the way of a healer. "Mister Hazelton, I don't know whether he had a partner or not. Tully's flat on his back and helpless, so someone's got to sit with him, and just in case there is another one, what harm can it do having Tully's sitter able to handle a weapon?"

"None," murmured the apothecary, and moved around behind his counter to retrieve something from a small tray. He held it out. "The bullet. I brought it along, but I won't really need it, if you'd care to take it along."

Lew only glanced at the outstretched hand. He had even less use for a spent slug, but all he said was: "Before you sink that bushwhacker, maybe you could get some boys to pack him up where Marshal Tully can take a look at his face."

Hazelton slowly put the slug back in the tray. Then he looked over at Lew Morgan, gently smiling. "You're an efficient man," he murmured. "I'd say that sometime, Mister Morgan, you've served the law. You think like a lawman."

The gunman delayed a retort while he ironically returned the apothecary's look. "Who are Andrew Tully's enemies?" he asked, and the sudden change in thought the answer required made Jeb Hazelton stare a moment at the far wall before speaking.

"As far as I know, Mister Morgan, he had no real enemies. But he's human, and therefore I'm sure he had some. Except that we just aren't that close. Ordinarily he don't take medicine and I don't care much about his kind of work, so we don't very often visit." Hazelton straightened up. "Walt, over at the saddle shop, or maybe Art Lane or Pete Moss, might be able to help you on that score. I surely can't." Hazelton glanced out where the snow was still falling. "If this doesn't stop soon, we're going to be marooned. Snowed in like we were my first year in Forrest. Then, we couldn't even get a freight rig into town, nor a stage, for ten days."

Lew Morgan went back out into the roadway deciding that if a man drank in this town, he probably had reasons. He then trudged across the road to the gun shop, and encountered old Walt Kenyon over there, leaning over a table watching a younger, thin, shock-headed man working with a Winchester he had clamped in leather-lined blocks. Both the gunsmith and the harness maker looked around when the door opened to admit Lew Morgan. Kenyon said: "Well, it's about time. Morgan, this here is Art Lane."

The shock-headed man nodded and offered an uncertain kind of small smile, then he picked up a cold pipe and tried to get the dottle to burn, but it wouldn't, so he put it back down, and Lew noticed that his work-stained, rough hands were not altogether steady. Maybe this gunsmith was a drinker, too.

Morgan went to the stove and planted his back to it. Jutting his jaw at the gun in the blocks, he asked if that was the assassin's weapon, and the shock-headed man bobbed his head. "Yeah. I was just lookin' it over, Mister Morgan. It's in pretty fair shape, for a stockman's weapon. There's no one takes worse care of guns than range men, you know."

Morgan hadn't known that. He watched Art Lane bend over the weapon, decided it was not as hot in the gun shop as it had been across the road in the apothecary's shop, and wondered why Lane's forehead was sweat-beaded.

Walt Kenyon asked about Andrew Tully. Morgan told him the same thing he'd told Pete Moss. "He looks alive." Then he swung his attention back to the gunsmith. "Whose weapon was that?"

Lane did not look up from his work at the blocks. "Well, Mister Morgan, like I said, it's in fair shape, and they usually don't come to me like that. And that there ivory bead on the front sight. . . ."

Kenyon gave a little start. "Hell," he blurted out, "I didn't notice that, Art. I seen something white but figured it was snow. That's one of your sights, Art!"

Lew Morgan, standing like carved stone before the stove, did not take his eyes off the gunsmith, and Art Lane did not lift his eyes to the husky man over in front of his stove.

The harness maker suddenly became stone-silent. Snow water dripping somewhere was a steady sound, but that was all, until Lew Morgan shifted weight, swept back his jacket with both hands on his hips, and repeated his earlier question, but in a flatter, softer tone of voice this time: "Gunsmith, whose saddle gun was that?"

Art Lane remained hunched over the gun in his blocks, moving both hands in a fluttery manner until Morgan left his position in front of the stove and walked to the table to look down at the carbine. It was the same gun he'd kicked away from the man he'd killed on the roof top, no doubt about that. Morgan turned slowly and put a dispassionate stare upon the old harness maker. "Walt, go on back to your shop."

Kenyon blinked his surprise and remained still for a moment, then abruptly turned and walked out—and slammed the roadway door.

Morgan reached to tap the gunsmith, now that they were alone. "I want his name, Mister Lane."

As the shock-headed man straightened up a little, it sounded almost as though he were sighing. He finally met Morgan's glance. "I don't like to give it to you," he said softly, "because these here guns get traded around an awful lot, especially in wintertime when riders run out of money and there ain't any work. I can tell you who owned it the last time I seen this weapon . . . which was when I put on that front sight . . . but that don't mean a damned thing, Mister Morgan, because the feller you killed on the store roof wasn't the same feller at all. So you see, this gun could have been traded or stolen or sold, or even. . . ."

"Yeah. Or even loaned to someone to shoot Marshal Tully with. Mister Lane, we're wasting a lot of time. Whose gun was it?"

"It belonged to Jason Blue when I put that sight on it, last summer."

Morgan thought back to the wiry, hard-faced old cowman in the leather works, and dropped his gaze to the Winchester. Eventually he said: "Now I want you to keep this strictly to yourself, Mister Lane. Don't tell a soul. Not Walt Kenyon or even Marshal Tully. You understand?" Morgan leaned, unscrewed the clamps, and lifted out the Winchester. "The minute I walk out of here old Kenyon's going to come back and ask a lot of questions."

Lane threw back his head to get a heavy coil of brown hair out of his eyes. "What will I tell him?"

"Tell him anything you like. Tell him you couldn't remember where you saw this gun before, but don't let him get any idea that you told me the name of the man who owned the gun." Morgan looked stonily at the taller man. "You understand me?"

"Yes. But if Jase's paw finds out I had anything to do with. . . ."

"He's not going to find out from me, Mister Lane, and I'm the only other man who knows, so, if he comes in here rattling his horns, you better lie like your soul depends on it, if you don't want him to know. And now tell me something . . . Jason Blue and his paw didn't like Marshal Tully?"

Lane fished forth a soiled old blue bandanna and wiped his forehead and upper lip before replying. "As far as I know, they were all friends. The old man . . . Hal Blue . . . used to set by the hour at the pool room playing pinochle with Andy. And Jase . . . well, I've never heard him say a word against Andy. Mister Morgan, as a guess, I'd say someone either stole that gun off Jase, or maybe bought it from him, or maybe won it in a poker game. When you meet Jase Blue, you'll see what I mean. He's not a bushwhacker."

Morgan already knew that, because the man atop the general

store had not been named Jason Blue. He took the carbine with him and walked out into the roadway. The snowfall had stopped. There were patches of clean blue sky overhead. It was still chilly, and there was now a little gusty wind blowing, but it looked as though, finally, the storm was going to break up. He buttoned his jacket to the gullet, re-settled his hat firmly, and plowed back to the opposite side of the road and went down the treacherously slick plank walk in the direction of the jailhouse. Some local people, including merchants, were outside with buckets of salt, sprinkling down the snow and ice.

He was not thinking about his promise to visit Pete Moss at the pool hall when he entered the jailhouse, but the man sitting in the chair beside Marshal Tully's bunk reminded him of that promise. It was Moss, and he was spooning hot beef broth into the lawman. He looked up and around, nodded at Morgan, then went back to his work.

Marshal Tully's head had been propped up with several old rolled blankets. His color was not as bad as it had been, and he swallowed the hot broth without spilling any. He did not look elsewhere until Lew walked over to the gun rack and propped the bushwhack weapon there, then his eyes fell upon the weapon briefly, with no show of recognition, before they raised to Morgan's face.

Pete Moss leaned back, bowl and big spoon in his hands. "You ate two-thirds of it," he told the lawman. "That's enough for now." He arose and went to put the bowl upon the desk. As he faced back around toward Morgan, he said: "Where you been? I waited around an hour for you."

Morgan told half the truth. "Tried to arrange with Jeb Hazelton to get someone to come down and sit with the marshal."

Moss grumbled about that: "No one's showed up yet." He was evidently in one of his bad moods, but Lew Morgan was not too concerned as he preëmpted the chair beside the cot and studied Tully's face.

"How do you feel?" he asked, and got that little crooked-lipped small grin again.

"Like a troop of cavalry rode over me."

Morgan smiled and settled back, shoved his hat away from his eyes, and sat for a while just looking at the lawman without speaking.

Pete Moss came over, scowling. "You know where he is?" he demanded.

Morgan raised his eyes. "Who?"

The black-eyed man snarled. "Who! The other one . . . who the hell do you think I'm talking about?"

Morgan's steady gaze lingered upon Pete Moss without wavering or blinking. He started to answer, then checked himself, waited a moment, then started again. "Pete, this thing only happened an hour and a half ago, and I'm not a lawman. I'm not even a good tracker, and I'm sure as hell no mind-reader. No, I got less idea than anyone else where he is. I also never saw this lousy village or any of you before. If you want a miracle, go hunt up a preacher."

Andrew Tully spoke in a tired-sounding voice: "The other one's probably ten miles away by now, Pete."

"No," said Morgan quietly, dropping his gaze to the man on the cot. "Not in two or three feet of snow." He arose, went over to the desk, and began dumping things from his jacket pockets. The other two watched until everything Morgan had taken from the dead man was lying scattered out, then Moss walked over and scowlingly watched as Lew Morgan began silently and intently examining a clasp knife, some folded greenbacks, a tin box of matches, a red bandanna handkerchief, and a large old-fashioned silver pocket watch.

Pete mumbled and made a little gesture of despair. "Is that all he had? There's nothing there."

Lew had to agree.

# VIII

The storekeeper was a pudgy, pale man named Aleck Trotter. He entered the jailhouse to say that he had been talking with Jeb Hazelton about Marshal Tully, and after a conference with Mrs. Trotter he had come to offer his house and his wife's care until the marshal recovered. Tully acted embarrassed, which Morgan could understand. No man liked to feel obligated, and no bachelor wanted to be tended and fussed over by a female. Tully said he was grateful, but he wouldn't impose, and, besides, it would probably be better if he remained at the jailhouse until the other renegade had been caught.

Aleck Trotter looked surprised. "I thought there was only one," he said, and Morgan saw the expression of apprehension tinge the storekeeper's round, pale face.

Pete Moss, over by the desk where he'd been minutely examining the dead man's personal effects, spoke up: "Maybe there was just one of them, Aleck, but the marshal and Mister Morgan figure there's another one around." Moss's black eyes went to Trotter's face. He stood looking at the larger, paler man, knowing exactly what was running through Trotter's mind, then he turned almost contemptuously and went back to rummaging through the effects atop the desk, and moments later Aleck Trotter departed. As soon as the door closed, Pete Moss said: "That bailed you out, Andy."

The lawman looked up at Lew Morgan to explain. "Aleck's sort of timid."

Morgan nodded. This was unimportant to him. Moreover he'd already guessed all he cared to know about the storekeeper from their encounter across the road moments after the shooting, so he acted as though Aleck Trotter had not been there by saying: "How does a feller reach the Blue cow outfit?"

Pete Moss's black eyes came up. "You want to ride out there?"

Marshal Tully, lying back with both eyes closed, sounded tired when he said: "It wasn't Jase. I know what you're thinking. I figured whose gun that was when you brought it in, but it wasn't Jase."

Morgan's response was blunt. "Yeah, I know it wasn't, or someone would have recognized him when they packed him down off the roof, Marshal. But that was his gun."

Pete Moss, looking back and forth, finally walked over to lift the carbine and inspect it, as Marshal Tully spoke again. "If you go out there, Lew, and old Hal guesses what you got in mind, he won't like it one damned bit."

Morgan had already guessed all he had to know about Hal Blue, too. Morgan was a good judge of men, and that look he'd got at the cowman earlier in the day had convinced him that Hal Blue would not be a good man to cross. On the other hand, he liked the marshal. Sometimes, with some men, it was not necessary to know a person a year or more to decide whether they measured up or not.

Pete gently placed the gun back against the wall and said: "I'll show you the way."

Morgan nodded. "I'll go fetch my horse from the marshal's barn and meet you out front in an hour." He went to the door, saw Tully watching him, and walked out of the building into a scuffling little low cold wind.

The sky was rapidly clearing. Its blueness had that intense shading to it that usually presaged cold weather. What was really needed to get rid of the thick snow was sunshine, and, although there was a sun hanging up there, its best efforts seemed to be inhibited by the cold wind. Morgan buttoned his jacket to the throat, yanked his hat down, and struck out for the lower end of town and the tracks leading from there out a half mile or so to the marshal's house and barn.

As he was passing the trading barn, a big, stooped old man muffled in a buffalo-hide coat with a thick woolen muffler around his throat lifted narrowed eyes from his position in the front of the log barn, eyed Morgan steadily, then nodded almost grudgingly when Lew stared back. Then the big old man turned and went into his barn.

The trail from the lower end of town through deep snow was well-trampled even though there had been more snow since Tully and Morgan had made it that morning. As he trudged along, he questioned the wisdom of making his horse plow through the deep snow and bitter wind to the cow outfit of Hal Blue. He could probably wait a day or two, until the sun had had a chance to melt things, making riding easier. But Lew Morgan had always operated on the principle that the man who held the initiative usually survived; he had it now, and, if he sat down to wait, it would slip away from him. Also, when the snow melted, it would not just be easier for him to travel, it would also be easier for that other man to travel.

He reached the barn, stepped inside to pause for a breather, and turned a slow glance roundabout. The blood bay gelding was gone. He stood a long while just gazing at the empty stall. The marshal hadn't taken the horse, because the marshal had not been out of Lew Morgan's sight since they had left the barn early that morning, and up until the time he had been shot down, and after he had been shot down, he sure as hell hadn't come out here to get the horse.

Morgan rolled a cigarette, turned back to gaze in the direction of the town while he quietly and thoughtfully smoked, then flung the smoke into a snowbank, and went after his own animal. As he saddled up, he glanced a couple of times at the empty stall where the blood bay had been. Of course, for all Morgan knew, the horse might have belonged to someone who'd had a legitimate reason for coming out here to remove him. It just did not seem likely.

Morgan turned his sorrel a couple of times, just in case the cold air and standing in a stall overnight and most of the morning doing nothing but eating might have given the sorrel ideas. Evidently it hadn't, because as soon as Lew was astride, the horse turned and dutifully followed the boot-track trail down in the direction of town. He had never actually been much to buck anyway.

That scuffling low wind seemed to be dying. At least when Morgan reached the south end of town again, it was blowing a lot less, and that pleased him. Morgan was one of those people who could stand most weather, but not wind.

As he walked his horse past the trading barn, that big old stooped man wrapped in the moth-eaten old buffalo-skin coat was whittling on a long stick, head down, in conversation with a shorter, thicker man who looked much younger, but not exactly youthful. Morgan surmised the identity of the thicker man by the mule-hide apron he was wearing: Jason Buell, the blacksmith.

The two men looked up, stared at Lew Morgan, then looked away to continue their conversation, and Lew made a spur-of-the-moment decision. He reined over toward the big, bare tree where the men were talking, hauled up about fifteen feet away, and nodded. The blacksmith spoke first, while the horse trader, in his mangy big old fur coat, stopped whittling and studied Morgan without even nodding.

Buell said: "How's Andy?"

Lew gave his stock answer. "Alive, I guess. He was the last time I saw him." He studied the stocky man. "You're Buell, the blacksmith?"

The burly man nodded. "Jase Buell." He looked quickly at the sorrel's hoofs, then nodded again. "He needs a new set, for a fact. If you'll tie him to the stud ring there in the tree, I'll get to him directly."

Morgan did not concede that his horse needed shoes, even though he knew the horse had been wearing the same plates about a month. He studied the older, stooped man. "Who are you?" he asked, and the horse trader's eyes, perpetually narrowed, showed a flash of quick resentment.

"I ain't Santy Clause," he answered testily. "And while I was growin' up, folks didn't come out with personal questions, neither."

Lew kept watching the big old stooped man. He thought he knew this man's type; most of the old-timers were like this, careful to avoid giving offence, and very quick to take offence. Morgan said: "I can see you're not Santa Clause, mister. Santa Clause would have dunked that greasy old coat in a creek once or twice."

Both the men stared. Morgan sat up there, looking steadily back at them. The blacksmith, receiving some sixth-sense kind of warning, forced a little smile. "He's Sam Evans. Owns the trading barn next door."

Morgan eyed the hostile big old stooped horse trader. "Sam, who took the blood bay horse out of Marshal Tully's barn a while back?"

The old man's nostrils flared. "I don't know. And if I did know, I wouldn't see where it'd be any of your concern!"

Morgan grinned. "I'll help you see, then, Sam, because everything that's happened since Andy Tully got shot this morning is now my concern." Lew kept smiling. He enjoyed old Sam Evans's discomfort. Men like old Evans were irascible, irritable, and sometimes bullying, but they knew exactly when not to be any of those things; the fact that they knew exactly when not to be that way was proven by the fact they lived this long. Otherwise, someone would have killed Sam Evans a long time ago, when there was even less law than there now was.

Sam said: "You the law, now?"

"Nope," replied the gunman. "I'm just a feller who don't like bushwhackers."

"What's that got to do with Andy's blood bay horse?"

"I don't know, Sam. That's why I asked who took him away. To see if maybe there is some kind of connection."

Jase Buell looked at the horse trader. "It couldn't be no secret, Sam. What the hell, maybe a half dozen folks seen him go out there from town and lead the horse back."

Evans lowered his head and made several vicious slashes upon the whittling stick without speaking. Morgan waited, then turned on the blacksmith. "Who was it?"

"Art Lane," replied the burly man.

Lew rubbed his jaw. "The gunsmith?"

"Yeah."

Morgan turned to gaze up the roadway in the direction of the gunsmith's shop. There was probably a perfectly reasonable excuse why the gunsmith did that, especially in broad daylight, as the blacksmith had implied. He turned without another word to ride on up to the tie rack out front of the jailhouse, where Pete Moss, wrapped in a blanket coat, was standing beside a saddled black horse. He hadn't quite kneed his sorrel when the old horse trader raised spiteful eyes to say: "Mister, you go ridin' rough-shod over folks in these parts, and they'll bury you here."

Lew said: "How? By bushwhacking me from a roof top?"

The horse trader said something that made Lew consider him in careful thought: "Maybe from a roof top. You're a friend of Andy Tully's, and you killed that feller up atop the general store. Mister, whoever is out to kill Andy's got plenty of reason also to want to kill you . . . now."

Up the road, Pete Moss sang out irritably for Morgan to hurry it up a little. The wind had entirely died by now, and for the first time in several days it was possible to feel genuine warmth from the sun. People were in the roadway again. Men were shoveling snow off the plank walk and salting the icy places, and several boys were trying to make rope harnesses for their dogs so that they could be pulled on their sleds. The dogs either avoided the boys, or, allowing themselves to be caught and harnessed, simply stood there, uncomprehending, wagging their tails.

Morgan reined up beside Pete Moss. "How far is it to the Blue outfit?" he asked, and got a wry look from the half-breed.

"Six, seven miles northwest." Pete swung into the saddle, shortened his reins, adjusted his carbine slung forward in its boot, and glanced out across the white range country. "But there's a trail by now. Couple of Blue's riders was in this morning, for some flour and the mail, and last night there was the old man and couple other fellers to town."

Pete was right in his implication. When he and Lew Morgan reached the turn-off lying south of the upper end of Forrest, they encountered a well-trampled trail, and that at least was a big relief. As they plodded along, Lew asked about the gunsmith. Moss, buttoning his blanket coat, then unbuttoning it as the heat increased, did not have a whole lot to say about Art Lane. "Come to the village five, six years ago and set up shop. He used to break and rein horses over in Idaho, so I've heard, and I know for a fact he's a top hand with horses, along with being real good with guns . . . fixing them, I mean, because I never yet seen him shoot a gun. That's all I know. Why, what's your interest?"

Lew explained. "He took Andy's blood bay from the barn this morning. I wondered who did it, and the blacksmith told me it was Lane. I was wondering why he'd do that."

"Probably figured someone'd have to look after Andy's animal, is all." Pete Moss turned his black eyes to the gunman.

"You're not trying to make Art out the other feller, are you?"

Morgan answered shortly. "I'm not trying to make anyone out to be the other feller, Pete. I'm just trying to figure out who he is, and I'll tell you why. That old sore tail who runs your trading barn here in Forrest thinks I'm the next target, for being a friend of Tully's and for potting that bastard on the roof top."

Pete smiled. "I think that, too," he said, and raised a coated arm to point ahead. "You see that smoke standing straight up yonder? That'll be the cook shack at the Blue place."

# IX

Pete Moss was correct. The smoke arose from the ranch cook shack, and, as the pair of riders left the snow trail and headed across into the large yard, where much activity had pretty well churned the snow into mud, a lean young cowboy looked back from the cook shack porch, eyed them a long moment, then ducked inside. As Pete led the way to the tie rack out front of the horse barn, which was lower-roofed and wider than the other log barn, the man Lew recognized as Hal Blue came forth upon the cook shack porch and stared. Evidently the youthful rider had said something about a pair of horsemen riding in.

Moss saw Hal Blue, and, as he stepped to his horse's head to loop the reins, he spoke quietly to Morgan: "Don't ruffle his feathers."

Morgan's answer to that was cryptic. "How many men's he got in there?"

"Four steady riders, his son Jase, that's all, but this is one outfit that don't hire greenhorns, and the men they keep on year around aren't fellers you'd want to lock horns with too often."

Morgan tied his reins, glanced at Pete Moss, and decided that for a cow outfit to have earned this much respect from a man as trouble-prone as Moss was, it had to be hardy.

Hal Blue came up, nodded at Pete, studied Lew a moment, then said: "We heard about Andy. How is he?"

"Holding his own," replied Pete Moss, and shot Lew Morgan a look.

The weathered, iron-jawed, wispy older man seemed relieved. "Sure glad to hear that." Then, fixing his stare upon the gunman, he also said: "You boys didn't just ride out to tell us that, did you?"

Morgan, who was also addicted to bluntness, appreciated it in the tough-faced old cowman. "No sir," he said, "that's not why we rode out here at all. Is your son handy, Mister Blue?"

The cowman's expression did not change one iota, but he answered slowly, after a delay during which he studied Morgan more closely. "He's in the cook shack. You want to talk to him?"

"Yeah."

"Is it private?"

Lew decided that it wasn't private, because even if he spoke privately to this man's son, before he and Pete Moss had been gone from the yard more than a few minutes, this tough, uncompromising old devil would know all they had discussed.

"It's not exactly private, no, Mister Blue. It's about a Winchester carbine your son had the gunsmith in town put an ivory sight on last summer."

Blue nodded curtly. "I remember. He was going up into the high country after elk, and in among the blasted trees . . . what about that gun?"

"It's the one someone shot the marshal with," said Lew.

Blue blinked, but otherwise his expression did not change. "Are you sure?"

Lew was positive. "Yeah. I'm the feller who potted the bushwhacker atop the store, and, when I got up there, that was the gun lying beside him. It's at the jailhouse now. I wanted your son to tell me the last time he saw that gun."

Hal Blue said: "What did the gunsmith tell you?"

Lew lied like a trooper: "Nothing at all. In fact, he wouldn't talk about the gun, but there was another feller who saw him putting the ivory bead on your son's Winchester. He identified the gun, Mister Blue."

Pete Moss's black eyes flipped from man to man as this conversation was taking place. Blue turned almost curtly and gestured. "Pete, go fetch Jase."

Moss walked away through the mud and slush in the direction of the cook shack. Before he reached the building Hal Blue had another question for Lew Morgan.

"What's your interest, mister? You a law officer?"

Lew gave the identical explanation he had given before back in town. "I don't like bushwhackers. That's my interest. No, I'm not a lawman. Seems to me in a mess like this, all a man needs is a feeling that a son-of-a-bitch who would try and kill someone from a roof top deserves to be caught."

Hal Blue slumped a little, moved over to lean upon the tie rack, and stare into the shadowy wide runway of the horse barn in front of him.

Pete returned across the yard with a lanky, raw-boned, square-jawed range rider who was wearing a thigh-length rider's coat with a tied-down Colt lashed below it on the right side. Jason Blue resembled his father in the face, but that was all; he was a head taller than his father, and rangier in build. When he acknowledged Pete's introduction to Lew Morgan, his eyes were hard and his wide, thin mouth was flattened. He was not hostile, but neither was he friendly.

His father turned. "Where's your carbine?" he asked.

The younger man looked briefly at his father, then back at Lew Morgan. "I left it at the trading barn three, four days ago by accident. It was beginnin' to snow and I flung my saddle on my horse to head for home before the snow built up. The damned gun would take another ten minutes to fix under the fender, so I leaned it in a corner of the grain room." The steady, unsmiling eyes took Lew Morgan's measure. "Pete told me it was my gun that downed Andy Tully."

Lew did not reply right away. He was thinking back to the look he had gotten from Sam Evans, before they had met and while he was walking past on his way out to get his horse. He also remembered the plain hostility of the older man after he had returned and spoken to the trader and the blacksmith. Most of all, he recalled Sam Evans's prediction about Morgan's being next.

Jason Blue said: "Well . . . ?"

Lew answered curtly. "Yeah, it was your gun that downed him."

"What's your interest?"

Lew gazed steadily at the taller, younger man a moment before saying: "The same as yours ought to be."

Jason Blue reddened, but his father broke in to say: "He's looking for the feller who had your gun, Jase, damn it all."

"Yeah?" snapped the raw-boned cowboy. "Then who the hell was it that he shot on Aleck's roof?"

Lew explained: "There were two of them. The one on the roof isn't going anywhere, but I want to know about the other one."

"And you think it was me?" demanded the big cowboy.

Morgan sucked in a long, deep breath before speaking. "You know," he said softly, almost casually, "you're making it kind of hard for me to like you, Jason. No. If I thought that other one was you, I'd take you back to the jailhouse."

Young Blue glared. Then he made a mistake. He took a backward step. To any gunman this kind of a movement, in culmination of frank antagonism, only meant one thing. Lew

Morgan jumped and swung, both at the same time. Jason Blue went over backward in the mud, lay there blinking, and behind Lew his father made a small sound as he pushed clear of the tie rack. That was also a mistake. Lew's right hand moved faster than Pete Moss could discern the draw and came up holding a cocked, ivory-butted Colt.

The father and the son did not seem to breathe for a couple of seconds. Jason was not injured, although he had taken that bony fist across the right-hand jaw and for a moment his mind had gone blank, but it was not blank now when Morgan said: "Get up!"

Jason rolled, planted both hands in the wrist-deep mud, and pushed, then he faced Morgan and shook icy mud off his hands and arms. He was soggy and dirty, and there was a faint stain of red along the lower right side of his face.

Lew said—"Get your horse!"—and flagged in the direction of the barn. When young Blue did not move right away, Lew reached, grabbed his gun, and flung it out into the mud, then he reached and also disarmed the cowboy's father. "Get your damned horse," he reiterated, "or you're going to trot ahead of me all the way back to town on foot!"

The elder Blue said: "Do as he says, Jase."

Pete Moss had not moved. He still remained in place, black eyes wide. Only when Jason Blue shuffled ahead to the barn did Pete move. He went along with the younger man, staying a yard or two behind him all the way. Pete was armed, and, for all Lew Morgan knew, he and Jason Blue might be partners or good friends, in which case the younger Blue would probably come back out of the barn shooting. Lew stepped half over, so that Hal Blue was between him and the barn opening. In this position he could also see the porch and door of the cook shack, where everyone else was eating their late midday meal in unsuspecting innocence.

The cowman waited a long time before he said: "He didn't shoot Andy."

Lew answered shortly: "I know that, damn it. I was there. I saw the man who shot him. But it was his gun."

"But he told you . . . he left it in the. . . ."

"Mister Blue, I'm not taking him back because I'm convinced he had anything to do with what happened to the marshal."

"Then why?"

Lew shot a look over the cowman's head toward the dark barn opening, before answering: "Because I don't like fellers who come at you, when you first meet them, like rampaging longhorn bulls, that's why."

"I'll be ten minutes behind you with my crew," stated the cowman. "We'll see what's going to happen."

"I can tell you what's going to happen, Mister Blue. You crowd me and make war talk, and you're going to get buried, maybe along with some of your riders . . . and maybe even that son of yours that you never took a harness tug to often enough when he was a child. Mister Blue, I don't bluff, not in cards, not in horse trades, and not in times like this."

The older man glanced over at the empty porch of his ranch cook shack, then twisted to look in the barn. He called over there: "Jase, hurry up with that damned horse, otherwise it'll be dark before you fellers get to town!" He swung fully toward Lew Morgan. "All right, mister, you take Jase along. I'll come into town in the morning. Now I'll tell you something else. Last summer someone shot a horse out from under Andy Tully when he was riding over east of town looking for some lost horses. I was on my way back, riding alone, after repping for our outfit at a roundup by the stockmen over there, and come onto Andy pinned to the ground by the leg. I got that dead horse off him, rode him double back to town . . . and he would not talk about that at all, not even to me who's been his friend for ten years.

Not then, and not later, and every time I tried to bring it up, he'd remember he had to go somewhere and do something."

Morgan saw movement in the barn opening and waited. Jase came walking out, muddy and with a more noticeable red mark on his jaw by this time. Behind him, unsmilingly herding the taller and younger man along, was Pete Moss.

Lew holstered his weapon, saw Hal Blue eyeing him, and scowled at the old cowman. "You're saying that Marshal Tully's got some kind of private feud going. Is that it?"

Blue flapped his arms. "I don't know. All I know is what I told you. Last summer someone tried to kill him and killed his horse instead. This year someone tried again, and this time you was handy, or he'd have got away again. If it's a feud, I'll be damned if I know anything about it. I'll also be damned if I can figure out why."

Lew stepped away and gestured for Pete and Jason Blue to mount, then he went over to his sorrel, wheeled the animal so that its body was between him and the others, then, after one final glance in the direction of that empty cook shack porch, he also swung up across leather.

Jase Blue said: "Paw . . . ?"

His father turned. "You damned fool," he said in monumental disgust. "Go on. You asked for it, and this time by God you got it. All he did was ask some questions." The old cowman turned his back and went hiking off in the direction of the cook shack, and Lew nodded for his companions to head out of the yard.

Young Blue did not speak on the ride back. He did not even look at Lew Morgan, but twice he put a reproachful glance upon Pete Moss, and the half-breed just shook his head, both times, as though to indicate that he had done what had seemed to him the best thing to do.

Morgan looped his reins, rolled a smoke, narrowly studied the village as it arose up out of the snow glare of the distance, and for the first time questioned his own part in this affair, which no longer looked like a simple case of bushwhacking, but like some kind of bitter personal feud, and, if that was indeed what it was, then he had no business being involved in it. He didn't know the people; he just barely knew the lawman. But, as Sam Evans had bitterly said, and as Pete Moss had also said, Lew Morgan was involved. The minute he dropped that ambusher atop Aleck Trotter's store, he was involved up to his gullet.

# X

The old horse trader was sitting with Marshal Tully when Lew and Pete walked in, behind Jase Blue. The man on the cot, as well as the big, stooped old frontiersman, looked up, stared, and did not open their mouths.

Lew got the cell-room keys from their peg behind the desk and, without speaking, took his prisoner on through and locked him in. When he returned, Pete Moss was explaining to Evans and Tully what had happened at the cow outfit.

Lew did not linger, and that puzzled the other men, too. He left the jailhouse office without a word to any of them, not even to Pete Moss who had been his partisan at the ranch, and walked southward through the waning light. The road was a millrace and every eave in town was dripping cold water. Two sets of deep, fresh ruts in the roadway indicated that a fairly heavy vehicle, perhaps a stage, had come into town from the south. Lew studied those tracks with more than casual interest all the way southward to the blacksmith's shop, and, when he entered, he asked Jase Buell if, indeed, a stage had reached town.

The blacksmith, in the act of cleaning his forge, a job he could only do when business was slack for a day or two, paused in the dusty soot to confirm that one of the coaches from down south had arrived in town about two hours earlier, and had gone on, after dumping the mail sack. For a while after this information had been volunteered, Lew Morgan watched Buell picking at the caked ash and clinkers. Apparently the forge had not been cleaned in a very long time, for all that insulating ash to have got that hard. Also, experienced smiths did not clean out all the ash; sometimes the firebrick lining on the bottom was burned out, and all that kept a forge from losing its fire through a rotten bottom were the layers of cement-like ash. Jase Buell did not gouge deep enough to put this notion to the test, and, while he was speculatively probing the possibility that his forge was burned through, Lew Morgan asked him if he remembered seeing young Blue ride into town, or out of town, three days earlier.

The blacksmith paused at his picking, mopped his sooty face, and answered affirmatively. "Yeah. I saw him ride out. I didn't see him ride in, though. That would be the day the snow commenced, and I was pretty busy in here that day."

"Old Evans was pretty busy that day, too," said Lew. "I guess folks figured they might be in for a storm, eh?"

Buell agreed with that. "Yeah, I expect that's what they figured. Sam Evans was like a kitten in a box of shavings. He had horses on the range he had to fetch in, and he had three teams he wanted snow shod with caulked shoes, and, if that didn't have him humping bad enough, his day man had quit the day before so he was short-handed." Buell looked up with a quick smile. "When old Sam's pressed, he gets cranky as hell. I was leading one of the teams over here through the back alley and he got mad because I didn't take 'em out the front way." Buell wagged his head and went back to his picking in the stone-hard ash. "It don't make any difference which door I use, this here shop's just as close one way as the other. But I knew what was the matter. I've seen old Sam get worked up before. Art

Lane was standing there and he just shook his head."

Lew rolled and lit a cigarette, watched Buell at his unpleasant chore a little longer, then walked out of the smithy, crossed the road, and headed northward up past Pete's pool room and past Walt Kenyon's harness shop. When he entered the little building next door, the gunsmith was replacing a pistol barrel in someone's old Colt, and could not look up right then, so Lew closed the door and went over to stand by the stove. As Lew stood and waited, he gazed out the window. It offered an excellent view of the southward roadway down as far as the jailhouse. Northward, the view was restricted, but outward, directly in front of the gunsmith's shop, it offered an excellent view, and if a man moved closer to the front wall, he could even see beyond town, southward—and also southwestward as far as Tully's house and barn, and even beyond that to the open country farther off.

Lane straightened up from his workbench wiping both hands upon an oily rag, and turned to face his visitor with an apprehensive look. "I saw you and Pete Moss heading out of town," he said, "like you was heading for the Blue outfit."

Morgan answered the question that had not been asked, but that clearly had been uppermost in the gunsmith's mind. "I told Hal Blue someone who saw you putting the ivory bead on the gun recognized it, and told me about you doing that work on it."

"That's no good," stated the gunsmith. "Old Blue is no fool."

Morgan shrugged. "It'll be up to you, if he comes around, but what I want to know at this moment is why you went out to Marshal Tully's place and led away his horse?"

"Because I knew there'd be no one to look after it," stated the gunsmith.

Morgan studied the taller man with frank skepticism. "Then why didn't you also lead away his pair of team horses? There wouldn't be anyone to look after them, either."

"Well . . . I might have gone back for them."

Morgan dryly said: "Yeah. You might have. But you didn't. What's special about the blood bay, Mister Lane?"

"He's one hell of a horse. I used to own him. I didn't like the notion of his being out there with no one to look after him."

Morgan did not take his eyes off the taller man as he stood for a while without speaking, and under this gaze the gunsmith seemed to wilt a little, seemed to grow nervous and apprehensive. "I'll tell you why you went out there and got that damned horse," stated Lew Morgan. "Because you were already down there below the jailhouse, Mister Lane. You were down there in the snowstorm somewhere south of the jailhouse, watching the jailhouse as well as the roof top across from the jailhouse, and, when the son-of-a-bitch on the roof top downed the marshal the way it was supposed to happen, you couldn't get back up here to your shop right away, because I came out and shot the feller on the store roof. So, to make it look like you had a legitimate reason for being down there, so far from your gun shop, you just hiked right on southward, out there to Tully's place, and brought back the horse, using him as your excuse for being down there in the first place. And folks believed you."

Art Lane stopped wiping his hands but still held the cloth as he stood mutely staring over at the man in front of his stove. He finally said—"That's the craziest thing I ever heard."—in a subdued tone of voice, and twisted to put aside the oily cloth. "Why would I get mixed up in anything like that bushwhack?"

"That's what I'm waiting to hear," said Morgan, and walked over to the door as he also said: "You think it over, and, when you're ready, come on down to the jailhouse." He reached for the latch. "Something else occurred to me this afternoon, Mister Lane. Who else in Forrest owns guns capable of firing one hell of a distance?"

Lane raised a hand to push away a heavy lock of hair. "What d' you mean? Of course I got rifles. That's my trade."

"I mean, Mister Lane, that last summer the feller who tried to shoot Marshal Tully was so damned far off when he pulled the trigger, that the slug dropped just enough to hit his horse instead. How do I know he was so far off? Because Hal Blue came along a minute or so later and found Tully nailed beneath the dead horse . . . and he did not see the bushwhacker, which he would have done if you'd been closer, and since he also did not hear the gunshot . . . which he would have done because he was only a minute's ride away, if you hadn't been so damned far off . . . it had to be someone with a long-range rifle, and the ability to use one."

"I'm not the only one in this country who owns a long-range. . . ."

"No, you likely aren't," conceded Morgan, without allowing the gunsmith to finish his statement, "but you're the only one who was also watching when the feller on the roof tried his ambush, and you're the only one who was at the trading barn three days back when young Blue rode out in a hurry, and left his carbine behind . . . who seems to have had a reason for taking that gun."

Morgan leaned on the door, holding the latch, while across the room at his workbench the gunsmith said nothing until he had picked up a wrench and turned his back on Morgan as he said: "You're wrong as hell. But go on down there and wait, if you like." As Lane leaned over the gun, Morgan opened the door, stepped out, closed the door, and cast a sideward glance at the sun, which was dropping away fast, and turning redder as it did so. Then he glanced southward in the direction of the jailhouse, did not look to his left in the gun shop window, and started away.

But he only went as far as the dogtrot south of the harness

shop. He ducked in, down there, and hastened through into the rear alleyway, where dusk had already arrived, and startled two foraging dogs, who tucked tail and fled at sight of Morgan. He eased up along the rear wall of Walt Kenyon's building, stepped back where three overflowing wooden trash barrels stood, and settled in for a long wait, watching the rear door of the gun shop, lying about sixty feet northward.

Those two dogs had ducked through rotten baseboards in an old fence along the opposite side of the alleyway. They poked their heads out to scan the area of their recent foraging, and did not notice the man in the gloom by the trash barrels, probably because Morgan was standing perfectly still, but as they began edging through into the alley again, a door opened on Morgan's left, Walt Kenyon stepped forth to fling out a pan of brown-stained water, and both dogs pulled back to disappear, this time without returning.

Kenyon would have seen Morgan if he had actually looked, but his brief glance up and down the alleyway was an instinctive thing, something he had been doing for many years and he actually did not notice particular items, only generalities. The shadowy gloom no doubt helped, also. Kenyon stepped back inside, slammed his door, shot the bolt, and Lew Morgan sighed, then resumed his vigil.

He was about to give it up a half hour later. Waiting like that, motionless and foot-weary, made a half hour seem like half a lifetime. Nor was there anything in the silent, empty alley to hold his attention. He wanted to roll a smoke to pass the time, but did not do it. He went back over in his mind all that he had said to the gunsmith, twice, then that also palled. Finally he started to raise a hand to tip back his hat when he heard a bolt being slammed back, hard. All his attention immediately focused upon the warped, weathered door in the back of Lane's shop as it opened slowly, the gunsmith stepped out without his apron and wearing both a rusty old black coat and a stiff-brimmed hat, then turned to lock the door.

Morgan palmed his Colt, took four big steps clear of the trash barrels, waited until Art Lane was pocketing his key and starting to turn away, then Morgan said: "Mister Lane."

The gunsmith whirled, right hand lost inside the old black coat, but he had no way under the sun to do it, so he froze in that position, looking from Lew to the ivory-stocked Colt aimed at his chest.

"The jailhouse is out front, and southward, not back here, and northward," said Morgan. "Bring the gun out, Mister Lane . . . with your fingertips . . . and drop it."

The lanky man did not obey at once. He looked past Morgan, looked at the gun pointing squarely at him, pulled himself slightly upright, then he finally brought forth his right hand, very slowly, and dropped a Colt Lightning six-shooter in the slush at his feet. It was a handsomely blued, new-looking weapon with a remade handle covered with fine-textured staghorn.

Morgan holstered his Colt as the gunsmith finally recovered sufficiently to say: "I live north of here. What's wrong with a man closing shop at five o'clock and heading for home and supper?"

Morgan's answer was bland. "Nothing. Only I thought we'd agreed you'd be coming down to the jailhouse, first."

"You said that!" exclaimed the gunsmith. "Not me. I got nothing to go down there about."

Morgan stared at the taller man. "Walk ahead of me. Head on south, out of here, and over to the jailhouse. And Mister Lane . . . you know better'n to try and run or do anything foolish, don't you? Move out!"

Lane walked past and kept on walking. He did not do anything reckless, nor did Lew Morgan expect him to. Lane was not a man who would be foolish with someone behind him carrying a gun. No gunsmith would be that foolish.

When they emerged from a side street below the general store and had the jailhouse in sight across the way, there was not a soul in sight on either plank walk, north or south. It was, fortunately for Morgan, suppertime in Forrest.

# XI

Marshal Tully was alone when Morgan entered with his latest prisoner, and did not rouse fully from his lethargic slumber until Morgan had locked the gunsmith in a cell, but as Morgan turned from replacing the keys upon their wall peg, the lawman was gazing steadily at him. Morgan sighed, pulled out his makings, took the chair Sam Evans had been using the last time Morgan was in the office, and loosened all over as he leaned methodically and thoughtfully to manufacture a smoke.

Andy Tully said nothing. He looked a little flushed, a little feverish, but his eyes were clear.

Morgan lit up, punched back his hat, leaned back to cross his legs, and, as he blew smoke, he said: "Marshal, it's been a damned busy day, and I still got to go out and feed your team before supper."

Tully got straight to the point. "Who did you just bring in? Wasn't it Art Lane?"

"Yeah, it was Lane." Morgan smoked, narrowly eyed the large man on the cot, and did not offer any more than that, so the lawman was forced to ask why Morgan had brought in the gunsmith, too, and Morgan's reply was spoken slowly. "Strange how things happen, Marshal. Now, when I first heard of this village, the fellers I was talking to were kind of questionable characters. I don't know whether the law wanted them or not, but they were on the fringe, by my estimation, and they told me Forrest was out of the way and quiet. Maybe they figured me to be on the fringe, too, for all I know. Anyway, I came up here . . . damned near didn't make it, too . . . but I came up here, and the first damned night, in your barn, I ran into trouble, and the very next morning, before my stomach was even settled, you were shot down in the snow out front. Marshal, I don't know the country or the people, and I don't figure to hang around long enough to make their acquaintances . . . but in one day I've picked up some information that just don't fit very well. For example, the feller who shot that horse out from under you last summer. Do you know who he was?"

Marshal Tully's gaze did not waver, but he did not utter a sound. He lay there gazing steadily at Lew Morgan as though he had been carved out of stone.

Lew sighed. "You know. You know damned well who he was. When you saw the Winchester I brought in this morning, you recognized it, too. Marshal, if you want to set yourself up as a sitting duck for someone who's out to kill you, I can't stop you, but my problem is that since I shot the bushwhacker across the road this morning, and roughed up old man Blue's son, and just now locked up the gunsmith, I'm in this just about as deep as you are . . . so you could sure help us both a lot if you'd give me some idea what's going on here."

Tully said: "Pete says the snow is melting off fast. Tonight'd be a good time for you to saddle up and ride on out."

Morgan inhaled, exhaled, and regarded the wounded man almost stoically. "Maybe," he conceded. "The trouble is . . . even if someone would let me do that, I'd be bothered all the rest of my life about your riddle."

"You'd better go," said Andy Tully. "A stage arrived in Forrest this morning from the south." Tully's steady gaze remained fixed upon the gunman, and Lew Morgan picked up the innuendo at once, because he had wondered about that stage arriving since he'd first seen the wheel marks in the roadway.

"What did it bring?" he asked.

Andy did not answer, did not even speak for a while, but eventually he said: "I'm obliged to you. The way Pete and I see it, Lew, if you hadn't jumped through the doorway this morning and nailed that bastard on the roof, he'd have shot me again, sure, and I'd have been an easy target the second time, snow or no snow. So I'm right obliged, believe me. But there's no need for you to hang around any longer, and the roads are all pretty well open by now. You could cover a lot of ground before sunup. You could even be up in. . . ."

"Like I said, Marshal, I'd always be wondering."

Tully finally moved his glance, let it roam to the far front wall, and up along the fly-specked ceiling. With one hand he groped for the pony of brandy, nearly empty now, and raised it to drain the last drop, and afterward made a face. "I don't see how Jeb drinks that stuff," he muttered, letting the little bottle fall to the floor at bedside.

Morgan shook his head. "You're not going to give me any answers, are you?"

Tully brought his gaze back to the other man's face. "All you have to know is that someone tried to bushwhack me, and you jumped him and shot him, which saved my life. Lew, most men live out their lives without ever knowing they've done that much. It ought to be enough. You came in here, got to be a hero, and rode on."

"Hero, my butt," stated the gunman, and leaned to grasp the arms of the chair as though to arise. "I'll get the answers, Andy. I've got two fellers in the cells, and one of them I know for a fact can answer some questions."

"Jase Blue?"

"No, damn it, not Jase Blue. He's just a disagreeable bastard who happens to be the apple of his paw's eye. Art Lane!"

"What can Art tell you?"

"Why he shot that horse out from under you last summer, why he was trying to kill you when he hit the horse instead."

Andy Tully's gaze raised again to the ceiling and remained there, fixed upon something. "Lew, what the hell are you trying to do? Art won't tell you anything, and neither will I. And neither will anyone else."

Before Morgan could reply the door opened and big, stooped old Sam Evans walked in, looked at the man in the chair from beneath shaggy eyebrows, looked at the man on the cot, then closed the door as he said: "Andy, you know what this feller's went and done? He got Art Lane just like he got Jase Blue. Now, by God, Jeb and me and some of the other folks think he's beginning to run the town, and, hell, for all any of us know, he could be . . . well, anyone at all."

The horse trader had changed that, at the last moment, when he saw the way Lew Morgan was looking at him. But he remained doggedly indignant, and stood back there by the door, looking bleak and defiant.

Tully did not even turn his head. "Go on home," he told the trader.

Evans straightened as much as his perpetual stoop would allow, his pale, malevolent gaze lying hard upon the injured lawman. "That's all you got to say? For me to go on home and leave this feller to raise hob with our community? Andy, we're not going to stand for it!"

Lew arose and ambled to the corner of the desk where he was closer to the old frontiersman. "Sam, according to Jase Blue, he left his booted carbine in the back of your barn three days back, when he left out of town in a hurry to get home before he had to plow through snowdrifts."

The old man's malevolent eyes swung. He looked like a gaunt old bear ready to spring, when he answered: "What of it? Folks are always leavin' things in my barn."

"Did you see that gun back there, Sam?" asked Lew.

"How do I know whether I saw it or not? I don't recollect seeing it, but, hell, I could have walked past it ten times. That was a busy day for me, and. . . ."

"You saw it!" exclaimed Lew Morgan. "You damned well saw it, Sam."

Tully turned his head; so did the old horse trader. They looked at Morgan without speaking, Tully, with strong curiosity, and Sam Evans with a glare that would have downed Morgan, if looks could have killed.

Lew spoke again, while the older men watched him. "Why did you raise hell with Jase Buell for taking horses out the back way, Sam? You didn't usually care which doorway he used. But you cared that day, and you got mad at him about it. Want me to tell you why? Because you knew Blue's Winchester was against the wall, back there, and you didn't want anyone else to remember seeing it there."

Tully's gaze raised slightly, seeking the face of the big old man in front of the door, but Sam Evans's malevolent expression faded before a sneering smile. "What the hell are you talking about, Morgan? You trying to make out that I had something to do with that bushwhack?"

"I'm just trying to fit a lot of pieces together to make some sense," stated Lew Morgan, "and so far about all I've done is get in a little deeper every time something turns up. But you knew that gun was there, Sam, and you'll never convince me otherwise, any more than you'll convince me that's not why you raised Cain with the blacksmith for not going out the front way of your barn."

Evans flung out both arms. "I shot Andy, then?"

Lew sighed. "Don't be funny with me. I've already got two cells full, out back, and there's not a hell of a lot more room . . . but I'll sure use what there is. Of course you didn't shoot him.

The bushwhacker's laid out in the icehouse. Just explain one thing to me, Sam. How did that bushwhacker get young Blue's Winchester?"

"How would I know anything like that?" snarled the old man. "I just told you . . . that was one hell of a day for me. My latest day man had quit the morning before, after only working three days, and there was the storm coming on, and I was swamped with things I had to do, and. . . ."

"And you knew that Winchester was there, Sam, and you didn't want Jase Buell to remember having seen it there. Why?"

The horse trader turned to glare at Marshal Tully. He seemed about to explode. Then he swung about, wrenched open the door, stepped out into the evening, and slammed the door so hard the crockery coffee cups suspended from pegs near the stove vibrated.

Lew leaned against the desk, gazing disinterestedly at the scattered contents of the dead bushwhacker's pockets, while across the room on his cot, Marshal Tully closed his eyes and lay perfectly still. Lew slowly raised his eyes from the dead man's affects, turned and gazed at Jase Blue's leaning carbine over by the gun rack, then he turned on his heel and walked out of the jailhouse, paused out front to lock the door from the roadside, and, when he turned, he peered southward down through the thickening darkness in the direction of the trading barn, but there was no sign of Sam Evans. He also scanned the roof tops across the road, before striking out for the opposite plank walk. Over there, he yanked loose the tie down on his hip-holstered Colt and walked up to the pool hall, which was completely empty except for Pete Moss, who was racking balls at one of the tables in preparation of the nightly trade, which would not be along until after supper. Pete did not straighten up, but he looked up when Lew walked in. Then he groaned loudly enough for Morgan to hear the sound, completed racking the billiard balls, and slowly wagged his head, black eyes fixed upon the gunman.

"You got the whole damned town upset," he grumbled, pushing clear of the table to head for the back of his little bar, where he set up two glasses and one bottle. "Folks don't know what to do, or what to think. Why'd you lock up Art Lane?"

"Because he's the one who shot a horse out from under Andy Tully last summer," replied Morgan, watching Pete pour their glasses full.

Moss raised surprised dark eyes. "He is? You sure?"

"Yeah. I'm sure enough."

"Well then, hell, he's the other one of those bushwhackers."

"Maybe," said Morgan, gingerly raising the glass so as not to spill a drop. He downed the liquor, gasped for air, drummed atop the counter with two fists, and, when Pete Moss got a pained and disgusted look upon his face, said: "It's not that bad." Morgan shoved the glass an arm's length from him. "Yes, it is that bad. It's awful. I've likely just been poisoned," he gasped.

Moss slammed down the bottle and swore, then he downed his straight shot without a quiver, but instead of pursuing the topic of his acidy, green whiskey, he said: "There was two of them. You got one atop Aleck's store. Art Lane tried to shoot Andy last summer. That'd be the other one. What more do you want?"

"I want someone to tell me why people want Marshal Tully dead," stated Morgan. "And I'll tell you something else, Pete. There were two men in Tully's barn with carbines and some notion of killing him. I spoiled that. Then one man got killed trying a bushwhack, and his partner . . . I'll give you the biggest odds you ever heard of . . . was Art Lane, but damn it all, somehow or other that old bastard who trades horses south of town had a hand in this mess, too."

Pete pushed his glass away, leaned down upon both arms, and with a strained look on his face that puckered his entire low, broad forehead said: "Sam Evans?"

"Yeah, Sam Evans. And maybe you, too, for all I know. But there sure as hell is a conspiracy in Forrest to kill Andrew Tully. Now, that's what I got to figure out. Why do so many people want him dead?"

The half-breed turned, regarded his offensive bottle of whiskey for a moment, then reached to refill his own glass again. He looked more baffled than irritable, for a change.

# XII

Lew left Pete's pool hall and walked directly to the apothecary's shop, but did not knock on the door. He instead hiked around back, through slushy, cold snow and cloying dark mud that caked so badly on his boots that he had to pause and find a flat stick to scrape his boots with. There was a light in one of the small rooms in the rear of Jeb Hazelton's shop. Lew considered it, then went over to the door beyond the lighted window, and gently knocked. Moments passed before the apothecary arrived and looked out. He was fully dressed, and, when he asked who was out there, his whiskey breath was strongly noticeable. Lew felt like swearing; for what he had in mind he did not need an inebriated apothecary. He said his name, then pushed the door aside, walked in, closed the door, and gazed at the man in front of him with the flushed face and glassy eyes. "Why in the hell," he said complainingly, "don't you just do your drinking before supper, instead of half the lousy night?"

Hazelton drew himself up erectly. "What are you doing here? What do you want?"

"I want you to come to the icehouse with me," said Lew, and reached to push the apothecary back in the direction of a small kitchen. "But first you're going to drink a pot of java."

"I am not going to do any such a thing," replied the indignant druggist.

Lew grabbed his coat, shoved him into a chair, and thrust a rigid finger into the apothecary's face. "Oh, yes, you are. Where is the lamp?"

Hazelton pointed to a table in a dark corner, and, when Lew started to move away, Hazelton arose from the chair. Lew could move very fast, as Jason Blue had discovered. He grabbed the druggist again, but this time he hauled him physically over where the lamp was, and slammed him hard against a wall.

"You're going to guzzle java, Hazelton, if I have to straddle you and pour it down your gullet!"

Hazelton did not flinch. He gave Lew stare for stare. But he also became resigned, and, when Lew found the pot and poked up a fire beneath it in the stove, Hazelton walked back to the chair and sat down. He watched everything Morgan did, then he said: "What in the world do you want to go to the icehouse for?"

"To look at that feller I shot on the store roof," Lew replied. "He's still there, isn't he?"

"Yes. You said not to bury him, didn't you? Of course he's still there. But what do you expect to do, looking at a dead man?"

Lew pulled up a second chair and sat facing the druggist. "You're drunk, but you're sure not fuzzy-headed."

Hazelton arched his brows and looked squarely at the gunman. "I'm never fuzzy-minded," he affirmed. "I am a person who can handle liquor."

Lew said: "Yeah. I've heard that before." Then he leaned a little. "Mister Hazelton, I need a name for that bushwhacker."

Hazelton sniffed. "You expect to get one from looking at his corpse in the icehouse, Mister Morgan? They don't talk. I'm sure you know that."

Lew waited for the druggist to say more, but Hazelton went silent, and boldly stared, with a hint of a cold smile around his lips. "Why would I know about dead men, Mister Hazelton?"

"Because, Mister Morgan, the stage came through from the south this morning . . . with last month's newspapers from the cities, and there is an article in one of them about a man named Morgan who served cattle interests in New Mexico Territory." Hazelton paused, but continued coldly to smile. "Would you care to see the newspaper? It's in the parlor. I can get it."

Morgan didn't care about the newspaper; he only cared that it had arrived with that article in it. The snowfall had insulated him for a few days. He had thought it might insulate him longer, perhaps for as much as a week. He said: "Don't believe everything you read in newspapers. I said I needed a name for that dead man. You're going to help me get it."

Hazelton was baffled enough to forget, momentarily at any rate, their previous topic. "How? At least two dozen people in town saw that body when it was brought down from the roof, and the man was a complete stranger. You heard that. What can I do?"

Lew went to the stove, filled a big china cup with black coffee, returned, and handed it to the druggist. "Drink," he commanded. "Down to the last drop."

Hazelton drank the coffee and Lew went back to refill the cup, but Hazelton held up a hand when Lew came back, with the cup held forth. "Morgan, one cup is plenty. I don't need any damned coffee, anyway. I'm not drunk." He looked around, then back at Lew again. "Not that drunk, anyway, not so drunk I can't go out to the icehouse with you." He arose from the chair as though to prove his point.

Morgan put aside the coffee. He preferred not wasting more time, so he would accept Jeb Hazelton at his word. He went over to the door, opened it, and looked back. Hazelton ambled over, sniffed the chilly night, then went over to a wall rack, took down a coat and hat, and put them on as he returned, and passed out into the darkness. As Morgan closed the door, the lanky, grizzled man lifted the hat, ran crooked fingers through his gray mop, replaced the hat, and eyed Lew Morgan with a skeptical regard.

"No one knew him, Morgan, and going over to the icehouse isn't going to help one damned. . . .'"

"Someone knew him," stated Lew, and gestured. "Lead the way." As the druggist turned to march up the alley, Morgan walked slightly to one side, and slightly behind, the taller man. "Someone had to know him, Mister Hazelton, because he didn't just drop from the sky onto that lousy roof top."

The druggist turned a withering gaze upon the gunman. "What are you talking about? He could have simply ridden into town this morning or yesterday, and. . . ."

"No one rode in, except me, Mister Hazelton, in that damned snowstorm, and I wouldn't have done it if I'd had any idea what kind of a place I was riding into. No one rode in, and that's pretty darned common knowledge. So . . . he had to be here already, didn't he? And if he was, Mister Hazelton, then he damned well stayed somewhere. He didn't burrow into a snowbank and den up like a bear, did he? Someone had to know him, didn't they?"

The apothecary halted and pursed his lips, staring into empty space for a moment. "I forgot," he said, starting forward again. "I forgot about the darned storm, Mister Morgan. You're right, no one would have ridden in, because the trails and roads were just about impassable. He had already to be here."

This fresh train of thought seemed to absorb the apothecary's interest the balance of their walk up in the direction of the low-roofed, massively thick, log-walled icehouse. He had nothing more to say until, in front of the icehouse door as he groped in a pocket for a key, he put a respectful look upon Morgan. "I've been underestimating you."

Morgan leaned slightly to look past at the massive brass lock. Hazelton had found the key and was also turning, moving a little as though he would have to stoop, when a blasting gunshot sounded, multiplied even in its roaring echoes, because of the hush of the star-bright night, and a bullet struck the door less than six inches from Jeb Hazelton's head, where he had just begun to stoop and reach for the lock. The bullet tore vertical splinters from the thick old door, showering both men with them. Hazelton was rooted in place with pure astonishment, but Lew Morgan reached with his left hand to give the apothecary a violent sideward shove as he himself sprang clear, drawing as he moved.

There was no second gunshot. Jeb Hazelton scrambled around the south side of the icehouse and crouched there while Morgan sought the background shadows of a shed belonging to a dark, two-storied frame house a few yards northward. He waited a long while before deciding the bushwhacker had fled, and even then he returned to the area of the icehouse very cautiously.

Somewhere not too distant, someone opened a stuck window with a mighty shove, but that was the only sound throughout town to indicate the gunshot had awakened people. By the time Morgan came up from behind the icehouse to where the apothecary was hiding, Hazelton had recovered from his initial shock and was frankly and suddenly very sober and shaky.

"My God," he whispered to Morgan. "He was trying to kill me."

Lew holstered his Colt, looking left and right and gradually beginning to accept the fact that the assassin had fled, as he said: "Maybe. And maybe he wasn't trying to hit you at all.

Maybe he wanted me. In either case, it was pretty damned close."

Hazelton straightened up, drew his coat closer at the neck, and his fear suddenly became righteous anger. "Why, that murderous son-of-a-bitch," he said a little breathlessly, glaring around him.

Lew told the apothecary to remain where he was, and walked up to the front of the icehouse, paused briefly, then crossed the alleyway heading in the direction from which that gunshot had come. The bushwhacker had been standing in some patchy, crusted snow on the north side of a store that fronted on the main roadway. His tracks would be much clearer in daylight, but even by star shine they were clearly readable when Lew found them, and slowly traced them down through to the front roadway, where they turned southward, but he could only track the man a short way once the tracks reached the plank walk by the gobbets of mud left behind. He stepped to the front of a store, made a close examination of the entire roadway, southward, saw no one at all, not even over in front of the pool hall, and finally turned back.

Jeb Hazelton hardly allowed Morgan to come up before he made an indignant announcement: "From now on, by God, I'm not going out at night without my gun."

Morgan did not comment; even if Hazelton had been armed, if luck hadn't been with him—with them both—that bushwhacker would have killed one or the other of them, and, as it was, it had been not only too close for comfort, but afterward there had been no target to fire back at, so Hazelton, with a gun, wouldn't have been any better off than he was now without a gun. Lew squinted at the star-bright sky, which had no trace of a moon in it, then shook his head. Usually he liked having a moon up there; tonight, thank the Lord, there hadn't been one.

The apothecary interrupted his thoughts with a question:

"Do you still want to look at that confounded corpse, Mister Morgan? Because if you don't, I'd like to get back home. I need a drink."

Morgan's answer was short. "Maybe tomorrow. Come along. I'll see you back down the alley."

Neither of them spoke until they reached the alley door of the apothecary's shop. Hazelton, stone sober and cold, addressed Morgan in a different-sounding voice as he stood with his back to the door: "I think it was you he was trying to kill, Mister Morgan. I think your poking and prying has got someone worried. Well, good night. If you want to go back up to the icehouse tomorrow, stop by and I'll go with you."

After they parted and Morgan was walking pensively back in the direction of the jailhouse to bed down, a horse neighed down at the lower end of the village, and over east of town somewhere a big dog barked in a booming way. Otherwise, Forrest was as quiet as it normally was this time of year, a few hours after nightfall.

Morgan entered the jailhouse, saw that Andrew Tully was sleeping, felt the chill in the room, and went over quietly to open the stove and toss in a couple more lengths of wood. He discarded his hat, turned the lamp down low, rolled a smoke, and went to stand in thought over at the front window, gazing out into the empty, soft-lighted muddy roadway.

Two, hell. There were three of them. The dead one, the locked-up gunsmith, and whoever that had been who had slipped along behind him, waiting for just the right time to kill him. He sighed. Tomorrow, he was going to wring answers from someone without much regard as to how he did it, or who he did it to. As long as the attack had been against someone else, he could afford to be restrained in his efforts to find out who—and what—he was up against in Forrest, but the moment he also became a target for assassination things changed drastically. Something else made him feel the need for a hasty resolution of this mess he was involved in—the arrival of those damned newspapers from the south. He now had very little time left.

# XIII

For many years Aleck Trotter had been arising very early, shortly before dawn in fact, eating his breakfast, then walking briskly to the store, summer and winter. It was his idea of a good exercise for a man who did not ordinarily get much exercise. This morning, as he hiked through the pale light, his footfalls echoing solidly, his alertly interested glance ranging left and right, he got a surprise. Lew Morgan was over beside one of the stores on the east side of the roadway, quartering around with his head down, like a bloodhound seeking a scent. Aleck slowed his gait a little to watch, but the moment Lew halted and raised his head, Aleck picked up the gait and looked directly ahead down the south roadway as though he had noticed nothing.

Lew saw Trotter, ignored him, and went on with his examination of the area where that assassin had been standing last night, when he'd tried to kill someone. When he was satisfied the spongy, snow-patched ground would yield no more secrets, Morgan went over to the plank walk where the gobbets of mud still lay, and gazed around at the awakening town.

Smoke was beginning to rise into the pale, clear air from dozens of stoves—cooking stoves and heating stoves. The scent of burning pine and fir was fragrant in the sharp, chill air of dawn. Morgan leaned and traced out the mud marks as far as they went, which was only about a hundred and fifty feet southward. He finally put his attention upon the steamy window of the café across the road, and southward—between the pool hall and the general store—and waited until a paunchy man wearing a soiled flour-sack apron opened the door, looked around, spat, then went back inside leaving his roadside door unlocked. Then Lew ambled over, kicked off roadway mud, and walked in.

He had seen no one enter ahead of him. In fact, he knew perfectly well no one had preceded him because he had watched the café man unlock his door for the day's business—nevertheless, Pete Moss was drinking a cup of coffee at the low wooden counter.

Lew walked up, straddled the bench, leaned down, and looked curiously at the half-breed. "How the hell did you get in here?" he asked.

Pete made an airy gesture. "Through the back door. He opens up back there first." Pete cupped both hands around the hot cup. "What were you doing across the road?"

Instead of giving a direct answer, Lew said: "Did you hear a gunshot last night?"

Pete shook his head, a frown forming on his low forehead. "No, but that don't mean there wasn't one. I sleep like a dead man."

"Some son-of-a-bitch took a shot at me . . . or the apothecary . . . out front of the icehouse."

Moss's black eyes widened to their limit. "The hell," he murmured. "Any ideas?"

"That's what I was doing across the road . . . trying to figure something out from where he was standing when he cut loose."

"And . . . ?"

The café man came, nodded woodenly at Lew, slid a big platter of fried potatoes, ham, and a matched pair of greasy fried eggs in front of Pete Moss, then he cocked an enquiring eyebrow, and Morgan said: "The same." As the café man padded back to his cooking area, Lew wagged his head. "I'm not all that good at reading tracks, Pete. What I need's an Indian."

Moss was picking up his eating utensils when he said: "How

about a half Indian?"

Lew grinned. "Not good enough. I don't need someone to read half the sign. I need someone who can read it all."

Moss smiled, then lit into his breakfast and did not speak again until Morgan's food had also arrived, and the gunman was also eating. Then Moss turned, one cheek distended with food, and said: "You didn't say whether you had any ideas about who tried to shoot you."

Morgan answered evasively: "What puzzles me is how he knew Hazelton and I were up there."

"Well, hell," returned the half-breed, "he followed you. What else would he have done? Maybe he'd been keeping an eye on you since earlier . . . maybe since you left the jailhouse when old Evans and I were in there talking to Andy."

Morgan shrugged. "Maybe."

"Well . . . who was he?"

Morgan turned a crafty smile upon the pool hall proprietor. "A tall feller with big feet who is a pretty fair shot with a Winchester, who doesn't want me to keep on sticking my nose in, and, when he ran away, he cut down through the village southward." Morgan's smile lingered as he studied the half-breed a moment, then said: "Pete, what happened around Forrest a year or two back?"

"What happened?"

"Yeah. Marshal Tully's been here ten or eleven years, then last year someone tried to kill him, and again this year, only this time they meant to do it bad. What happened that stirred folks up?"

Pete Moss glanced over where the café man was working and turned back a moment later to say: "I don't know." Then he twisted fully around at the sound of mounted men out in the roadway, looked through the steamy window a moment, and settled forward with a dry comment. "Your friends from the

Blue cow outfit just rode in. They're tying up across the road at the jailhouse."

Morgan reached for his coffee, gulped it down, jumped up, and tossed a silver dollar atop the counter. Pete Moss also arose. As Morgan headed for the door, Moss called after him: "It's the whole crew! I'd better come along."

Morgan said nothing one way or the other, but when he emerged from the café, old Hal Blue was just finishing at the hitch rack, stepping from the muddy roadway to the muddy plank walk. One of his riders mumbled something, and the cowman slowly turned, looking squarely over where Lew Morgan and Pete Moss were heading over toward him.

The sun had arrived while Morgan had been inside the café. It was still too fresh actually to send forth much warmth, but the promise of a warm day was in whatever light heat it was now projecting. Probably, by evening or tomorrow morning, the snow would be restricted to a few white patches here and there, on the lee side of trees or boulders or buildings. Early springtime did not last very long, even in Colorado, before late spring and summer arrived. Morgan shot one glance at the position of the sun, just before moving out and around the saddle animals and reaching the plank walk, near Hal Blue.

Pete Moss, who had said the Blue outfit did not hire novices or weaklings, moved in nearby and said something in a light tone to one of those four weathered, roughly dressed Blue range riders. The cowboy nodded gravely at Pete Moss, but did not answer. He, like the other three armed range men, were concentrating their full attention upon their employer—and the husky man beside him, who had that ivory-stocked Colt in his holster.

Hal Blue said: "Well, Mister Morgan, you got your other bushwhacker?"

Lew considered, then turned to lead the way inside. He did

not look at the range riders, and neither did Hal Blue. They remained outside with Pete Moss.

The office was warm because Lew had piled wood into the stove a couple of hours earlier, and Marshal Tully, looking either flushed from his wound, or from the excessive heat in the office, turned his head and gazed at the pair of men who had entered his jailhouse. He said: "Hal, I wouldn't have locked Jase up."

Blue smiled thinly. "I know you wouldn't have, Andy. But at least a man gets his rest in a jail cell." He walked over, looked at the inert man on the cot, and said—"You need a shave, Andy."—and smiled.

Lew Morgan, watching, felt a first stirring of liking for Hal Blue. Whatever his faults, and he certainly had them, any man who lived as tough a life as Blue lived, had faults. Blue smiled at his old friend on the jailhouse cot, and teased him, which was in Lew Morgan's view a lot better than sympathy any day of the year. When a man felt bad, he didn't need long faces and soft voices to make him feel worse.

Morgan took down the cell-room keys and wordlessly went through the cell-room door to release Jason Blue. Art Lane, leaning upon the front steel straps of his cage, owlishly watched until Jase was released and was moving away with Morgan, then he called out: "Hey, why release just him? I got a right to. . . ."

"You just sit down and sweat a little," interrupted Morgan, herded young Blue out to the office, closed the door, and tapped the rangy, tall cowboy on the shoulder to make him turn. "The next time someone tries to make a conversation with you, Jase, you better act civil, because the next time the other feller might just kill you."

Jason Blue stared stonily at Lew Morgan. For a while it did not seem that he would respond at all. Then he slowly inclined his head. "About that carbine of mine," he said. "What I told you at the ranch is all I honestly know. I left it in my hurry to get home, and I haven't any idea what could have happened to it afterward."

Morgan pointed. "That's the gun, against the wall yonder. But you'd better just leave it there for now. Until all this damned mess is unraveled."

From the cot Marshal Tully said: "Lew, did you see that gunman who tried to kill you last night?"

Morgan strolled over and gazed at the man on the cot. "How did you know anyone had tried that last night?"

"Simple," said the lawman. "Only a few minutes after you walked out of here . . . maybe an hour or less . . . there was a carbine shot from up north somewhere. I told you. The best thing a smart man would have done last night was get the hell out of this village. Well, did you get a look at him?"

Morgan said: "No, just some tracks."

"Where did he try it?"

"I was out front of the icehouse with Hazelton."

Marshal Tully's eyes widened a little. "Out front of the icehouse?"

Morgan brushed the lawman's curiosity aside. "I'll go get you some breakfast, Marshal." He turned, caught Hal Blue watching him, and shouldered on over to the door where he turned, facing young Blue. "Nobody was out to make trouble for you yesterday, Jase. They still aren't. It was your gun, but you didn't use it atop the store. Making that war talk just made more trouble for me . . . and for you." Morgan nodded and walked out where Pete Moss and the range riders were idly enjoying the warming morning brilliance as the climbing sun sent along layer after layer of very welcome springtime heat.

The cowboys stared in frank interest at the man with the ivory-stocked six-gun, but they said nothing. Pete Moss had a remark to make, however. Jerking a thumb at a lean, youthful cowboy, the half-breed said: 'This here is Quentin Holworth.

He was just telling me about a feller who came by the ranch couple days back looking for some of Sam Evans's loose livestock."

The lanky cowboy, evidently disliking Moss's casual handling of when, exactly, he had spoken to the rider, said: "It was the day before the storm hit. That's three days back, not a couple of days."

Morgan gazed at the cowboy with no comprehension. "Well, what of it? I'd guess that before the storm hit there were lots of riders out."

"This feller had a name burned into the leather on the back of his cantle," stated the cowboy. "Jase."

Morgan turned very slowly and saw Pete Moss's expression of ironic amusement. Pete was one of those people who enjoyed seeing other people get disconcerted, apparently. But actually Lew Morgan was not really all that astonished. He had his reasons for not being, and right now he did not mention them. He wouldn't have mentioned them in any case, but now he did not get the chance because Pete Moss spoke. "Quentin was just describing this feller, and you know who he sounded like, Morgan?"

Lew stared at Moss. "The feller in the icehouse?"

Moss's expression weakened. "How'd you guess that?"

Morgan did not say how he'd guessed it. He said, instead, for Quentin and Pete to come along with him, and turned to lead the way up the roadway in the direction of the apothecary's shop. The other range riders looked at one another, then without discussion they went trooping along, too. Whatever impended evidently was likely to be more interesting than standing around out front a damned jailhouse waiting for their employer to emerge. They were dead right.

# XIV

Jeb Hazelton had finished breakfast, had his shop open for business, and near at hand while he worked at bringing some untidily kept records up to date was a small glass of sherry. When Moss preceded Morgan into the shop, Jeb casually reached and set the sherry upon a counter shelf out of sight. Lew saw, and said nothing as the cowboy Quentin Holworth edged into the shop, also, but the other range men stopped just short of the doorway, looking in and listening but making no effort to crowd inside, which was just as well since the apothecary's shop was not very large. At least the professional, front part of it wasn't.

Lew smiled stiffly and said: "The key to the icehouse, Mister Hazelton."

There was no argument. Hazelton took the key from a pocket and placed it upon the counter within Morgan's reach as he looked around for his coat, and picked it off a chair back. When the other men turned to depart, Hazelton went along with them, locking the shop after himself.

Across the road Walt Kenyon was standing, immobile, before his harness shop window, watching with intent interest as that group of men headed around through the softening mud for the alley. His interest was only interrupted when Aleck Trotter entered carrying a folded newspaper, that Aleck proceeded to unfold to disclose a column on the front page around which someone had drawn a red border, and put this opened paper upon Walt's cutting table. He thumped it with his fist to get Kenyon's undivided attention.

"Read this," he told the harness maker. "You never read anything like this in your life, Walt . . . and that's the man over across the road leading Hal Blue's men into the alley."

Kenyon, pulled both ways, decided finally that whatever it was in the newspaper that had got Aleck so agitated must be more interesting than the range men across the road, who would shortly disappear into the alleyway, and went to his workbench, while the men he had been watching, and who had been neither aware of Kenyon's vigil nor especially susceptible to the shakes as a result of it, followed Lew Morgan right up to the icehouse door, and there, when Jeb Hazelton twisted to look steadily all around, his face tinged with an expression of apprehension, the range men did not even notice.

Morgan flung back the door. An icy darkness greeted the men close to him, and someone muttered something about this being a hell of a place to keep a dead man as Pete Moss growled for the men to stand aside so whatever light might reach inside could do so unimpeded. Not everyone was anxious to enter, anyway, and not just because it was cold and dark and musty in the icehouse.

Morgan nodded at Quentin Holworth and entered with the cowboy. Behind them, Pete Moss fumbled on a shelf until he located what he sought—a thick, stubby candle—and, when Pete moved over close to the rough-board table where the corpse was lying, he had the candle lighted. It was neither a pleasant scene nor occupation. Quentin Holworth turned to look wistfully out where his companions were standing in the welcome sunshine. He also looked at the big blocks of ice, sprinkled with sawdust, in the back of the eerily lighted, ghostly room, and, when Lew Morgan murmured something and Pete Moss held the candle forward and low, Quentin turned and looked steadily at the blue-gray, waveringly lighted face on the plank table. He looked a long time, then turned away heading for the door. Morgan and Pete Moss followed along. As Pete replaced the candle, Morgan went out into the sunshine, tapped Holworth's arm, and arched an eyebrow.

The cowboy said: "That's him. That's the same feller as sure as I'm a foot tall."

Morgan smiled his thanks, waited for Pete to close the door, hoist the hasp, and snap the lock closed, then he stood loosely and comfortably in the contrasting new day warmth and rolled a smoke. He did not say a word, not even after they were all trooping back through the mud to the front roadway.

Out there, the range men headed for the jailhouse, where their employer was untying his horse out front, leaving Pete and Lew with Jeb Hazelton, near the apothecary's shop. Hazelton did not linger. Evidently the cold, the grisly sight in the icehouse, and his interrupted, leisurely sherry sipping motivated him to leave. Lew waited until Jeb was entering the shop, then turned to Pete Moss to say: "Well, it wasn't Jase Blue and it wasn't Jase Buell."

The half-breed's answer was curt. "It never crossed my mind there'd be a third one. Privately I figured it was Jase Buell."

Morgan flipped the smoke into a runnel of chocolate-colored water in the roadway. "Why him, Pete?"

"Damned if I can say, for a fact, Lew, just that I never believed it would have been Jase Blue. He didn't have a damned thing to gain by killing Andy."

"Did Jase Buell?"

Moss looked pained. "No, not that I can say, but at least he's here in town, likely to be mixed up in whatever's behind the shooting."

It was an open-ended discussion and Morgan realized it, so he ended it by saying: "Well, Buell's out of it now, too. And someone else is in."

"Yeah. A corpse in the icehouse. Wonder who he was?"

Morgan studied the hawk-faced man sardonically. "Not the feller in the icehouse. He did his part, and he damned well paid for doing it. The man he worked for was Sam Evans. The reason Evans had no hostler at the barn the day of the storm was because he'd already sent Jase whatever-his-name-was away, sent him out on the range to look for horses . . . at least that was their story . . . only he didn't just look for horses, did he? He slipped back into town under cover of the snowstorm, got onto the roof, and damned near killed Marshal Tully. Let's walk down and talk to Sam Evans." As Morgan started to turn southward, he casually added: "Incidentally that's who took the shot at me last night."

Moss stood stockstill. "Sam Evans?"

"Yeah. Come along."

Moss fell in beside the other man. "How do you know it was Sam Evans?"

"By the boot tracks out back, and, when we get down to the trading barn, we'll verify it by his fresher tracks."

Hal Blue, watching the approach of Moss and Morgan from the saddle out front of the jailhouse, with his raw-boned, unsmiling son beside him, leaned with both gloved hands atop the saddle horn and spoke as Lew Morgan came on up. "Quentin solved the riddle for you, Morgan. Now it might be a good idea if you did like Andy suggested . . . rode on out."

Lew returned the older man's unwavering regard. "No doubt about it, Mister Blue, it'd be a good idea. But I got a few loose strands still dangling. Then I'll ride out." He nodded curtly and walked on, with Pete Moss saying nothing and walking at his side.

Hal Blue lifted thin shoulders, and dropped them. Then he turned his horse to ride up northward out of town, and only got two-thirds of the way when Aleck Trotter, hiking briskly back from the harness shop in the direction of his general store, called and waved a folded newspaper. Hal Blue reined over, accepted the paper, unfolded it, and puckered his forehead as he laboriously read the red-bordered article. Afterward he slowly refolded the newspaper, handed it down to Trotter without a word, but looking bleak in the face and, still without speaking, turned back as far as the tie rack out front of the pool hall and swung down. He ignored the watching storekeeper to say: "Get down Jase, and the rest of you. No sense in riding all the way back on an empty stomach. We'll kill an hour or so eating breakfast."

None of the range men looked especially surprised, and none of them looked the least bit disappointed as they swung to earth and led their animals on up to be tied. The sun was steadily climbing and at the same time pouring molten heat down upon the village. Men shed coats and jackets, the sky was clear blue, the last of the snow was turning to run-off water.

Down at the lower end of town when Lew and Pete Moss halted near the blacksmith's shop, Jase Buell came to the door, wearing his shiny old mule-hide shoeing apron, and smiled as he said: "Damn, that sunshine feels good, don't it?"

Morgan was brusque. "Have you seen Sam Evans this morning?"

The blacksmith's smile began fading as he looked from Lew to Pete Moss, then back to Morgan before answering: "Yeah, he was around a while ago." Buell leaned as though to peer in the direction of the trading barn. "But he was around kind of late last evening, so maybe he's went back home to rest for a spell."

Morgan gazed at the blacksmith. "He worked late last night?"

Jase Buell nodded his head. "Yeah. I seen his lamp on in the barn when I was locking up to head home, and I got all involved with a busted buggy axle and didn't close up shop until well past suppertime. Sam's lamp was still burning when I left."

"Did you see him in there?" asked Morgan, and got a negative reply from Buell. "Not exactly. No, I didn't actually see him, but for quite a few years, whenever there's a light over there after supper, Sam's working."

"By any chance did you know that hostler who quit him the day before the storm hit town?" asked Morgan.

Buell looked almost dolorous over his reply. "He told me

he'd hired a feller, but sometimes I got no business over there for days at a stretch, especially if I got a lot of my own work to turn out. No, sir, can't say I knew that feller. Sam said he'd hired a man. But you know how those hostlers are. They come and go, like the birds, here today an' gone tomorrow. Mostly they're drifters or drunks."

Morgan exchanged a glance with Pete Moss. Pete seemed slightly more baffled than enlightened by all the blacksmith had said. Morgan turned in the direction of the trading barn, saw the side and roof of Andy Tully's log barn farther out, about a half mile, and suddenly remembered that he had completely forgot to go out there last night and feed the team horses. He fished in a pocket, dug forth a silver half cartwheel, and offered it to Jase Buell, if he would walk over and fork down some feed and water for the marshal's stalled harness animals. It was a lot of money for a slight chore, and Buell took the coin gladly. Then Morgan and Pete Moss headed on around to the trading barn.

There was not a soul in the runway so they went to the harness room, which also served as an office. But there was no one there, either, so they went down the row of stalls looking in. Someone had fed the animals, including Morgan's sorrel, but when they got down to the alley way opening and looked over in the direction of the public corrals, they still found no one.

Pete scratched his head. "Don't know where Sam'd be, unless maybe he's up at the café."

"How about being up at your pool hall?" asked Morgan, and got a strong negative look from the half-breed.

"Not Sam. He hasn't been in my place five times since the first of the year, and even those times it was at night. I've never seen him shoot a game of pool, nor sit in a serious poker game."

Morgan caught sight of movement from the edge of his eyes and turned. But it was Jase Buell, without his shoeing apron, briskly walking past, out front, heading for the marshal's log barn to earn his half dollar. They went out back, southward to the edge of the barn, then paced up along the south wall to the front roadway, and still did not find any trace of Sam Evans. Morgan was more annoyed than puzzled. He had no reason to believe the horse trader was not around. Jase Buell was the only visible moving thing, and he was hiking up the well-worn little path in the direction of the Tully place, his stride and bearing purposeful and brisk.

Pete Moss said: "Hell, he didn't just disappear. He's got to be around here somewhere. Sam's a businessman. He wouldn't go off and leave this place unattended."

Morgan was skeptical of this. "Then where is he?"

Pete had an inspiration. "The jailhouse! I should have thought of that before. Sure as the devil he's up there."

Morgan glanced northward, noticed the cow horses tied over in front of the pool hall, paid slight attention to this, and started walking. "You might be right. Let's go see," he told Pete who walked back with him. "I didn't know Evans and Marshal Tully were that close. In fact, my opinion of the horse trader is that he wouldn't be very close to anyone."

Pete smiled ruefully. "He sure enough gives that impression, but he's not young any more, and seems to me most old gaffers get sort of sour on life . . . and folks."

Lew looked around. Philosophical pool hall proprietors who also happened to be half-breeds were new to him. Moss caught the look and was slightly embarrassed, so he did not speak again until they walked into the jailhouse.

# XV

Sam Evans was not in the office, but Morgan got a surprise when he and Pete Moss entered, because the gunsmith was seated in the chair beside the cot where the lawman was lying.

The four men stared at one another. Andy Tully said: "Aleck was in a while ago and I got him to let Art out."

Morgan could not really rebuke the lawman for releasing a prisoner from his own cells, since Tully, not Morgan, was the law in Forrest, so he shoved back his hat, asked if Sam Evans had been in, and, when Tully replied that he had not seen the horse trader since the previous day, Morgan went to check the stove, stoke it a little, and turned to find the gunsmith balefully looking at him.

Pete Moss sank upon the wall bench near the front door, impassive and silent, content to be a spectator when Lew Morgan said: "Lane, I was going to get around to you directly, anyway."

Marshal Tully eyed Morgan, but like Pete across the room, Tully was content to be an observer. At least for the time being.

The gunsmith, though, was not as calm as the other two. He eyed Lew Morgan with more misgivings than he'd shown before. He seemed to want to speak, but did not make the attempt as his eyes remained fixed on the gunman. Even when Lew strolled to a chair and had to pass behind the gunsmith to reach it, Art Lane twisted completely to keep his eye on Morgan. Another time it might have been funny. Right now Lew Morgan was not in a smiling or chuckling frame of mind. When he eased down, he said: "Where's Sam Evans?"

Lane's gaze wavered when he replied. "I have no idea. How could I know, anyway, me being locked in a cell since yesterday?"

Morgan did not press it. "What's the last name of the feller in the icehouse, Mister Lane?"

"You mean the feller you shot?"

Lew did not speak. He sat there gazing steadily at the lanky man next to the marshal's cot. Lane looked around at Pete, got a stone-steady black stare from that direction, and sat forward upon the edge of his chair as though he might spring up and run, except that he did not do so. He said: "I don't know what his last name was. All I know was that his first name was Jase. That's the gospel truth."

Morgan did not press this, either. "I heard you call him Jase the night you two fellers were in the marshal's barn with your carbines."

The gunsmith blinked his surprise.

"You were a little nervous that night, gunsmith. You wanted to head out, but Jase didn't want to go. I'll guess why. Because he'd been paid to assassinate Marshal Tully."

Lane still sat forward without speaking, his eyes fixed on Lew Morgan.

"Want me to tell the marshal who hired that dead feller to bushwhack him, gunsmith? Want me to tell him who got that carbine and handed it over to the bushwhacker, and who was down here, the morning of the bushwhack, to make certain Marshal Tully got killed?"

Art Lane's tongue darted out, around his dry lips, and back. He still did not speak, so Morgan shifted his attention to the man on the cot.

"Now you know who the pair of them were who happened to come into your barn the night I was bedded down in the loft, Marshal. This one, and the feller in the icehouse, whose first name was Jase. And if you'd like to know who took that shot at me last night . . . it was Sam Evans, which is where Pete and I just came from . . . the trading barn . . . only he wasn't down there, so we thought he might be up here. Marshal, I got a feeling that you were lucky as hell when I walked in here, when Evans was visiting you. If I hadn't, you probably wouldn't be able to hear me now. And that might hold true this morning . . . right now with Lane."

Marshal Tully raised his head slightly in order to look back where Lew was sitting, but he only glanced at Morgan; his main interest was the gunsmith. He stared so long without speaking that Lane got nervous.

From over by the door Pete Moss quietly spoke: "Art, what the hell's been going on?"

Lane acted as though he had not heard Moss, and Lew Morgan arose, walked to the desk where he could see the lawman on the cot, and made a suggestion to the gunsmith: "You can talk, or I'll lock you back in the cell. But I think that if I was in your boots, I'd talk, gunsmith, because as soon as I can find the horse trader, he'll talk. Then it'll be worthless for you to try it. And there's another thing I'd worry about, if I was in your boots. Evans knows you're in here. He probably has it figured that I'll stamp it out of you sooner or later. It wouldn't surprise me one damned bit if he tried to kill you."

Andy Tully sighed, and shook his head at Lew Morgan. "Sam's not going to do anything like that."

Morgan shifted his glance to the man on the cot. "Why isn't he?"

"Because. . . ." The lawman paused, looked at the man sitting beside his bed, then quietly said: "You going to tell him, Art, or shall I?"

Lane arose stiffly, eyed Pete Moss beside the door, turned toward the stove where he could see Morgan head on, and began speaking: "He's my uncle."

Morgan nodded, but Pete Moss looked astonished.

"Four years ago he come on to two shot-up fellers in a dry camp. They died. What he had to do with that, I don't know. But I do know that when he tried to ride back into town that night . . . with two fat saddlebags . . . he didn't risk it because it was Saturday night with everyone in town and a lot of cowmen down at the public corrals. So he rode over to Andy's place and cached the saddlebags somewhere. I always figured he'd cached them in the barn." Art Lane let his gaze wander over to Pete, who was staring back. Finally Lane went on speaking. "He kept tryin' to get the bags back, but Andy was always either at his place, or here in town, too close for my uncle to make it over there and back with the saddlebags without running a hell of a risk getting caught."

"What," asked Lew, "was in the saddlebags?"

"Nineteen thousand dollars."

Morgan and Pete Moss stared. Marshal Tully was already staring at the gunsmith.

"It came from a bank robbery over in Denver where those fellers got shot up pretty bad during the robbery." Lane returned to the chair, but turned it so he would not have to look at the man on the cot. "My uncle come to me last year. He wanted me to help him. Promised me five thousand dollars if I'd get Andy out of town and bushwhack him. . . . I got him to ride the east range looking for lost horses, and I was out there, waiting. But it was no accident when I hit the horse. That was what I aimed at. I didn't want to kill Andy. I just wanted him pinned down out there until my uncle had a chance to get out to the barn and get back those lousy saddlebags. It would have happened that way, too, if that damned Hal Blue hadn't come up moments later and rescued Andy. My uncle saw them come into town. He came to my place that night, raising hell. I told him I'd shot from a long ways off. I'd hit the horse instead of Andy. He was mad for two weeks." Lane looked briefly at the wounded lawman. "He tried every way to get you out of town for a few days, and like a damned fool you stayed right here. I don't know where he found Jase, that feller who was at the barn for a couple of days, but anyway he sent me with Jase the night Morgan was in your loft to show Jase where your house was, and all like that."

"To kill him?" asked Pete Moss. "To kill Andy, Art?"

"Yes, damn it."

Pete said: "Would you have let him do it?"

The gunsmith looked stonily at the floor without answering for a moment, then he ignored both Pete and his question to say: "Morgan was behind us where I didn't expect anyone. He gave us both a bad start and we loped back to town, to the barn, where my uncle was waiting in the dark. We told him Andy had someone in his barn loft, so my uncle sent Jase to the alley out back of Aleck's store to climb to the roof top and shoot Andy from up there, in the snowstorm. You know the rest of it."

Lew fished out his makings and quietly went to work making a cigarette. When he had it lighted, he put a thoughtful look upon the lawman. "How much of it did you know?" he asked.

Tully slid his eyes down from the ceiling to Morgan's face. "The part about the saddlebags full of money, because I found them three years ago when I was making over some feed troughs in one of the stalls in the barn. I quietly set out to learn where the money came from. I found out. Then I sat back waiting for someone to come for it. And to be right honest, Lew, when you showed up in my barn that morning of the snowstorm, I was sure you were the man I'd been waiting for. That's why I never left town, nor spent any time away from my place. But it never crossed my mind someone from right here in town . . . someone I knew as well as I knew Art and Sam . . . would be involved, because I had the full descriptions of those two bank robbers from Denver. I was waiting for them. That's why I never wanted to talk about the time someone shot the horse from under me, neither. I figured they'd come, and I waited for them." Tully turned his head a little to look at the gunsmith. "Art?"

The gunsmith would not look at the man addressing him. "I didn't like any of it, Andy, and that's the truth. But with five thousand dollars, you see, I could have gone down to Arizona. That's why I did it. You ask Jeb . . . I got the consumption, and unless I live in a dry, hot climate, I'm not going to make it for more than maybe another couple of years." Now, finally, the gunsmith turned to look at the wounded man. "I wasn't going to let that bastard shoot you that night from the barn. Just maybe wing you, or scare you off. That's a fact, Andy."

The roadway door opened and Jeb Hazelton walked in, very erect, very ruddy-faced, and with bright, alert eyes. He smiled around, then announced that he had come to change the marshal's bandage and look at the wound. Morgan was half the width of the room away, but he knew Hazelton had been drinking. He shrugged. If he hadn't learned much else in Forrest, he had learned one thing. Some men who drank functioned better with a load aboard than they would have functioned stone sober. He got off the edge of the desk, walked over where Pete Moss was sitting, still staring at the gunsmith, and said: "Let's go find Evans."

Moss roused himself, arose, and jutted a thumb in the gunsmith's direction. "What about him? Lock him up again?"

Morgan turned to watch the apothecary approach the bed. Hazelton had no inkling what he had just interrupted. He was looking and acting very pleasant and very professional. Morgan met the gunsmith's stare, and shook his head. He did not say it, but he was thinking it. The chase, like any excitement, had been worthwhile right up to the point where the sordidness and the culmination arrived, and now he didn't give a damn about the participants, except for the one he still had to catch. He also had another thought. Of all the people around, who were not qualified to lock up someone else for breaking the law, he was probably top man.

He did not answer Pete. He simply jerked the door open, just as Jeb Hazelton called his name, and he turned sideward at the exact moment someone outside fired into the room from across the road. The bullet came within an inch of Morgan, sped past, and made a meaty, tearing sound as it caught the gunsmith directly over the heart. Lane had one second to register complete astonishment, then went over backward, chair and all.

# XVI

Pete Moss stumbled along the front wall so suddenly that his knees caught the bench he had been sitting on, and rather than fall he sat down again on the bench. Elsewhere Hazelton did as he had done once before under similar circumstances; he froze in place, mouth sagging, his eyes fixed on Art Lane on the floor with his chair overturned beside him. Andy Tully and Lew Morgan reacted differently. Andy told Hazelton to get away, to get clear of that opened doorway, and Lew Morgan sailed through to land out front on the drying plank walk, moving constantly as he searched the roof top across the road, the recessed doorways north and south of the general store, and finally the interior of Trotter's store through the windows for some sign of a man with a gun.

Everyone in Forrest had heard that gunshot, but the general reaction was to stay in place, or to retreat into shadows, because in less than a moment the entire length of the roadway was deserted. Lew made it to the opposite side of the road before Pete Moss had regained his feet and had leaned to peer out front. Lew entered the general store with his Colt lightly swinging. He was doing a reckless thing, but not all the advantage lay with the bushwhacker. Aleck Trotter's wispy old clerk was motionless against a far wall and the storekeeper himself was rooted in the doorway to his little office area, also staring at the man with the gun. He saw the gun swing toward him and blurted out some words.

"He isn't in here. I don't know where he shot from, Mister Morgan, but it wasn't in here."

Lew kept moving swiftly. He looked behind each counter,

looked into every shadowed corner, then went to the door leading to the roof top, but it had a newly installed brass hasp and lock in place, so he turned and hastened back to the roadway, raking the sun-bright emptiness in both directions. Across the way Pete Moss whistled, then pointed rigidly southward, and Lew turned in that direction, still moving.

Pete Moss started southward, keeping as close to building fronts as he could get. He had his Colt fisted, and moved with silent caution. Lew, who remained upon the opposite side of the road, gauged his chances, if he did as Pete was doing, decided he could not make it, and spun to run through Trotter's store and out into the rear alleyway. There, he ran again, southward this time so as to arrive down in front of the livery barn about the time Pete got abreast of Buell's smithy.

The town was totally quiet. The sun was pleasantly hot, the sky was burnished blue, there were a few patches of snow remaining here and there, in shadow, and off to the southwest Marshal Tully's log barn shone darkly against the greening, rolling rangeland. Someone up in the vicinity of the pool hall let out a yell. Lew did not look around, as he edged forward alongside a building where he was able to see the north roadway. He didn't know who was up there, and didn't care, his full interest was upon the shoeing shop and, beside it, the trading barn.

Pete had stopped at the southernmost corner of Buell's shop, looking for Lew. When he saw him, he raised his left hand slightly in acknowledgment. Lew did not respond. He inched ahead, half exposed, until he had the trading barn runway in sight. But it was dark down in there; it was always dark in the runway, summer or winter. Except for the front and rear openings, there was no way for daylight to get inside for more than a yard or two.

Pete finally leaned to peer around the corner of Buell's

smithy. He could see nothing; Lew knew that, because in his better position, he could see nothing, either. Several men cat-called back and forth from up the roadway, northward, and someone in a waspish voice yelled an order to them.

"Get out back! Don't let him escape out back!"

Lew felt like swearing. Not because he was not appreciative of Hal Blue's support, but because in this kind of an encounter the fewer intruders there were, the less chance there was of the wrong person getting killed. But there was nothing he could do. Even yelling out for the range men to keep out of it would not deter a man like Hal Blue. Perhaps as a result of the range men taking an interest, perhaps as a result of natural curiosity, a number of townspeople began to appear here and there up the north roadway. The moment Lew Morgan got to the edge of the building where he could see in both directions, north and south, he saw them. He did not recognize them, did not even know them, in fact, but he knew they were from the stores and shops and residences of the town, and it irritated him to see them out there, taking a completely unnecessary risk.

Pete was gesticulating, making an encircling motion. Lew, watching the runway, decided he might as well consent to what Moss was silently proposing, so he nodded, and the moment Pete ducked back down through the blacksmith shop to get out back, Lew filled his lungs, then sprinted as hard as he could for the opposite side of the road. Fortunately village roadways were rarely as wide as town roadways. He was more than two-thirds of the way across before someone fired at him. He heard the blast, saw the dust spurt a yard back, and knew the shot had originated from within Sam Evans's trading barn. He fired back, straight down through the runway with no idea at all of hitting anything; all he wanted to accomplish was a distraction. He wanted to make old Evans duck, and that would give Lew enough time to clear the roadway.

It must have worked that way because Evans did not fire again. Lew sailed up against the wall of the blacksmith shop, and out back someone with a high-pitched voice bellowed: "Evans, you damned old bastard, come out of there!"

Lew did not hesitate but a moment as he entered the smithy. It was empty. Buell was obviously still on his errand. Lew reached the rear of the shop, looked out, saw two men pressing against the north wall of the trading barn, and recognized one of them as Pete Moss. Pete was arguing with the other man, a lanky, sorrel-thatched range rider, evidently one of Hal Blue's men.

Lew whistled, then ran up to those two. Pete turned and said: "God damned cowboys all over the place." He was monumentally disgusted. Lew was also irritated, but he said nothing to the range man. He edged past him to the corner and peeked around there. No one was in sight. He kept on moving, gliding along the back wall to the edge of the doorless rear opening, then he halted. This was as close as he was going to be able to get, until he entered, and the moment he did that, all hell was going to break loose and he damned well knew it. He could have called in to Sam Evans, but he didn't. There were several things he could have done, as alternatives to what he ultimately actually did, but he did not even consider them. Maybe Andy Tully would have reasoned with the horse trader, and without a doubt most professional lawmen would have offered Sam several chances to extricate himself without having to die. Lew Morgan did not even consider any of those things. This was Sam Evans's game; he had begun it; he had established all the rules for it, and it was not Lew Morgan's fault that Sam had missed him in the jailhouse doorway. Sam had tried hard to kill him, and now it was Lew's turn.

He dropped to one knee, looked elsewhere, saw no one close by, leaned and eased his gun hand halfway around the log wall.

Nothing happened. He shoved his entire fist with the gun in it around, and that time a Winchester half deafened Lew from inside the barn. A slug ticked doorway wood and its breath was lethally noticeable as Lew twisted his wrist and thumbed off a shot. Then he swung the gun a fraction and fired again. He did that three times before withdrawing his gun and leaning to snap back the gate and hulling out spent casings and plugging in fresh ones. He did not speak. Neither did the man inside the barn. Nor did anyone else anywhere around, and Pete and that cowboy were looking around their log wall corner, watching Lew. Farther back, beyond the alleyway and upon both sides of it, several other armed men were intently watching when Lew raised the Colt and shoved it around again—then yanked it back instantly.

Evans fired. There was no gun there after he pulled the trigger and had to lever up his next load, but by the time he was half ready Lew was prone in the dirt looking in from the lowest corner of the alleyway opening. He saw jerky movement and heard the oily parts mesh as Evans completed levering up. Lew fired. He did not have Evans in sight, but he knew about where the sounds had come from, and he fired a second time.

Evans bawled, fired his carbine, levered up again, and fired again, shooting away raw segments of the back wall. Lew rolled in closer, fired once more, to draw some muzzle blast, and, when it came, he drilled two fast shots dead into it, one, inches to the left, the other one, inches to the right.

There was no more carbine fire. Lew lay prone, straining to hear a body sinking down, or a Winchester skittering against a log wall. All he heard was someone up the roadway calling out for the men down by the barn to be careful. He could cheerfully have found that loud-mouth and cracked his jaw. The man's yells completely overrode any sounds that might have originated inside the barn.

Lew looked over his shoulder where Pete Moss and the cowboy were intently watching him. He gestured for Moss to go around front, and, as Pete turned, so also did the cowboy. Moss turned on him with a savage curse, and the cowboy remained where he was.

The sun was almost directly overhead, and heat was filling the alleyway as Lew carefully reloaded his weapon for the second time, then leaned down in the dirt and mud again, one ear as close to the doorway as he could risk putting his head.

Out front, someone called distinctly to Sam Evans. It was not Pete Moss. Lew Morgan was positive of that. The caller said: "Give it up, Sam! Hal Blue's outfit is completely around you, and Pete Moss is up here, while that Morgan feller is out back."

Lew raised up a little, puckering his forehead. *That Morgan feller* did not sound very complimentary. He tried to imagine who that might be up front, and decided finally not to bother himself about it just yet, and leaned to listen again. A moment later he pushed his gun hand ahead, wiggled it, then rapidly withdrew it. This time, he drew no gunshot. He edged along trying to make a shadow also to draw fire, but the sun was wrong; he could not make a shadow. Finally he arose to one knee, leaned, listened, glanced elsewhere, saw the cowboys watching very intently, and suddenly sprang to his feet, swinging sideward as he hurled himself into plain sight in the wide opening. One second there was absolutely nothing. The next second dully shining steel was swinging to bear. He fired down that gun barrel, fired under it, and to both sides of it, thumbing off shots so fast it sounded like one continuous long drumroll of gunfire. The carbine exploded, roof shingles parted with a burst of dust, and directly overhead sunlight streamed down through where there had never been sunlight before.

Lew Morgan's ears were ringing when he let go with his last shot. There was one bullet left in his gun. He cocked the weapon and walked forward until he could see over the feed sacks. Sam was lying in a corner, hurled there by violent impact. At first, Lew saw no sign of the wounds, but the longer he stood there the better he was able to see. Evans had been hit three times, hard. At least one bullet had slammed him against the wall, and perhaps the next slug hurtled him sideward as he was falling.

Lew reached, retrieved the Winchester, leaned it upon the feed sacks, methodically holstered his empty Colt, then picked up the carbine, and walked out into the alley where men were standing like stone, eyes glued to the doorway, scarcely breathing while they waited to see which man would emerge.

Pete Moss walked in, looked long at dead Sam Evans, then went out back where Lew was pausing for a deep-down lungful of pleasant fresh air. Lew turned at Pete's sound, saw who it was coming up behind him, and slowly said: "Pete, you got quite a village here. When you need help, you couldn't blow them out of hiding with dynamite. When you don't need them, they're falling over each other, getting in everyone's way."

Moss agreed. "Nothing more worthless than a herd of cowboys in a fight, anyway," he said, "unless it's teats on a boar."

Lew looked past at the empty doorway. "You see him in there?"

Moss had. "Yeah. Busted like a rotten melon. Now what, Lew?"

Morgan jerked his head without speaking. The pair of them walked unaccosted up as far as the jailhouse, and, although half the town was in the roadway by this time, no one called over to them or attempted to delay their progress to the jailhouse.

Inside, Aleck Trotter was mopping his face on a clean apron, and Hal Blue was standing beside the cot where Marshal Tully was lying, looking steadily toward the door.

Lew crossed the room without speaking, leaned Evans's

carbine against the foot of the cot, and said: "How do you feel, Andy?"

Tully smiled toughly. "Well . . . better now, I reckon. Who was it?"

"Sam Evans. You knew it would be."

"I expect I did. Is he plumb dead?"

"Can't get any deader, Andy," replied Morgan, raising his head a little to look from Trotter to old Hal Blue.

Marshal Tully said: "Hell of it is, Lew, neither of them could have got those saddlebags back anyway. Not Art and not Sam Evans. I returned that money to the authorities up in Denver two years ago. They did all this for nothing. For absolutely nothing at all. And now look where they are."

Lew glanced down again. "A man'd have to pucker his eyes pretty hard against the heat, to look at where they are now, Andy." He smiled, turned, and without another word walked out of the jailhouse, heading southward again, in the direction of the trading barn where his sorrel was stalled.

A stage rolled up to the very edge of town before slackening speed, then its driver tooled it dead ahead with his hitch at a walk, and no one paid any attention at all. For once, something far more interesting than the arrival of a stage had happened in Forrest.

# XVII

There was not a soul in the barn when Lew led forth his sorrel and went after the saddle, but when he emerged from the harness room, several men had drifted southward and were standing over across the road, looking down into the barn where Lew methodically saddled up. He had bridled the horse and was making his customary final inspection when two large men walked in out of the warm sunlight, both of them wearing bowler hats and dark suits, both of them resolute in bearing and obvious purpose. They saw Lew, and one man stopped back in the doorway, a hand inside his coat on the right side, while the other one, still dust-mantled from his long stage ride, walked ahead.

Lew turned, studied the pair of strangers, and reached for the slack reins when the oncoming man said: "Hold it right where you are, Morgan." He stopped, legs wide. "We got a warrant for you from Tularosa."

Beyond the second man, out in the sunshine between the roadway and the barn opening, several armed men drifted in casually. From northward, up by Jase Buell's blacksmith shop, several more men walked over solemnly, and halted back a couple of yards behind the bowler-hatted big man in the doorway. The stranger turned, very slowly, and stared as that loosely assembled body of range men and townsmen steadily increased, when more men drifted on up.

Down midway in the barn, Lew and the second stranger stood face to face. The stranger said: "Drop the gun, Morgan, and be damned careful. Two Pinkertons equal one gunman any day of the year. Now drop it!"

From out in the sunlight old Hal Blue called ahead: "Mister . . . you down there in the bowler hat! Come on back out of there."

The man in the doorway, still with his right hand beneath his coat, did not seem to be breathing, as still more men strolled up out front. Jase Blue, shaggy-headed, raw-boned, and mean-looking, softly said: "Take your hand out of there. Keep 'em both in plain sight!"

The Pinkerton detective obeyed, as he turned back, very carefully, to stare down where his partner was still facing Lew Morgan. "Hall," he quietly said. "Look out here."

The man facing Morgan turned a little, stepped sideways in order to have Lew still in sight, and saw all those armed men out in the sunlight. He stiffened. He was a big, powerful man. "You fellers disperse!" he called. "This here is the law's business. We got a warrant for Morgan from the justice court down in Tularosa."

Pete Moss, leaning in the doorway, answered that. "Mister, no damned New Mexico warrant is any good in Colorado. Unless a U.S. marshal serves it, or the Army. Who are you fellers?"

"Pinkerton detectives," snarled the powerful, large man. "And our warrant is good enough."

Pete shook his head. "Naw. Not in this town, not in Colorado. Anyway, who d' you think you're arresting?"

"Lewis Morgan. Wanted in New Mexico for shooting his way out of a jailhouse, wounding two deputies, and. . . ."

"Well, mister," spoke up old Walt Kenyon, the harness maker, holding his shotgun two-handed, "you got the wrong man. That ain't Lewis Morgan. That there is his twin brother, Lemuel Morgan."

For five seconds no one spoke. Every eye was fixed upon the old harness maker, who grinned now, and raised the twin barrels of his shotgun until they bore steadily upon the Pinkerton detective in the doorway. "Mister, you make an attempt to arrest ol' Lem, and I'm going to cut your partner in two, and at this distance, mister, even an old feller like me can't hardly miss, can he? Now you come on out of there!"

Hal Blue, with his riders behind him, walked over to the nearest Pinkerton detective and held out his hand. "Your gun," he said quietly.

The large man down the runway swore and lunged up in the direction where his companion was handing Hal Blue his nickel-plated revolver. Pete Moss straightened off the door jam and stepped ahead. So did Jase Blue and three lanky range riders, plus four townsmen, all armed and all deadly serious. They stopped the big private detective in his tracks.

He glared, red in the face with fury. "That man down there is Lewis Morgan. We got pictures of him. He had a moustache then, but it's the same man. You fellers are obstructing justice, damn you. I'll call in the Army and the U.S. marshal!"

Old Kenyon grinned in the face of the large man's anger. "Mister, that there is Lem Morgan. Didn't you know Lew Morgan had a brother? I've heard tell they're twins, but I wouldn't know about that. And Lem never wore no mustache. And he's been working the cow outfits around here for ten, eleven years. You can go ask our town lawman, if you doubt me. He's known Lem as long as the rest of us. Not a man here won't stand up in court and say that's Lem. . . . By the way, mister, what was Lew Morgan in that jailhouse for, before he busted out?"

"For hiring out to cattle interests against the settlers in the New Mexico cow country," snarled the detective.

The men turned and looked at one another, then turned back toward the Pinkerton men. All the country around Forrest and elsewhere in southern Colorado for hundreds of miles in all directions was cattle country. Hal Blue motioned for his son to disarm the large man, and Jase moved ahead, rammed his cocked Colt into the detective's middle, stared straight into his face, and reached beneath the dusty coat to pull away the second nickel-plated weapon. Hal then said: "Come along, gents, we'll go up and talk to the marshal at the jailhouse."

The big man tried to turn, to protest, and Jase grabbed him as three other cowmen stepped up to shove him roughly. The entire body of men walked away. All but Pete Moss and old Walt Kenyon. Walt was grinning wider than ever as he and Pete walked down where Lew had turned his horse and was swinging up across leather.

Pete said: "They're going to figure you'd go north."

Lew nodded. "Yeah, I know. I'll head due west toward Idaho. And damned if I'll ride into another town between here and there." He smiled at Moss. "Going to miss you, Pete." He looked at the old harness maker. "You, too . . . shotgun and all."

Old Kenyon beamed. Every man was entitled to finish out his years with one moment of glory, and old Kenyon had just had his moment.

Pete said: "We'll keep 'em here for a day or two. You shouldn't need more time than that." He considered Morgan's tough face a moment, then wagged his head. "Sure a funny partnership . . . you and Marshal Tully. Well, good luck, Lew."

Morgan turned, rode out into the empty alleyway, angled southward until he was beyond the village, then he pointed his sorrel due west and did not even glance back until he was several miles out, atop a low, grassy little hummock beside a squatty old tree. He sighed, shook the reins, and told his horse they'd ought to have their damned heads examined if they entered another town until they were so far off in the mountains of Idaho that folks had never even heard of range wars.

The sun was slanting away slightly, high and brilliant and blessedly warm. Springtime was fast fading into summer, the best time of year for a man to be saddle-backing half across a continent.

★ ★ ★ ★ ★

# Gunman's Moon

★ ★ ★ ★ ★

# I

The way it happened was not especially unique, unless the fact that one of two women, a mother or her daughter, were accused of Bolley's murder, where ordinarily, since Ralph Bolley was anything but a woman's man, it might have been expected a man, or perhaps more than one man, would have stood accused. The fact remained. Katherine Willard, the mother, and Georgia Willard, the daughter, were in Robert Lefton's jailhouse charged with murder. The way that killing actually occurred wasn't at all complicated or disputed. Ralph Bolley had died from the results of a shotgun blast that had literally shredded his upper body from a distance of perhaps no more than twenty or thirty feet. Of course there was speculation. For one thing, Ralph Bolley was a known gunfighter. Then how was it that he had permitted anyone, certainly least of all a woman, to get within twenty or thirty feet of him with a shotgun that was loaded and cocked. It didn't make much sense.

"Oh, yes, it makes sense," said Stan Oldfield, proprietor of the Texas Belle Saloon uptown in Mandan, winking. "It makes sense when you look at those two. I swear Kate's the finest-looking mature female in the whole countryside, an' her daughter's got more of everything girls ought to have than a man can see anywhere else in three weeks ridin'."

But the rebuttal here was simply that Bolley had never impressed anyone as being a woman's man. At least not the kind of women the Willards were: respectable, decent, upstanding ranch folk, Kate widowed and Georgia orphaned two years earlier when Justice Willard's horse fell with him in a dead run.

"Then he was out there to rob them," suggested Stan Oldfield. "How would I know what he was doing out there? Maybe they sent for him. Maybe they got someone pickin' on 'em the rest of us here in town don't know anything about." Stan raised his big hand and waggled a thick finger at the men along his bar. "But I'll tell you one thing I do know. Bolley's dead, and Deputy Bob Lefton's got Kate and her girl locked up in his jailhouse, which is the first time in my recollections a female's ever been put in the jailhouse at Mandan."

The way Kate and her daughter had told it, Ralph Bolley had come out to the Rocking W late at night, waving his gun in the air and yelling drunkenly. Kate ordered him off the ranch. Bolley just laughed, walked up onto the porch, and said he'd kick the door down. Kate fired. She said she'd been standing just behind the parlor window with the sash raised and her scattergun's twin barrels pushed out. When Bolley aimed his second kick at the door, she let him have that load of lethal turkey shot from the buckle up.

It was one of those arrests big Bob Lefton would have preferred had been made somewhere else, preferably a good distance from Mandan, by some other peace officer. He didn't like the idea of having women in his jailhouse. He didn't like, particularly, having handsome Kate and her beautiful daughter. He didn't like having to press an investigation into an affair where the whole cussed community was better off because Ralph Bolley was dead. And finally it frightened him, thinking what would happen if Kate and Georgia were somehow found guilty of murder. Big Bob Lefton was a Montanan who'd drifted north after delivering some bulls down to northern Arizona, back toward his home stamping grounds, and had been caught in Mandan by the first blizzards of fall—seven years before.

He'd never gotten any farther north. For three years he'd punched cattle for the Wyoming Cattle Company, Sawyer Given's huge, powerful, very rich cattle outfit. The next three years Bob had served, first, as Mandan town marshal, then as local resident deputy sheriff.

He was a pleasant, efficient, youthful man of thirty with a good head atop his shoulders and a fast right hand. He was slightly above six feet in height and weighed close to two hundred pounds. If Bob Lefton had a fault, it was perhaps attributable to the fact that he'd been a mature, tolerant human being long before he became affiliated with the law. As folks sometimes said, Bob Lefton thought like a cowboy, acted like a very common man, and behaved like a peace officer, but not a good peace officer. In other words, what folks meant was that big Bob Lefton was not hard, or fierce, or thoroughly dedicated to separating the right from wrong. Bob's reply to that, one time up at Oldfield's saloon, had been dry: "Wrong is always what the other feller doesn't think you should do, and right is what you always think you're doing." That was a little abstract for the folks around Mandan, but they quoted it every time the subject came up of whether Bob Lefton was a good peace officer or not.

No one ever questioned his courage or his gunmanship, or even his ability to wade into a saloon brawl and thin out the battlers, and, when his admirers were backed to the wall, they always dragged out a spectacular single-handed apprehension he'd made several years back of four villainous Mormon horse thieves from Utah Territory who'd hit a herd of fine horses belonging to Sawyer Given. That affair had done two things for Bob Lefton; it had raised his stock in the eyes of the folks around the Mandan country, and it had made hard-bitten Sawyer Given his friend. In a man's lifetime he only had one or two chances to have the kind of friend rich Sawyer Given made.

Given was a short, burly, hard-eyed man in his mid fifties who'd been battling all his life one way or another. It had been Indians in his early years, outlaws after that, and all manner of slickers who hovered like birds of prey after his wealth came. He'd spent every waking moment scheming how to expand, how to grow, how to create his cattle empire, and he'd created it. Thirty-five thousand acres of good land, ten thousand cattle, three hundred horses, ten fulltime range men, and in summertime as many as twenty on the payroll.

When folks mentioned Sawyer Given, they said Mr. Given. That went all the way up to the governor's mansion, too. But no one, including Bob Lefton, expected Sawyer Given to pay any attention to a simple matter of a saddle tramp named Ralph Bolley getting himself made into mincemeat out at the Rocking W place. For one thing, Rocking W was only three thousand acres and four hundred critters. For another, Sawyer Given hadn't known Ralph Bolley, and just barely knew who the Willard women were. And finally, as Bob Lefton told Art Flannagan, the blacksmith, it was pretty much of an open and closed case of self-defense. There wasn't anything to it but routine investigation, routine trial, routine acquittal for Kate and her lovely daughter, so why should Sawyer Given, with ten thousand head of cattle to worry about in the hot summertime, get involved in it at all?

Art, who'd been a Given cowboy for five years before breaking loose to start up his smithy in town, said he knew Sawyer Given as well as most folks, and he could solemnly say that Mr. Given didn't miss much. When something happened anywhere in the Mandan country, he made it a point to know about it. "Like he told me one time," Art explained. "When a feller's interests are vitally affected one way or another by everything that occurs, it pays him to damned well keep one eye lookin' backward, an' to keep one ear to the ground."

But Carl Hicks over at the general store had a radically different view of both Sawyer Given and what had happened out at the Rocking W Ranch. He told Bob Lefton that the way he saw it, and speaking strictly from thirty years' experience in the Mandan country, if Kate Willard lost Rocking W, Sawyer Given would pick it up. "That's how he got hold of every section of land he owns, Bob, you can take my word for it. I've watched Sawyer Given grow from the first year he come here. When others went under, died off, or drifted on, there he was, like a buzzard, waitin' to jump on the remains. He'd do the same in a minute, if Kate and Georgia Willard lost their ranch."

"How would they lose it?" Lefton inquired. "The land's clear. They got four hundred cows and bulls."

Carl cast a jaundiced eye up at the taller and younger man. "Easy," he said. "They hire lawyers to keep 'em from being found guilty. Not just this time, but every time they get into more trouble. Pretty soon the lawyers eat 'em up, land, cattle, horses . . . the works."

Lefton gazed at Carl, thinking the older man was warped somehow. "Every time Kate and Georgia get into trouble," he repeated. "Carl, a widow an' a beautiful girl like Georgia . . . they aren't the kind to get into trouble."

Hicks evilly grinned and murmured: "If I got this figured right, Bob, you'll see. Next time you'll see how they can get into more trouble. An' when that happens, remember one thing. I told you so. Maybe Sawyer Given's got you hoodwinked like he's done to most of the other late-comers around here, but I'm not the only old-timer who remembers back a few years to when he wasn't rich or powerful. Then he was an altogether different Mister Given."

Bob caught it from both sides and all around. Everyone had some pet theory. Mostly they added up to just one thing. Bolley had been drinking; he'd gotten to thinking about those two

women out there all alone in the night, and had decided to visit them. Actually Bob himself believed that was all there was to it. He'd had trouble with Ralph Bolley ever since he'd drifted into the Mandan country a year before his death. He was an aging gunfighter, mean, sly, unpredictable, vicious in a fight, and a heavy drinker. His string was just about played out one way or another, when he got himself killed. No one mourned his passing, and, when they'd hauled him over to the little graveyard hill southeast of town in a livery wagon and planted him over there, exactly three people were present—the two laborers who'd been hired at town expense to shovel in the dirt and Deputy Sheriff Bob Lefton.

As for Kate and Georgia Willard, Bob did everything he could to see that they were comfortable in his jailhouse. He wouldn't have kept them in there five minutes if there'd been any legal way not to, but since there was no writ of *habeas corpus* in the Mandan country for the elemental reason that there was no resident attorney to draw it up, and because in Wyoming Territory murder was not admissible to bail, Kate and her daughter languished in custody.

Deputy Lefton had sent an urgent message over to the county seat for the circuit judge to take the first stage to Mandan and resolve the dilemma of his female prisoners. But the judge was in the midst of an involved suit over misbranded cattle and couldn't arrive in Mandan for at least another week. Bob read that reply to his appeal, pocketed it, and went up to Stan Oldfield's place for two strong shots of rye whiskey for the easing of his frustrations.

Stan asked how his investigation was progressing. Bob's reply was gruff. "What investigation? You knew Ralph Bolley as well as I did. What is there to investigate?"

"Yeah," said Stan soothingly. "When's the hearing?"

"Not for another week, and maybe not even then. The judge's

bogged down in another case and can't get here."

"Oh?" murmured Stan. He was a dark, solid man with battle scars over both eyes from twenty years of running brawling saloons. "You figure to keep Kate and Miss Georgia locked up until then?"

"That's the lousy law," said Bob, pushing his glass abruptly forward to be refilled. "You can't let 'em out on bail if the charge is murder in this territory."

"I didn't know that," muttered Stan, refilling the glass. "That's pretty tough on those two women, wouldn't you say?"

"Well, I didn't make that law, Stanley."

"I didn't mean it like that, Bob. I was just. . . ."

"Here's to the law," growled Lefton, and downed his second straight shot. "Here's to the law an' the damned idiots who serve it!"

"Yeah, sure," murmured Stan, and walked away, leaving disgusted Bob Lefton to himself.

# II

During the cattle-working months, usually from March until September in Wyoming Territory, range riders came and went in a sort of blur of names and faces. In wintertime this wasn't so in the Mandan country. Then only owners or steady hired hands were around. But in summertime this did not apply at all, and, because the restless range-riding fraternity came and went, the ranch riding crews constantly changed. Not that anyone cared; they didn't, as long as things were more or less orderly, but now and then some grinning cowboy would hook old Carl Hicks down at the general store, depart the country leaving an unpaid bill, and the storekeeper would moan to the highest heavens how folks certainly weren't as honest as they'd once been. That was how Bob Lefton met Walt Patterson. Walt was an oldish man for a cowboy, at least forty and perhaps closer to fifty, but it was impossible to tell. He was a large man. At one time his six-foot-two-inch frame had been bone and muscle; now it ran somewhat to tallow, especially around Walt's thickening middle. His nose had been broken at least once, and badly reset. His hands were scarred from fights, rope burns, and bruises galore. Walt was an unkempt individual with little sunk-set blue eyes. His hair usually hung from beneath his old hat, straight as a string, and, when he talked, it was in a deep-down, rumbling way that left the immediate impression that old Walt didn't even have a very high regard for himself.

He'd worked for all the worthwhile outfits at one time or another. No one actually had ever complained that Walt Patterson didn't know his trade. He knew it all right; in fact, he knew it so well that sometimes he just got plain bored, quit, and drifted into some town to drink for a spell. When his cash ran out, he then went back to work again. It was one of those times when his cash was gone that Bob Lefton met him, up in the Texas Belle, in fact, at the fretting insistence of Carl Hicks, who'd sworn up and down that he knew Walt meant to skip without paying the bill he owed.

Tackling a man over a bill was nothing Bob liked. It'd always seemed demeaning to him, in the first place, and in the second place he was not especially tactful, which a man should always be when broaching the sensitive topic of past-due accounts. He bought Walt a tall beer and sat at a corner table with Patterson, also sipping. In a way, there was something sad about a cowboy growing old. Within another four or five years, old Walt just wouldn't be hired on. And even an ugly, battered, raffish old coot like Walt Patterson had feelings. Perhaps if Bob had guessed just what actual feelings Walt possessed, he wouldn't have felt so nervous about bringing up the subject of that past-due bill down at the general store. But he didn't know, so he said. "They tell me you're fixin' to ride on, Walt."

Patterson's deceptively mild eyes lifted and clung to Deputy Lefton's smooth-shaven, handsome features. He said in that rough, rumbling voice of his: "Now, Bob, I know why you bought me this beer. Old Man Hicks is stewin' himself into a froth over that seven dollars I owe him."

Bob said nothing. He tipped back his head, drank beer, and waited. When he put the glass back down, Walt spoke again, sounding more aggrieved than annoyed.

"Hell, Bob, I'll pay him. After all, a man's got his pride, y' know. I wouldn't beat that stingy old scrawny skinflint outen his just dues. You ought to know that. I been comin' back to the Mandan country eleven years, each summer, ridin' for the outfits hereabouts. Folks know Walt Patterson. They know he wouldn't willingly run out on no debts."

Bob's eyes twinkled. "How's your memory, Walt?" he asked, and right away the heavier and older man's little eyes puckered warily.

"What you aimin' at, Bob?"

"Two years back, Art Flannagan. . . ."

"Oh, that," said Walt, and managed a slight flush as he grinned, abashed. "Well, I'll tell you how it was, Bob. When a man gets into his thirties, y' see, sometimes he sort of forgets. But I'd have remembered in time. He didn't have to brace me out in the roadway like he done. After all, it was only two dollars, an' I wasn't figurin' on beatin' him out of it. Just a little slip o' the memory was all."

Bob smiled. Thirties! Why Walt Patterson was right close to the stage where he'd never again see his forties, let alone his thirties. Bob finished his beer. "You got the seven dollars on you, Walt?"

"No. I'm a mite short today. But commencin' next week I go to work for Mister Given again. Range boss on his southeast sections. I'll have the money next month, an' I'll make it a special point to see Mister Hicks gets it. That satisfy you, Bob?"

"It doesn't have to satisfy me, Walt. Just satisfy Carl. I don't like being asked to do this kind of stuff."

"Sure not," said Walt, then, as Lefton jackknifed in the chair as though to arise, Walt said: "Say, you goin' to keep Miss Kate and her girl in that jailhouse of yours much longer?"

Bob sighed and settled back, pushed his long legs far out under the table, and said: "Walt, don't tell me you, too, have a theory about Ralph Bolley getting killed."

Walt's eyebrows shot upward like a pair of startled caterpillars. "Theory? What theory?" he asked. "Bolley got just exactly what he asked for. Who says any different?"

Bob shrugged. How did a man explain the intricacies of the law to anyone as thoroughly elemental as Walt Patterson? The answer was they didn't. "There's some talk," Bob murmured. "There always is in a killing."

"What kind of talk? Who's makin' it? I tell you, Bob, I knew Ralph Bolley here in Mandan, and elsewhere on the ranges. It's a pure wonder he lived this long. He was as thoroughly no-good as any man I've ever known, an' let me tell you . . . I've known a heap of men. But that ain't the point, Bob. The point is how much longer you goin' to hold those ladies in that jailhouse of yours?"

"Walt, I can't do a damned thing about releasing them until the court tells me to."

"All right. What's holdin' up the court?"

"The judge. He's up to his ears in a trial over at the county seat. His best guess is that it'll be maybe another two weeks before he can get over and commence a hearing."

Walt's eyes widened. "Two . . . weeks? You mean to tell me Miss Kate's got to . . . ?" Walt stopped speaking, pushed away his beer glass, and began idly drumming on the table top. His little eyes were nearly hidden in rolls of weathered flesh. Finally he said: "Bob, that just ain't right. It ain't natural. A fine woman like Kate Willard settin' in that jailhouse of your'n just because she killed a man like Ralph Bolley. It just plain ain't right."

Bob wearily nodded his head in sober agreement. "But it happens to be the way the law's written," he said, arose, turned, and ambled on out of the saloon, bound down toward Carl Hicks's general store to relay what he'd learned about Carl's chances of getting his $7.

Carl was waspish, which was about usual for him. He said: "I didn't expect much else, to tell you the truth, Deputy. Patterson's a deadbeat an' then some. I recollect over ten years back when he killed a man out there in the roadway. Folks who saw that fight said Walt never even give the other feller a chance. Just drew an' killed him."

Lefton was interested. He'd known Walt Patterson ever since he'd been in the Mandan country; he'd heard stories of Walt's periodic, fabulous drunks, and even now and then of his brawls. But this was the first time he'd ever heard anyone intimate that old Walt wasn't a perfectly fair fighter.

"Who was the other man?" he inquired, and old Hicks shrugged both bony shoulders.

"How should I remember? I just told you, it was ten years back or better. Some other unwashed cowboy, as I think back."

"You didn't see it, Carl?"

"No. I was in the store. I heard that one shot, though, and there was some talk afterward."

"How come Walt wasn't arrested?"

"Humph! He was arrested all right. We had a right upstandin' marshal here in Mandan in them days. But Walt wasn't even tried, except for a hearin' held over in the jailhouse the mornin' after. Then he was handed back his gun and the marshal held the roadway door open for him to walk out, a plumb free man."

Bob regarded the garrulous old storekeeper steadily. "You got something else in your craw," he observed. "OK, Carl, spit it out."

"Sure I'll spit it out. I can tell you in one word why that hearin' didn't amount to a damn, Deputy. In one word."

"I'm waiting, Carl."

"Sawyer," spat out Carl Hicks, spearing Bob with a narrow stare. "Sawyer. You understand now?"

"Yeah, I reckon I do. You're implyin' Mister Given got Walt off."

"Implying! Implying, hell. I know he got him off. Deputy, I was in the jailhouse sittin' on a bench when they had that hearin'. It was the dangedest miscarriage of justice you ever seen in your whole life. Mister Given says to Walt, he says . . . 'Walt, was that feller makin' his play?' And Walt said . . . 'Mister Given, he had his hand on his gun an' was drawin' it when I shot him.' And Sawyer says to the marshal, he says . . . 'Marshal, clear case of self-defense, don't you see it that way?' "

"Go on, Carl," urged Bob Lefton.

"Go on? Go on for what? Walt's still walkin' the roadways, isn't he, cheatin' merchants outen their honest dues? Of course the marshal says he seen it that way. Then he walked over an' opened the door an' nodded his head as Mister Given an' Walt Patterson walked out. That, Deputy, was the whole trial from start to finish." Now, old Hicks leaned far over his counter, piercing Lefton with a fierce look. "You want to know how I know Patterson lied? I'll tell you, Mister Deputy Sheriff. I was Mandan's undertaker then, just like I still am. When the fellers fetched the dead man in to be boxed and planted, his six-gun still had the tie down fastened. He couldn't have been drawin' when Patterson shot him! Now stick that in your pipe an' smoke it!"

Lefton watched old Hicks turn and stamp off toward a waiting customer, wondering how much of what he'd just heard had been prompted by spite, and how much had been gospel truth. He'd never known Carl to lie before. It was a fact, though, that old Carl didn't like Sawyer Given. Just as obvious, too, was the fact that neither did he have any use for Walt Patterson. Eventually, as Deputy Lefton drifted on out of the store, heading for the café to get a couple of trays of supper for Kate and Georgia Willard, he resolved his private dilemma by telling himself that something that had happened a decade earlier hardly concerned him now. But one undeniable fact about gossip, true or false, is simply that it sticks in a person's mind, and later on, when the same target comes under mental scrutiny again, those unconfirmable tales pop up to color a man's thinking.

He got the trays of food and went back to his jailhouse, ruefully reflecting that what had initially been a very simple matter of two unprotected women fighting off a would-be assaulter—or whatever Bolley'd had in mind that night—had now become everyone's personal affair authoritatively to form wild theories about, and plague hell out of the local deputy sheriff with them.

Art Flannagan, whose smithy was on the south side of the jailhouse building, the same as the café was on the north side, was standing out front cooling off, when Deputy Lefton came along with the trays. He saw that Bob had both hands full and sprang over to get the jailhouse front door for him.

"I'm obliged," Bob said, smiling. He and Flannagan were longtime friends. Like a lot of other local men in Mandan, they'd both gotten their start with the Wyoming Cattle Company, Sawyer Given's outfit.

" 'S'all right," said Art, his rough, scarred features creasing into a pleasantly boyish smile. "Anything new?" He meant about releasing the Willard women, of course. That seemed to be all anyone—at least the male anyones—around town thought about these days.

"Not a thing," Lefton said, and stepped inside, side-stepped, kicked the door closed, and advanced across toward the cell-block doorway where he set the trays on a wall bench, fished for his keys, and unlocked the steel-reinforced, oaken door, built so long ago it was black all over, iron, steel, wood, even the hand-made T-hinges.

He was bending to lift the trays when someone opened the roadside door, poked a head in, and said: "Deputy, letter for you." The head of that speaker belonged to Frank Eberly, the Mandan Stage Line's local superintendent. Frank was holding up a long, yellow envelope with some kind of scroll work upon the upper left hand corner.

Bob put the trays down again, went over, and took the envelope. Frank still leaned there, watching. "From Judge Heber," he said, "over at the county seat."

Lefton looked down his nose. "Thanks a lot," he murmured. "I was just ciphering it out for myself, Frank."

Eberly reddened, nodded, withdrew his head, and closed the door as he departed. Lefton opened the envelope and read the letter. It said that Judge Horace Heber, Wyoming Territorial Second District Appeals Justice, would arrive in Mandan to hold a hearing concerning the matter of the late Ralph Bolley two days hence.

Lefton nodded at the letter, pocketed it, and went back over to take up the trays again. He knew Horace Heber; he was a wizened gnome of a man with a flying mane of gray hair and the disposition of a whelping bitch, who took instant umbrage toward anyone at all who even attempted to discuss cases with him that he was to hear. Judge Heber, in short, was a prickly, dogmatic, fiery old stickler for law and order.

Lefton sighed, picked up the trays, and walked on into the cell-block where his only two prisoners shared adjoining cells. That was the trouble; with Heber, no one could ever be sure how the verdict would read.

# III

Katherine Willard actually wasn't forty; she was thirty-eight years of age. She was, to all but the young bucks around the countryside who didn't know anything about mature beauty anyway, the finest-looking specimen of a female in Wyoming Territory. At thirty-eight she was five inches over five feet tall, weighed around a hundred and thirty pounds, and had that solid weight better distributed than most girls of her daughter's age. Moreover, she had hair the color of a desert sunset—darkest auburn red—and green eyes with the arched brows to match that could melt stone or freeze fire when she looked at a man with them. She'd been a widow two years by the time she killed Ralph Bolley, and right up until the past six months she wouldn't even return a range rider's smile if she suspected there was anything beyond pleasant friendliness behind it, which of course meant that she seldom smiled, because a woman such as Kate Willard did things to men, even to married men, let alone the bachelors of which there were plenty in the Mandan country, including dried up old prunes like Carl Hicks, the storekeeper, Deputy Sheriff Bob Lefton, the blacksmith Flannagan, and darkly battered and bold Stan Oldfield. Of course there were the other bachelors, too; men like unkempt Walt Patterson and Sawyer Given, one of which wasn't even remotely eligible, and the other of which knew Kate Willard existed, and left it right there.

Georgia favored her dead father. She was long-legged, had taffy-colored blonde hair, and direct blue eyes. At eighteen she was high-breasted and lean-hipped, and did more cowboying on the Willard home place, the Rocking W, than a lot of Sawyer Given's paid riders. She was open and warm and friendly. She was also the cause of more than one cow-camp brawl without ever suspecting that she was, and could've had her pick of the top hands, if she'd wanted them. In fact, the thought occurred to Bob Lefton as he placed the trays on a table outside those two cells, if he'd sat down and deliberately tried to pick someone to lock up who'd have the whole sympathy of the menfolk for five hundred miles in all directions, he couldn't have done a better job. About womenfolk, that might ordinarily have been a different thing, for the ranch and town women had turned green in years past just at the mention of the Willard name. But even that had changed, after the slaying of Bolley. Women just naturally rallied to the support of some unfortunate fellow female who'd been treated harshly by a man. When it happened also to be a widow, who'd been nearly attacked, that made it even worse.

Bob opened Georgia's cell first and handed in her food. He didn't look up until he'd relocked the door. She was watching him, her lovely eyes solemn, her beautiful face totally still and expressionless. He tried a little grin. "You don't have to look like that," he said. "It's not your last supper."

Kate met him at the door for her tray. He looked straight at Kate. She was seven or eight years his senior, but for some inexplicable reason, when Kate was around he couldn't see Georgia for shadows.

"Thank you, Bob," she said, and turned to set the tray aside. "Any word yet about the judge?"

"Yes'm. He'll be here day after tomorrow."

She kept an assessing gaze upon Lefton, then said: "You don't look happy about that, Bob. What is it? Do you like having women in your jailhouse?"

"You know better," he replied, relocking her door, also. "This judge is old Horace Heber. He's a bear for the law."

"Well, I should hope so," stated Kate, keeping her green eyes upon Bob's face. "We wouldn't want any other kind of a judge.

After all, the law states that people are in the right defending themselves and their homes."

Lefton reached up to thumb back his hat. Outside, the afternoon was wearing along. Inside, there were only two small, high little barred windows set deeply into the back wall. The light failed fast in Mandan's cell-block. It shadowed Kate's lovely features, softening them toward him, turning them sweet and desirable and girlish. "I reckon," he said quietly, thinking different thoughts. "Kate, I sure wish you 'n' Georgia well."

Her stare became very still. "Why do you say that?" she asked. "Bob, is there something I should know?"

"No," he muttered. "No. Only I'm not as green around the law as you are, so I know how the simplest things sometimes get turned all around, twisted out of shape and reason."

Kate took one forward step, placed both hands upon the bars, and said: "Is there something wrong?"

"Nothing's wrong, Kate. All I'm saying is, look him right in the eye, tell it just like it happened, and for the life of me I don't see how he can hand down any other verdict than justifiable homicide."

Kate nodded very gently. "Thank you," she murmured, and stepped over to the pallet where she'd put her supper tray. Over in the adjoining cell Georgia, watching those two and listening, looked longest at Bob Lefton, as he turned and ambled back out front to his office, closed the door, locked it, and pocketed the key as he strode across to leave the jailhouse and make his last round of the day.

Outside, he paused to draw back a big breath and carefully expel it. Kate Willard, eight years difference in their ages or no eight years difference, was the kind of a woman who could draw a man against his will, who could smile in passing, and fifty years later in his rickety old age a man would still hold that fleeting smile as clearly and vividly in memory as the day he'd first received it.

"You look tired," said Art Flannagan, heading for home with his coat thrown over one brawny shoulder. Art had washed at the blacksmith shop. It was very easy to see precisely where the soap and water had reached, and where it hadn't. His face and neck were startlingly pale, while his arms and exposed shoulders were grimy with sweat and coal dust, forge smoke, and just plain honest dirt.

"Yeah," said Bob.

"Meet me at Stan's in a couple hours and I'll stand the first round."

"Fair enough," agreed Lefton. He and Flannagan both lived on the second floor of Mrs. Daily's rooming house, where in fact most of Mandan's bachelors resided. "Maybe a little stud poker later on."

Art nodded, then licked his lips and cleared his throat. "Anythin' new this afternoon?" he inquired.

"Trial'll be day after tomorrow," grumbled Lefton, stepped out into the roadway, and tramped across toward the harness shop opposite his office, where he usually commenced making his evening rounds.

News traveled fast in Mandan, particularly when it was concerning the impending Willard trial. Before Lefton had completed his patrol, which was an evening ritual established by the Lord knew who in years past, he met two local men who confided in him that the trial date for Kate and Georgia Willard had been officially set for two days hence. If it got around that fast in town, he speculated, by the day of the trial it would have also spread to all the outlying cow outfits for miles around.

He was correct. When Judge Heber arrived, sneaked one quick one up at the Texas Belle, beat roadway dust off himself on his way down to the town council's quarters that also doubled as courtroom upon occasion, among other civic functions, Mandan was full of range men from as far off as the Wyoming Cattle Company's northernmost ranges, and from as far southward as the Ute Agency, where Indian Bureau employees—one with the most elegant lavender sleeve garters ever seen in Mandan—came all the way to town in wagons.

Deputy Lefton had all the depositions in order. He presented them to the court, who smelt fragrantly of Stan Oldfield's mountain dew, and withdrew at the court's direction with instructions not to open the doors until one hour hence, which would permit the court to get familiarized with the facts.

Frank Eberly from the stageline office, with a necktie on and a celluloid collar, was outside, standing with old Carl Hicks, who'd combed his scanty hair to cover that shiny spot on top. Even Stan Oldfield was among the folks waiting to go inside and take seats. Mandan hadn't had a decent trial in three years. The last one, as a matter of fact, no one liked to recall, for thirty minutes after the judge had departed on the afternoon stage, popular opinion had reversed the judge's verdict; the horse thief had been taken out of town quietly and lynched. No one had ever been arrested for that crime. No one had ever willingly discussed it afterward, but because the horse thief had been as thoroughly a worthless individual as Ralph Bolley had also been not one shred of guilt was displayed.

The crowd was milling by the time the court had decreed Deputy Lefton could fetch over the prisoners and throw open the roadside doors. There were nearly as many women as men, too, which was unusual. Ordinarily womenfolk didn't meddle in things like trials.

When Bob returned with the Willards, a low, quiet sound passed up and down the room. Judge Heber peered over the top of his glasses, peered again, then removed the glasses and admiringly stared. Kate walked in front, young Georgia several paces behind her mother.

There was no jury. In fact, this wasn't actually a trial, but rather a hearing. If a hearing found sufficient evidence to warrant an official trial, then the case would be remanded to a higher justice. If no such evidence was found, then the prisoners would be released, the case would be dismissed, and nothing more would be officially said of the matter.

Judge Heber asked Kate to testify first. She told him precisely what she'd told Bob Lefton the day he'd fetched Kate and her daughter into town under arrest for suspicion of murder. Heber's gnomish body was hunched forward. His lined, decidedly acid features never once turned away all the time Kate was speaking. When she'd finished, he thanked her with a courtliness that made Bob Lefton stare hard at him in surprise, then asked Kate's daughter to step forward and tell what she'd seen. Georgia's testimony, although spoken in a subdued, low voice, was audible all over the room. There wasn't a sound among the crowded people seated on the benches.

Judge Heber thanked Georgia in the same courtly way, and told her to return to her bench. He put on his glasses, inched them down his nose, and peered over a paper in his hands at Bob Lefton. "Who embalmed the deceased?" he asked.

Lefton turned, sought out Carl Hicks, and said: "Mister Hicks, Your Honor. He's the storekeeper . . . and undertaker."

"*Ah* yes," murmured Heber, squinting out at Carl. "I'm glad to see you Mister Hicks. It's been some time, hasn't it?"

"Some time," echoed old Carl, reddening under the stares of spectators.

"Tell me something, Mister Hicks," said Judge Heber in a very gentle voice. "This man Ralph Bolley . . . was he badly shot up?"

"Your Honor, he was a mess."

"But you embalmed him, Mister Hicks?"

"No, sir, Your Honor. I don't bother embalmin' 'em if we got a ready hole over at the cemetery, and I got box that'll fit 'em. Just nail 'em in, get the wagon from the livery barn, an' have 'em hauled out an' planted."

"I see. One last question, Mister Hicks. This Ralph Bolley . . . he was a gunman, wasn't he, a dissolute person, troublemaker, brawler, drunkard?"

"You left out some of it," said old Carl, and the spectators started to laugh. Bob Lefton winced for them.

Judge Heber snapped erect in his chair, struck the table top hard with a gavel, and flashed a furious eye out over the room. "In case you folks hadn't been informed," he said angrily, "this is a court of law, not an amusement theater. No one laughs in a court of law but ignorant fools! Do it one more time and I'll have the deputy clear this room!"

The silence returned deeper than before, and, if several dozen dark-stained faces glared cold venom at the judge, Horace Heber appeared not to notice it. "Thank you, Mister Hicks," he said to old Carl. "You've been right co-operative." He seemed to have finished. But suddenly he leaned over, stabbed a finger at old Carl, and said: "I want the truth from you. Did those pellets hit Ralph Bolley from in front or from behind?"

Carl's mouth dropped open. Heber's fierce tone and stabbing finger seemed to freeze the storekeeper where he sat. He blinked up toward the table behind which Judge Heber sat hunched forward, batting his eyes like a person who'd just walked out of a dark room into bright sunlight.

"Well, Mister Hicks. From in front or from behind?" Heber lowered his hand, removed his glasses, and leaned back. "Oh, come," he said, dropping back to his normal tone of voice again. "That's a very simple question to answer, since you're the one who cleaned up the corpse and boxed it."

"Your Honor," stammered old Carl, shaken to the core. "I told you, Ralph Bolley was a complete mess. I rolled him into the coffin and. . . ."

"Mister Hicks! I want an answer to my question right now! Was Ralph Bolley, or was he not, shot in the back?"

Carl crumpled. He was more than frightened now; he was thoroughly confused and befuddled. Around him, startled spectators stared. They were just as astonished at this turn in events as Bob Lefton himself was.

"It could've been . . . either way" whispered old Carl. "Your Honor . . . sir . . . he could've been shot from either in front or behind."

Judge Heber smiled frostily and turned his bleak eyes. "Deputy, remand the prisoners to jail pending a trial by a higher court. This hearing stands adjourned!"

Bob Lefton couldn't believe his ears.

# IV

Poor Carl was a frayed wreck two days after that hearing. He'd tried to explain a hundred times why he'd said those things, and what it boiled down to was simply that it just hadn't occurred to him that anyone would ever question how Ralph Bolley had been shot. "An'," he confessed to Bob Lefton, "Horace Heber put the Injun sign on me. I swear, Bob, my mind just went blank. I couldn't think of the right thing to say. I just plain couldn't think of anythin' to say. He put them words in my mouth, and I was too danged upset 'n' confused 'n' fuddled to do anything about it."

The indignation throughout the Mandan countryside was so fiercely intense Lefton was glad Horace Heber had departed the afternoon of the trial. He'd have been mauled at the very least, and at the worst he'd have been lynched, if he'd still been in town when the shock and astonishment had passed. Worst of all, for Bob Lefton, was the way Kate and Georgia looked at him when he brought them their meals. It wasn't what they said; they were scrupulously civil to him. Frigidly civil, in fact. But they regarded him through their bars as though he'd done something unspeakably treacherous. As he told Stan Oldfield up at the Texas Belle that second night: "I could walk under a snake's belly carrying an umbrella, I'm so damned low in their eyes, Stan."

Oldfield wasn't very sympathetic. In fact, even Art Flannagan began avoiding Lefton. By the end of that first week a pall had settled over Mandan. The town resembled some kind of divided camp, while actually there was no real division at all. It was simply that people had stopped quite trusting their law officer, and even looked at one another with some doubt.

Unkempt Walt Patterson rode into town one early evening and washed up over at the public trough, then led his horse on down to the jailhouse tie rack when he saw Bob Lefton seated out there in the pleasant shade in front of his office, under the warped old wooden overhang awning.

"*Whew,*" rumbled Walt, clumping over to sit down beside Bob, "she sure was a hot one today. I rode the east ranges lookin' for Mister Given, never even seen his dust, an' liked to've croaked for a little water before I got back to town."

"I thought you were going to work for him a couple of weeks back," said Bob without looking around at the larger, heavier man. "That's what you told me up at the Texas Belle."

"Well, sure I was, an' I still am, only he don't know it yet 'cause I ain't havin' much luck findin' him to tell him," said Patterson, who now dug out a wicked-bladed clasp knife and began to pare his fingernails diligently. "Say, how're them pretty prisoners o' yours, Bob?"

"Pretty still," replied Lefton dryly, "and still pretty."

"You been told yet when that there higher court'll try 'em?"

"Nope. They keep a calendar. They enter each case on it, and, when your turn gets close, they let you know."

"That's interestin'," murmured old Walt. "Y' know, I was in the back o' the room when Judge Heber held court over here that day, Bob, an' I been wonderin' ever since what that paper was he picked up an' read just before he surprised old Hicks half out of his wits with that dang-fool question about whether Bolley was shot from in front or from behind." Walt stopped paring and lifted his small, clear eyes. "You got any idea what that paper said?"

Lefton shook his head. He hadn't given that aspect of the trial more than a passing thought in the two ensuing weeks. "Probably one of the depositions Kate or Georgia made to me. Or maybe some paper having to do with his next case for all I know."

"No," contradicted old Walt slowly, resuming his fingernail carving. "No, it wasn't none of the papers you'd given him, Bob."

Lefton raised his head, looking skeptical. "How do you know that, Walt?"

"Well, them other papers on his desk wasn't folded. They didn't have no creases in 'em like the one he read when he hit old Carl with them questions was. That one looked to me like it was a letter. It'd been folded a couple of times like it'd been stuffed into an envelope."

Lefton kept staring. Walt Patterson looked upward from beneath his shiny old hat brim and grinned over at the deputy with just his eyes. He was holding that big wicked knife blade so that the late-day sun struck it, burnishing the steel to a reddish hue.

"Feller learns to observe things," Walt said, sounding almost apologetic, "when he's had the close scrapes I've had in my years o' living, Deputy. Sometimes, just seein' how a leaf was turned, in the old days, or which way the grass had been bent, kept a feller from ridin' into an ambush an' maybe losin' his hair."

"Never mind all that," said Bob. "You're hinting that Judge Heber'd received a letter from someone saying that Ralph Bolley'd been perhaps shot from behind . . . murdered?"

Walt ran a hand under his long, crooked nose, sniffled, and said: "Well, Deputy, a feller gets to puzzlin' things through sometimes when they puzzle him. I figure old Heber had some reason to ask that question of Carl. I figure a man who's been sittin' in on other folks' miseries as long as old Heber's been doin' it, don't make up accusations out of the whole cloth. I figure, Deputy, someone planted that thought of Bolley gettin' it from behind in Judge Heber's mean little mind. They done it by sendin' him a letter. That was the same letter he was lookin' at when he surprised Carl with them questions."

Lefton sat for a long time regarding the big, slovenly old cowboy without saying a word. He went back in time to the trial, trying hard to recollect whether that paper Heber had been studying when he'd thrown Carl Hicks into confusion had been folded or not. As Patterson had said, the papers Bob had presented to Heber hadn't been folded; he'd made them out on his desk and had carried them across the road unfolded. He always did it that way when a trial was held in Mandan. He'd never folded a paper he'd presented to the court since he'd been making them out. It was a small thing. So insignificant in fact that he hadn't even thought about it. Until now. But what Walt was inferring didn't make a whole lot of sense, either. Why would anyone want to stir the troubled waters?

"Spite, maybe," muttered old Walt, closing his pocket knife and holding up one set of thick, splayed fingers to examine his paring job. "You know how folks are sometimes, Deputy. Mean without no real reason for bein' that way. Vicious an' spiteful." He pocketed the big knife, dropped his hand, and said: "Or maybe it wasn't just spite. I been reflectin' on it this past week. Maybe it was someone who stands to profit some way if Miss Kate an' her daughter get convicted in this mess."

"Who?" asked Deputy Lefton. "With all this figuring you've done, you'll have come up with more than just this much, Walt."

"No, as a matter o' fact, y' see, I been too busy tryin' to get hold of Mister Given so's I can get back to work." Patterson heaved a big sigh, stood up, indifferently shoved his baggy shirt into his sagging trousers, and looked up the road wistfully toward the Texas Belle. Without gazing around, he said: "Deputy, you wouldn't have a couple of dollars on you a feller might borrow for a few days, would you?"

Lefton gave him the $2 and remained out there on his jail-house bench until dusk was descending, turning the matter of that folded letter over and over in his mind. He didn't come out of this reverie until the late-day stage spun into town from the north, and that event reminded him that he hadn't made his rounds, so he arose and went ambling on over toward the harness works where he usually started checking things.

The last patrol of the day deliberately ended out front of the Texas Belle. It ended out there this night, too, but before he had a chance to enter the place, Art Flannagan strolled up, freshly washed and dressed, and said—"Too bad about that mole of a judge."—and would have barged on past but for Bob's blocking arm.

"What judge?" he asked. "You mean Heber?"

Flannagan turned back, his face smooth, his eyes dead level. "Sure. What other judge's been around here lately?"

"What about him, Art?"

"Why, someone let him have a blast from a shotgun yesterday when he was ridin' through on the morning coach. Hell, I thought everyone'd heard about that by now."

Bob was stopped cold. "I hadn't heard," he said. "Who told you?"

"Some of the fellers. The news came in with the evening stage."

Deputy Lefton turned on his heel, stepped off the sidewalk, and went hiking down toward the stageline office where an orange lamp was brightly burning upon a battered counter where Frank Eberly, still wearing his eye shade, was making entries in a large book. When Lefton walked in, Frank looked up, his pen poised. The look on Lefton's face kept Frank from saying anything right away.

Bob leaned on the counter. "Who brought that tale about Judge Heber being shot?" he demanded.

Eberly carefully lay aside his pen, removed his eye shade, and said: "The driver an' guard on the late stage. Why? Don't you believe it?"

"I don't believe rumors or gossip, Frank."

Eberly stepped away, stepped back with a yellow slip of paper in his hand, and dropped it atop the counter in front of Lefton. "See for yourself," he said, slightly offended. "Those are the details as told by the driver of the coach old Heber was ridin' in. The coach was proceedin' southward from the last stop. They'd slowed the horses because they had a long uphill grade to make. A feller stepped out from behind a big rock at the side of the road, called out, an', when Horace Heber poked his head out, the killer let go with both barrels of a shotgun. It's all right there, even the driver's name an' the shotgun guard's name. No one had a chance to fire back. That killer just stepped out there, called to Heber, and let fly, then he jumped back behind his rock and disappeared."

Bob read the crisp, blunt report, then he reread it. Eberly had summarized it very well, except for one fact. Judge Heber had been southbound for Mandan.

Lefton put the yellow paper down and squinted at the far wall. To his knowledge there was no reason for Heber to be returning. In fact, he didn't think it was wise for the judge to show up around Mandan again, so soon after remanding Kate and her daughter to jail pending a superior court trial.

"What's the matter?" asked Frank Eberly.

"He was coming here. It says so right where it lists the number and date of his stage ticket."

"Well, he had to be going somewhere, Bob."

"But why Mandan? He'd already done all the damage around here he could do. Besides, I don't have any other prisoners to be heard."

Frank reached over, picked up the yellow paper, and put it back on a spindle on his desk. He then closed the book he'd been making entries in with a loud slap of finality, and said: "Can't say I'll shed any tears over his passing. Well, unless you've got something else on your mind, I've got to close up."

Deputy Lefton went back outside where darkness was closing in, turned, and ambled down toward his jailhouse. He'd fed the Willards earlier, and he'd finished his evening round. Except for his customary couple of drinks up at Stan's bar, he was finished for the day. Ordinarily he'd have headed for Mrs. Daily's rooming house, but it was still a little early for bed so he entered his office, crossed to the cell-block, and went down where the old backless chair was, out front of Kate Willard's cell, and wordlessly sat down.

Kate and Georgia had been brushing one another's long hair through the bars, but when Bob appeared, they desisted, and turned to watch him. He pushed back his hat, eyed the pair of them, and said: "Someone killed Judge Heber."

Georgia didn't make a sound but her mother said: "Oh, Bob, I'm sorry. What happened?"

Lefton told them as much as he knew, then he said: "Kate, I

want you to be plumb straightforward with me. Can you think of an enemy you might have who'd want to see you convicted of Ralph Bolley's killing?"

Kate's arched brows gently lifted; her large green eyes got perfectly round in the guttery light of the single overhead lantern. "We have no enemies, Bob," she murmured, watching his face closely. "At least if we have any, I surely can't imagine who they'd be."

"But you've wondered about Judge Heber remanding you back here to be held for a higher court."

"Yes, of course."

"And you've wondered why he'd try and make out that you'd shot Bolley in the back, committing murder, instead of killing him in self-defense like you said."

"Yes. But, Bob, he's a judge. It's his job, I suppose, to be suspicious. To want a complete investigation made. To be thoroughly satisfied it wasn't murder."

Lefton glanced over at lovely Georgia. She was watching him with a puzzled little expression. He slapped his legs and stood up.

"Well, I don't think you murdered Bolley. What motive would you have? He had no money, and that's usually what folks murder other folks for. Besides, he just wasn't the kind of a man who could very easily be murdered. He was a gunfighter. He knew every trick of his trade." Bob paused, resettled his hat, then said: "But I'll tell you one thing. This isn't going to end so simply, after all."

"No? What are you thinking?" Kate inquired.

"I'm thinking that whoever killed Judge Heber did so because he'd been brooding over how the old cuss tried to railroad you two."

"Railroad us, Bob, but why?"

Lefton shook his head. "I can't imagine, Kate. But I aim to

find out, and I aim to do it before you're tried, too." He hooked both thumbs in his shell belt and stood a moment looking straight down into those large green eyes. "Why couldn't it have been just a simple case of aggravated assault and self-defense?" he growled.

# V

The murder of Judge Horace Heber gave folks in Mandan something fresh to speculate about. Because of this, they began to forget that they'd been a little cold toward Deputy Lefton. Even old Carl Hicks, whose caustic disposition had been subtly altered by the looks of disapprobation that had been leveled at him since his agonizing moments at the hearing, began to perk up again, not as much on the defensive as he'd been before. Trade picked up a little, too, at Carl's general store, because people wanted to hear the opinions others might have to express. Actually, except for Bob Lefton, the range men and townsmen both surmised that someone had killed old Heber over his decision in the Willard case, but they didn't reason beyond that. Bob did because it was his job and his training to do so. But when it came to pinning down who might have given old Heber those two barrels of buckshot, he had the entire countryside to suspect, and even farther, because many of the spectators at the Willard trial had come from even farther off than the generally conceded environs of the Mandan range. As he told Stan Oldfield the day after the news of Heber's murder had hit town: "How do you narrow it down, when you never really know what a man'll do when he's upset? I've seen 'em go off the deep end over a lot less than this and so have you. Hell, Stan, some fellows'll shoot to kill just over being accidentally jostled right here at this bar."

"Amen," assented Oldfield quietly. "I know what you mean."

"So it could've been anyone. It could've been you, in fact."

"Oh, no," responded Stan vigorously. "Heber got it day before yesterday. You just ask around town. I was right here in my saloon all the time. I can name thirty fellers who came in here between ten in the mornin' an'. . . ."

"I didn't mean you, really," broke in Lefton. "What I meant was, anyone could've done it. I've got no way to narrow it down."

An apprentice who worked in the harness shop poked his head in and said: "Deputy, there's some fellers over at the jailhouse want to see you right away."

Lefton finished his drink and departed. It was dark out, otherwise he might have been able to recognize those bunched up horsemen standing down there in front of the jailhouse. As it turned out now, though, until he was even with the front door of the café that adjoined his building on the north, he didn't recognize any of them. One man stepped over onto the sidewalk as he saw Lefton striding over. It was Sawyer Given himself.

Lefton looked out by his hitch rack where the others were standing with their mounts. There were five of them. One in particular he knew—Buzz Hilton, Given's range boss for the whole ranch. The others he knew by sight; mostly Sawyer Given's permanent hands did not get down this way very often. His mountain range was the place where his riders had to be kept in camps during the grazing season, and, because this particular stretch of range was so distant from Mandan, those men usually made the towns on across the mountains.

"Want a word with you," said Given, swinging to head on over to the jailhouse door. He was his customary brusque self, short, heavy, decisive, the way he moved as well as spoke.

Lefton led the way inside and looked back. None of the range riders out at the tie rack made any move to come inside.

"Never mind them," stated Given bluntly. "They'll wait."

Bob closed the door and went across to sit at the desk. His

visitor dropped down upon the edge of a bench and said: "I've got a feeling, Bob. There's something going on."

Lefton grunted agreement. "There's something going on all right," he assented. "But as far as I can see it doesn't concern your outfit."

"Why doesn't it?" snapped the older man, thrusting his jaw out. "Anything around here affects me. Anything at all, an' don't you forget it."

"Just how would the murder of a court judge affect you, Mister Given?"

"I'll tell you how. Heber was on his way down here to see me. That's how."

Bob rolled this interesting bit of information around in his head a moment, then said: "Mind telling me what he wanted to see you about?"

Sawyer Given was a man who shot straight answers at anyone he happened to be conversing with. He did that now. He said bluntly: "I hired Horace Heber two years ago to represent me in some civil matters. Quiet title to land I acquired a long time ago that had uncertain deeds or clouds on the titles. He was to visit me at the ranch yesterday with a report of the progress he'd made."

"I see. Well, Mister Given, tell me this. Who knew he'd be visiting you?"

"Who'd know? How the hell can I answer that? I knew, and maybe Buzz Hilton knew, although I don't recall telling him. But whoever Heber might've told he was coming down here is anybody's guess." Given's flinty gray eyes turned speculative. "If you're thinking someone from my outfit did that, Bob, you're all wrong. No one'd have any reason to."

"That," stated Lefton bluntly, "is what we won't know until we catch the killer, Mister Given. Who can say what motive prompted that killer to blow a hole in Heber? I'll tell you this for a fact. When he ordered Kate and Georgia held for further trial, he made half the riders and townsmen and visitors at that trial mad clean through. Now you tell me you don't have any men in your employ who've gone for their guns on less of an excuse than that."

Sawyer Given heard Lefton out, eased off, and leaned back with his thick shoulders upon the solid wall between Bob's office and the cell-block. For a while he simply regarded Lefton with a thoughtful, steady stare, then he said: "All right, Bob. You're makin' sense. I won't say none of my men killed Heber, but I will say that I can't imagine which one would've done it. I've been home most of this past couple of weeks working out some shipping-weight tallies, and in that length of time I've seen every man who works for me at least twice, right there in the yard of the home place. If one of them could ride over to the eastward trace, waylay a coach, and return in one day, I'd sure like to know which of my horses he was riding."

*"Whoa,"* said Bob suddenly. "Back up just a minute. You said you were at the home place all of the past two weeks?"

"Yes. What of that?"

"And all your men knew you were there?"

"What the hell are you getting at?"

"Just answer my question, Mister Given."

"Yes, confound it, my men knew I was at the home place. I told you . . . in that length of time I saw every man at least a couple of times."

Bob leaned back in his chair and gazed over Given's head at the wall. Walt Patterson had lied. He'd said he'd been hunting Sawyer Given to get a job, and hadn't been able to find him. It had to be a lie, because if Given had been at his home all that time, and all his men knew he was at the home place, then Patterson either hadn't ever gone to Given's headquarters ranch, or hadn't talked to any of Given's riders, which made him a liar because he'd told Bob Lefton sitting right outside the office on that old bench that he'd hunted high and low for Sawyer Given and hadn't been able to find him.

"Well?" demanded the powerful cattleman. "What're you starin' off into space for? You got some clue or something?"

Lefton didn't directly answer any of the questions. He said: "You need any more men?"

"No, in fact, as soon as the boys're finished drifting steers down from the mountain ranges, I'm figurin' on lettin' the extra gang go. Why, you know someone who wants work?"

"Walt Patterson, Mister Given."

The cowman slitted his eyes and hung fire over his next remarks. Finally he said: "Send him out to the home place. I don't really need anyone, but I've known Walt Patterson since we were both young men. I'll find a bunk for him."

"Thanks," said Lefton, arising. "I'll do that."

Given made no move to arise. "We're not through talking yet," he growled.

Lefton resumed his seat. "What else?" he inquired politely.

"That trouble I said I could feel buildin' up when I first came in here," replied Given, "has to do with cattle, Bob."

"You're losing stock again?"

"No, I'm gaining stock." Given snapped his thin-lipped mouth closed for a moment to let that enigmatic statement sink in, then he said: "I've got a bunch of prime two-year-old steers in my home place gather that got my brand but which don't belong to me."

"How can you be sure they don't?"

"Easy. My critters are all marked when they're calves, usually under six months of age. These big steers are still showing pink scars. They were branded not more than a couple of months ago. Some of 'em still have scabs."

Bob was stopped cold. He sat gazing over at Sawyer Given

trying to imagine what kind of a stunt this was. Given wasn't lying, he knew that. Given had no reason to lie. "How many head?" he asked.

"Couple hundred I'd say offhand. We haven't found 'em all yet."

Lefton nodded about that, too. If a man such as Sawyer Given had set out to steal other people's steers, he wouldn't stop at two hundred head. He didn't even think of cattle in lots of less than a thousand head.

"What have you figured out about this?" Bob asked.

Given lowered his head. "Nothing," he said. "Why would someone use my brand? Years back men occasionally did something like that to cause bad blood among neighboring cow outfits, but hereabouts I own most of the land. My neighbors are little ranchers, most of them running only a couple hundred head and less. These cattle didn't come from them or you'd have heard by now that someone was losing cattle." Given shook his head at Lefton. "You haven't had any such complaints or I'd have heard of that, too, by now."

Whether Bob agreed with Given's implication that he'd have heard or not, one thing was true. No one had complained of a cattle loss. Also, what Given had said about most of his neighbors being small ranchers was also true; if any of those people had lost as many as two hundred steers, not just Bob Lefton but the whole countryside would've heard about it by now.

"It doesn't make very much sense," agreed Bob.

Now, finally, Sawyer Given stood up. "Keep your ear to the ground," he said gruffly. "Sooner or later someone's going to want to know what became of two hundred head of prime two-year-old steers. When you hear, let me know, Bob. It's not the cattle. I'm curious as all hell as to what's going on."

Lefton accompanied Given back outside and watched as he

and his riders got astride, loped up the road as far as the Texas Belle, whirled in up there, and got down again. As they were trooping inside, a sudden startling thought struck Lefton squarely between the eyes. He stood stockstill, staring up toward the Texas Belle Saloon. A full minute passed before he stirred, then he struck out for the livery barn, got his private animal, and rode out of Mandan westbound.

The night was faintly star lit. It was a warm night, and pleasant to travel through. There were stars as big as hen's eggs overhead and a good fragrance rode a low breeze down from the upland country where pines and firs and cedars grew in great abundance. Sawyer Given's Wyoming Cattle Company's range ran southward on both sides of Mandan, but directly below town was the open range of several other cattlemen. Mostly Given's ranges were north, east, and west. It was over this great expanse of westerly range that Lefton was now riding.

There were some fringe ranchers several miles out, where Given's land dwindled down to a long contiguous front with these people. Mostly these fringe ranchers grazed to the southward. Occasionally, because of poor patrolling either by the fringe outfits or Given himself, some of the settler cattle got up onto Given range. In the recent past this had caused no trouble; one side or the other always rode out, rounded up the strays, and pushed them back where they belonged. It was said, though, by folks who were old enough to remember, that in the early days Given's tough riders shot strays as a warning to settlers to stay off Wyoming Cattle Company range.

The Willard place was one of the first fringe ranches a rider passed over after he left Mandan, riding west. It was actually surrounded on three sides by Sawyer Given's range. When Justice Willard had been alive, there'd been no trouble. In fact, Bob could recall seeing Justice and Sawyer set up drinks for each other at Oldfield's saloon on more than one occasion. Willard had run his cattle southward, down where the fringe outfits shared something like fifteen thousand common open range acres. Justice Willard was a good cowman; in fact, he had been one of the more successful small cowmen in the Mandan country.

When Bob topped out over a low land swell, star shine showed the Willard ranch buildings on ahead. They reminded him of Justice Willard. They were strong buildings, set squarely on their fir log foundations, well built and well kept. Although they looked forlornly deserted now, as he approached them, they nevertheless still had that honest, strong aura to them.

He tied his horse and went around behind the barn into the corral network back there. He had a hunch the snubbing post would reveal fresh marks of wire-taut lariats on it. No cattle, to his knowledge, had been worked through these corrals in the past two years. Not since Justice had been killed. He'd heard the neighbors say how they'd brought in Kate Willard's critters with their own and had worked them at their home places, being neighborly, because there was no man at the Willard ranch any longer to do it for Justice's widow.

The snubbing post was a mighty cedar log set four feet deep into the ground, squarely in the center of the round, or working, corral. After two Wyoming winters and summers it still showed the deep scores where smoking ropes had bit hard down with a thousand pound critter at the other end. A lot of cattle had been worked through this corral, but now one gate sagged in the grass, and moonlight showed that quiet neglect was otherwise also taking its toll.

He ran a hand over the snubbing post, encountered fresh, raw slivers, and bent closer to look. When he slowly straightened up, he slowly paced his way back and forth through churned dust and trampled weeds. He had not only his answer to the fact that these corrals had been used often, and comparatively recently, too, but he thought he now knew where those two hundred misbranded steers had come from, and why no one had complained of their loss. No one could complain; the owners of those steers were locked up in Deputy Lefton's jailhouse back in Mandan!

He got back astride, turned, and pointed his horse back toward town, let the beast choose its own trail and its own gait, and fell to thinking some unkind thoughts about someone.

# VI

He didn't bother Kate and Georgia that night, but the following morning, while they were eating the breakfast he'd fetched, he stood outside in the little narrow alleyway that ran down in front of the cells and smoked a cigarette while idly talking.

"Kate, a couple of months back, did you and Georgia take a trip anywhere?"

Kate Willard was sipping coffee. She gazed out at Lefton. "Yes," she said. "We went down to Denver for several days. There are some friends down there Justice and I knew in the East years ago."

"Any other recent trips, Kate?"

"Now and then an occasional visit or shopping trip to Cheyenne or Laramie, or . . . why, Bob? What are you driving at?"

He ignored the question to ask Georgia how much riding she'd done previous to the killing of Ralph Bolley. She shrugged lovely, rounded shoulders. "Not as much as I did earlier in the spring, but when the neighbors rode out to check drift or hunt strays, if they let me know in advance, I'd go along."

"One final question," the deputy said. "When did you folks figure to make your annual gather?"

"Not until September," replied Kate. "Perhaps August, Bob, when the others got ready to trail their two-year-olds to railhead." Now Kate put down her coffee cup and gazed hard at Lefton. "Is it the cattle?" she quietly asked.

"Appears like it," he answered. "But I can't say much more until I know more myself." He started to turn away.

Kate called him back. "Bob . . . ?"

"Yes'm."

"Buzz Hilton paid us a visit two weeks before Bolley came by. He said his men had pushed some of our steers down off Mister Given's range and they were unbranded."

"Two-year-olds?" said Bob. "Will you explain something to me? How come you to have two-year-olds that weren't branded?"

Kate and Georgia exchanged a blank look, then the older woman said: "I didn't know we had any that weren't branded, Bob."

He nodded his head at her, saying nothing but thinking privately that the biggest mistake a man could make was to leave two women to operate a cow outfit, even a small one, by themselves. He returned to his office where morning sunlight flooded the place, killed his smoke, and picked up a cooling cup of coffee he'd brought back with him when he'd fetched breakfast for his prisoners. As he sipped, he turned over in his mind the few strong suspicions he'd had thus far. They didn't add up to a very impressive array, but at least they formed the framework for some pretty solid suspicions to be hung upon. One thing, someone had stolen and rebranded Kate Willard's two-year-olds. For another thing they rebranded them with Sawyer Given's mark, but Given had straightforwardly said this had happened, so it was highly improbable that it was Given who had ordered the rebranding.

Lefton put the coffee cup down. At least all this was deliberately set up to look exactly as it appeared. On the surface, Given had rebranded the Rocking W critters. Lefton strolled to a window and gazed out into the roadway. Rebranded wasn't the right term since the animals hadn't been marked in the first place. And that, also, was interesting. The neighbors had overlooked a sizeable bunch of Rocking W steers when they'd altered and marked for the Willards. He knew the neighbors, each and every one of them; there wasn't a dishonest man among them. And that, he told himself emphatically, made the matter of those two hundred unmarked animals even more interesting. Who, for instance, had been taking a slice off the Willard herd for at least a year and a half, and hiding it, holding it up in the hills, perhaps, or so far out on the communal southward range no one could find it?

He rubbed his jaw, went to the desk, and sat down over there. Someone, he told himself, had planned this whole affair a long time ago. Before Justice Willard died, in fact, and since its inception he—or they—had kept it working as smoothly as silk. Given? He got up and restlessly paced the room. What Carl Hicks had told him of Sawyer Given was still there, just below his immediate awareness, to shape and color and influence his thoughts. He'd known Given a while, and they were friends. He'd worked for him, too, but that didn't mean anything because Sawyer Given's hired men never seemed to get as close to him as those outside his ranching activities did. Was he after Kate Willard's ranch? If so, where did those stolen cattle fit in, and what possible scheme could Given have devised to utilize all these loose ends—and dead ends—Bob was coming up with?

Art Flannagan walked in from the roadway. He had his mule-hide shoeing apron on. He'd obviously been at work next door in his shop. He said: "Bob, I was just talkin' to a couple of fellers who ranch on west of the Willards. They said they were headin' homeward last night pretty late and saw lights at the Willard place."

Lefton gazed straight at Flannagan. "Lights? Hell, Art, I was out there last night."

"What time? Those fellers said it was past midnight."

"It couldn't have been me, anyway. I didn't light any lamps." Bob arose, skewered the blacksmith with a hard look, and said: "Come along. Show me those fellers you talked to."

Flannagan didn't move. "They pulled out an hour ago. I been tryin' to get over to tell you ever since, but it's been one thing after another."

"Well, they'll be around town somewhere, won't they?"

"No. They were heading for home. I'd guess they're maybe two, three miles out over the range by now."

Lefton pursed his lips in thought. He could, of course, chase after those men, and probably overtake them, but if all they'd told Flannagan was that they'd been passing by and had seen lights, then that was also all they'd be able to tell him. "Thanks for telling me, anyway," he said, and ushered Flannagan outside. The blacksmith was full of curiosity. He wanted to know who it could be, out there at the Willard place, but since Bob Lefton hadn't the faintest idea who it was, he didn't have much trouble ending their discussion. Then he went straight into his cell-block and asked Kate who might be visiting her ranch late at night. She didn't know and couldn't imagine; in fact, she seemed disturbed about it.

"We locked the house, Deputy, before you brought us here. It must be a thief of some kind. There's just no other explanation. We have a few small things of value out there. Please, Bob, don't let them rob us, too."

He reassured the Willard women and went out to make a round of the town. It was a very agreeable morning. Even old Carl was about as cheerful as he'd been in the past forty years. He finished tying some bolt goods for a ranch woman, said—"Wait a second."—and rushed over to attend to another female customer at the tinned goods counter.

Bob waited. He wasn't going any place in particular until after nightfall anyway. Outside, rigs, gray old wagons ground through the powdery dust. A few riders came or went, passing in front of Carl's front window in Lefton's view. Buzz Hilton, Sawyer Given's range boss, loped past with what looked like a bundle of newspapers sticking up out of one saddlebag.

"Hey," said old Carl, having got rid of his customer and returned, "I got somethin' for you, Deputy Sheriff."

Bob turned. Old Carl rolled his eyes like an anarchist conspirator to make certain they were alone. He leaned over his counter and dropped his voice to a faint, excited whisper: "Judge Heber was a-comin' here to see Sawyer Given." Old Carl said that like it was a pronouncement that was destined to shake Bob Lefton to his roots. Afterward he straightened up and beamed in solid triumph. "How d' you like that, for half solvin' the killing?" he demanded.

Bob calmly eyed the storekeeper without saying a word for a long time, then he let out a long breath. "Just tell me how that half solves the murder," he said, "and I'll be indebted to you."

Hicks was disappointed; the deputy hadn't shown any astonishment at all. It seemed almost as though he'd already known Heber was coming to see Given when he'd been killed. "Well," he said, "I told you before, Sawyer Given is a land hog. The way I got it figured, he's out to get Rockin' W. He somehow got old Heber to tie them ladies up in legal monkeyshines while he moves to claim their land."

"Where does that leave Judge Heber, Carl?"

"It's plumb plain, Bob. Given had him killed to keep him from ever tellin' how he was bought off, to tie Kate and Miss Georgia up with the law."

"Oh," said Bob, and turned as several chattering women entered the store. "See you later," he said, using the newly arrived customers as an excuse to escape.

Back outside again, he sadly wagged his head. In every killing there was always at least one Carl Hicks. He struck out up the road for Oldfield's saloon. It was really too early in the day for serious drinking, but it was warming up, so a beer wouldn't taste too badly.

There were only three men at the bar of the Texas Belle. Two were freighters, recognizable by their rough attire. The third man, talking with Stan, was just as obviously a stranger. He was a grizzled, burly man with a lined face and hard, suspicious eyes. When Bob entered, Stan looked relieved. "Bob," he said. "Come meet a newcomer to Mandan." Lefton strolled on up, unsuspecting, ready to smile and extend his hand. Then Stan said: "Deputy Bob Lefton, meet Jack Bolley."

Bob stopped, his smile died, and he didn't offer his hand. "Bolley?" he murmured.

The hard-eyed rugged older man looked Lefton straight in the eye, fished in a vest pocket, and palmed a dull little steel badge. "Deputy sheriff in Animas County, Colorado," he said. "Ralph Bolley was my brother."

"Oh," said Bob, having a little difficulty in reconciling what he knew of Ralph with that badge in the other Bolley's heavy hand.

Jack pocketed the badge. "I been talking to Mister Oldfield," he rumbled in a voice like distant cannon fire. "When I heard about Ralph, I got leave to come up and plant him. But I understand you took care of that already."

"Yes," murmured Bob Lefton. "It happened some time back."

Jack Bolley nodded. "Have a beer, Deputy," he rumbled, and made a gesture for Stan to fetch it. Stan moved to obey reluctantly, as though wishing to remain and hear what those two had to say to one another. Jack eyed Bob bluntly. Lefton could see a little of the dead man in his brother, the same toughness, orneriness, willingness to fight. But there seemed to be more to Jack than there'd been to Ralph. Bolley said in that deep, hard voice of his: "I can guess what you're thinking, Deputy. Well, you write down to Animas County and verify who I am. As for Ralph, he's had it coming for twenty years. He had to end up like that sooner or later. I didn't come up here to shed any tears. Only to see that he was buried decent-like. That was the last thing I had to do for him. We haven't spoken in ten years. The last time was when I whipped him and run him out of town. He swore he'd come back someday and kill me. Well, I reckon he meant it when he said it, but after all, opposite sides of the fence or not, we were still brothers. You understand?"

"I reckon," assented Bob, trying to imagine Ralph Bolley keeping his word about anything at all, or being influenced by sentiment, either, for that matter.

"Mind showing me his grave?"

"No, I don't mind."

Stan returned with their beers. Bolley picked up his and said: "Drink 'er down, Deputy."

Bob obeyed. Jack Bolley, at least in this respect, was like his brother. He didn't invite folks to drink with him; he ordered them to.

Stan leaned on his bar, hoping there would be more talk, but there wasn't. When Bolley had downed his beer, he put the glass down, dropped some coins beside it, turned, and started for the door. Bob finished his drink and turned also to depart. Stan was left to wonder and to speculate.

# VII

At the cemetery southwest of town on its little hill, Jack Bolley didn't remove his hat as he stood flintily gazing at his brother's grave. After a while he said: "I'm obliged, Deputy, for the decent way you folks did it. It's a damned sight better grave than I expected him to wind up in, and it's a damned sight better grave that he deserved." He looked around the graveyard, then turned and surveyed the view from that little pleasant hill. "Big country, up here," he murmured, "lots of good cow country." Without altering his tone or looking back, he then said: "How did he get it? The barkeep back there in town said he was trying to break into a house west of Mandan where a couple of women were alone."

"That's about it," Bob agreed. "He tried to kick down the door. He was drunk. He caught the full blast of a shotgun head on."

Jack Bolley listened and afterward stood still for a while, his back to his brother's grave. "He wasn't above it, I reckon," he eventually stated. "Only, Ralph wasn't the kind to get caught head on by a shotgun blast, Deputy. Drunk or sober."

Bob had also wondered about that, when the killing had occurred, but he didn't encourage Jack Bolley by saying so now. He stood there, watching the fleecy clouds play back and forth in front of the high, golden sun.

The gruff, rough man beside him finally turned, gazing straight at Deputy Lefton. "What were your opinions?" he asked. "They tell me Ralph'd been hanging around Mandan some time before he got it."

"He had," agreed Bob. "Frankly, Mister Bolley, I wasn't too surprised. About the only thing that I wondered a little about was him going out there in the first place. He'd been around Mandan for a spell, like you said, but I'd never noticed he was much of a woman's man before."

"He wasn't," stated the Coloradoan. "I'll let you in on a little secret, Deputy. My brother had no use for women, not even pretty ones. He never did have. When we were half grown kids back in Missouri, he was contemptuous toward girls. I used to wonder about that, but that's how he was."

"He was drunk that night, Mister Bolley."

"Just plain Jack, Deputy. All right. Maybe being drunk made him remember these here women. It sure enough changed him, being drunk. But Ralph was a gunfighter, Deputy. Did you ever know a gunfighter as old and seasoned at it as Ralph was to walk straight into the face of a shotgun?"

"No, I never did," agreed Lefton. "But I'm not sure he knew Kate Willard had a shotgun, that night."

Bolley thought on that a moment, then said: "Where's this Kate Willard? She can damned well settle that for us right sudden."

"In my jailhouse awaiting arraignment."

Bolley's eyes widened. "You mean it wasn't called self-defense?"

Bob shook his head. "I think it was self-defense, and I reckon everyone else does hereabouts, Jack, but she was bound over, along with her daughter, to be tried by a higher court."

Bolley's heavy, dark brows gradually dropped until his weathered, leathery face was creased into a puzzled scowl. "Hell, Deputy," he murmured, perplexed, "the court had to have some evidence it was murder to bind her over. What came out at the trial?"

"That," replied Bob, looking straight into the older man's eyes, "is what's bothering me right now. Nothing came out. The judge simply bound her over. He didn't give his reasons. All he said was that no one knew whether your brother had been shot from in front or from behind."

Jack Bolley kept staring hard at Lefton. "Well," he growled, "let's go talk to this judge, Deputy. He'll tell us. I'm surprised you haven't already talked to him."

"Be kind of hard to do, Jack. Judge Heber was murdered coming down here on a stage."

Bolley's dark scowl deepened with puzzlement. He finally said: "Deputy, I'm beginning to understand that sort of preoccupied expression you wear on your face. This isn't just a simple matter of Ralph getting killed after all, is it?"

Bob shook his head and started walking back toward town. Bolley moved out beside him. For a time neither of them said anything. Off in the northwest a dust banner rose from beneath the loping hoofs of several town-bound horsemen, far out. The steady, fluting ring of a struck anvil down at Art Flannagan's shop sounded musical in the warm day. A big freight rig drawn by sleek mules left Mandan, riding high on its springs, evidently empty. A man upon the high seat was singing a rollicking cowboy song in a surprisingly good voice.

Jack Bolley said: "Lefton, what's the rest of it?"

Bob wasn't ready to make any confidences. Furthermore, while he didn't doubt Jack Bolley's claims, he shied clear of discussing the dilemma any further than he already had with the brother of the dead gunfighter. "I'm feeling my way," he said. "It's beginning to unravel a little. I'm keeping both eyes peeled and both ears to the ground."

"All right," Bolley conceded, understanding that Bob wasn't going to confide in him, and probably understanding the reasons why he wasn't going to, also. "But tell me this. Could Ralph have been shot from behind?"

Bob Lefton had a vague theory about that which he hadn't mentioned to a soul, hadn't, in fact, really dwelt upon with himself to any appreciable extent. "He could have, Jack, he could have."

"Who by?"

"That's all I'm going to say for now," Bob replied, then looked closely at the older, thick-set, rough-looking man. "How'd you like to take a little ride with me tonight?"

"Got something to do with my brother's killing?"

"Maybe. Maybe not. But at least we'll be going out to the place where he was killed."

"You got yourself a pardner," rumbled Jack Bolley. "You expecting a little trouble, maybe?"

"Maybe," said Jack as they stepped up onto the plank walk in town again. "Keep it to yourself and meet me at the livery barn right after supper."

He veered off, leaving Bolley gazing after him as he struck off for his jailhouse. He turned once, as he entered, saw Jack Bolley striding along back up toward the Texas Belle, and thoughtfully closed his office door, digging for the keys to his cell-block.

Kate and Georgia were quietly talking when he approached them. They broke off to glance upward through their bars. Bob said: "Kate, that shotgun you used the night Bolley was shot is outside in my rack. You recollect I fetched it to town with us?"

"Yes. For evidence, you said," replied the handsome woman.

"Kate, think back now. Did you load that gun yourself?"

Those lovely green eyes widened. "Load it? Why, no, I didn't load it. It was already loaded when I fired it."

"But did you know it was loaded when you picked it up?"

Kate hesitated a moment. "I didn't open the breech to see, if that's what you mean, Bob. It'd been in the wall rack with all Justice's other guns since he died. He never kept an unloaded gun in the house. He used to say when a person needs a gun he doesn't very often have time to load one."

Bob nodded and turned away. "I'll go fetch your dinner," he said, and walked back out into his office, stopped beside his desk for a second, then left the jailhouse. But he didn't head for the café; he struck out straight across the road for the general store.

Carl had several customers. Bob fidgeted as he waited, watching roadway traffic and nodding at the townsmen who strolled along outside on the plank walk who glanced in at him. It was a long wait. He leaned there on the counter, speculating on that vague theory he'd thought of once or twice but hadn't actually concentrated upon until now. Both Ralph Bolley and Judge Heber had been blasted at close range by shotguns. That was unique in a land where men used carbines and .45s, but not unheard of, except that in both cases the killer or killers had to take unnecessary chances to get close enough to fire, for a shotgun had a very limited range. At least in the case of Judge Heber, the killer'd been exposed to the risk of a return fire from the stagecoach driver and guard. Also, even though Ralph Bolley had been drunk, the killer'd had to get close to him, too, and as Jack Bolley had pointed out, his brother—even drunk—was a very dangerous man with a gun. There was one advantage to a shotgun. It killed without any question, up close, and, if the first barrel missed, there was always that other barrel.

Carl finished and walked over. He was wiping both hands on his apron when he halted and raised his eyebrows. "Don't tell me you need some bolt goods," he murmured. Until he said that, Bob hadn't been aware of being at the bolt goods counter.

He smiled. "Thought about whipping up a new shirt," he said jokingly, then sobered. "Carl, I want you to think back very carefully, then answer the same question for me you never quite answered for Judge Heber."

"You mean . . . was Bolley shot from in front or from behind?"

"Yeah."

Carl dropped the apron and glanced out his roadway window, answering slowly, solemnly: "Bob, I've thought an' thought about that ever since Heber asked it." He paused, swung his eyes straight over at Lefton, and said: "I believe he was shot in the back."

"You thought that at the time?"

"No. Like I said at the hearing, Bolley was such a mess when he reached my back room that I just rolled him in a blanket and put him in the coffin. I never really thought about it at all, until the day Judge Heber asked me that. And the day after . . . and also the day after that. Until finally recollectin' all the details, I got convinced Bolley had been caught from behind." Old Carl wagged his head back and forth as though the recollection were distasteful to him. "But let me tell you somethin' else, Bob. A feller shot up close like Bolley was, with a scatter-gun, isn't anything a feller wants to stand there gazin' at a dang' bit longer'n he has to."

"I appreciate that," stated Lefton. "But it's more important now than it was before, Carl. Are you plumb satisfied in your mind that the slugs cut into him from behind?"

"Yes," stated Hicks without any hesitation at all. "An' if I was in court right now, I'd give that as my opinion. I'm no coroner nor medical man, but I'm an old man an' I've seen enough dead men in my time who stopped lead to know how they stopped it. With Bolley . . . well, I didn't have any use for him to start with, an' I was right busy that day, too, so I just dumped him in the coffin an' got him out o' the way as soon as I could."

"Thanks," Bob said. "I'm obliged, Carl. One more thing. Keep this to yourself."

Hicks snorted. "Do I look like a fool? If someone cut Bolley down from behind, and Kate was in the house with her daughter, then she couldn't have done it because he was facin' her. So . . . that leaves a murderer still wanderin' around, doesn't it?"

Lefton nodded. "That's exactly what I'm also thinking," he said.

"Then you don't have to worry none about me tellin' the world what I figure really happened out there that night. Even us old duffers get sort of attached to life."

Bob left the store with afternoon shadows beginning to form here and there throughout the town. He went across to the little hole-in-the-wall café one door northward from his jailhouse, ate a good meal, then ambled on up to the Texas Belle where Stan welcomed him with a slight roll of his head, indicating a gloomy corner table where Jack Bolley morosely sat playing solitaire, his hat pushed back, his legs thrust out, dour-looking in the face but otherwise quite obviously killing time, and thoroughly relaxed. He didn't even glance up as Lefton crossed to the bar where Oldfield set up two beers, one for the lawman, one for himself, and said in a low half whisper: "He hasn't said a word since he came back in here. Just got a deck of cards and commenced playin' solitaire over there."

"What's wrong with that?" asked Lefton. "Solitaire's a good one-handed game."

Oldfield frowned. "You know perfectly well what I'm gettin' at. What's he waiting around for? Ralph's dead and buried. That's the end of it as far as his brother or anyone else's concerned."

Bob said mildly: "Good beer, Stan. You make a fresh batch?"

Oldfield straightened up, drank his glass empty, and set the glass down, hard. "All right, play games with me," he growled. "But deputy sheriff or not, I'd just as soon that bird found himself another perch. Word'll spread quick enough Ralph Bolley's brother's in town. All that can mean is trouble. Either way, trouble, Bob. You see if I'm not right."

Bob took his time with the beer. He had nothing more to do until after nightfall, except think. Stan Oldfield's bar was ordinarily a good place to do that thinking, but with Stan in his present garrulous frame of mind, what had been true in the past was not necessarily true now.

But at least Stan eventually changed his tack. He said: "Heard anything about when the Willards will be tried again?"

"No. But I ought to get the letter any day now. They tell me court calendars over at the county seat are chock full this summer. Still, I'd hazard a guess that maybe they'll be tried within a week or two."

"It ought to be some trial," said Stan, turning pensive. "Half the Mandan countryside'll troop over there to sit in."

"Yeah, I reckon so."

"Bob? You heard anything about who killed Horace Heber?"

"Nope. It didn't happen in my end of the county, so I won't hear anything you won't read in the newspapers, Stan, when the next batch comes through on the stage." He put a coin beside his empty glass, nodded, and walked out of the saloon. Outside, the sky was darkly reddening. Evening wasn't more than an hour or two away. He headed this time for the livery barn.

# VIII

When Jack Bolley came along, Lefton was already saddling. The man from Animas County got his horse and began also saddling up. They appeared to be alone. Bob thought the night hawk had probably gone to supper. At least, when Bolley started to speak, that's what the deputy told him, but he also said it'd probably be better if they didn't talk until they were beyond town.

They didn't. They were two miles out, as a matter of fact, before Bolley opened his mouth again. Then he said: "I been sittin' and listenin', Deputy. You know how it is. A feller rides into a strange town an' goes to the cowmen's hang-out, gets a deck of cards, a corner table out of folks' way, then just sits an' plays solitaire by the hour . . . an' listens."

Bob said: "Get to the point, Bolley."

"No point in particular, Deputy. I know who Sawyer Given is. Even down in Colorado we've heard of him. He's a right powerful man. There were some of his Wyoming Cattle Company riders in the Texas Belle this evening. They were talkin' about some recent branded two-year-old steers."

Bob gazed over at Bolley through the intervening shadows. The Coloradoan was smiling at him. Bolley didn't know everything, but enough to make it pointless keeping the rest of it from him. "All right," said Bob Lefton. "Did they say it was a little mystery who branded those critters and why?"

"That's all they said, Deputy. I got the distinct impression Sawyer Given was as mystified as anyone."

"He seems to be." Bob lifted an arm and halted his horse at the same time. He was pointing far ahead through the night toward a little square of orange lamplight. "That's the Willard place," he said, and dropped his arm. "That's where your brother was killed."

"I see. An' that's where we're headed now."

"Right. But there's not supposed to be anyone there. I've got Kate and Georgia Willard locked in my calaboose back in town."

Jack Bolley lifted his reins as though to ride on, and said: "Who're we expectin' to be there, Deputy?"

"I have no idea. But last night some cowmen who live out this way reported a light at the Willard place as they passed through."

"You're figurin' he might be . . . ?"

"Let's wait an' see," interrupted Bob. "Now follow me out and around. We'll come in on the blind side behind the barn."

They rode leisurely but alertly. It was a pleasant night, warm, star-lighted, fragrant from the sage and sumac. They had the whole area to themselves, or so it seemed, because they did not encounter so much as one head of livestock. Bob, who knew the area well, had no difficulty at all in leading them up to the rear of the log barn where the corral network lay off to the south, or on their left as they swung down.

Lefton tied his horse in a stall inside the pitch-dark barn. So did Bolley. They moved up to the big front opening and halted there.

"He's sure not tryin' to keep his presence much of a secret," said Bob, and Jack Bolley mumbled in agreement. Bob stepped out and started across the yard. Bolley strode along a little distance to Bob's right, the way a gunfighter might have accompanied another gunfighter; it made anyone who chose to fire at them change stance after getting off one shot, which in turn gave the surviving gunfighter an even break.

But nothing happened. They got to the very edge of the porch and Bolley wrinkled his nose. "Cookin' his supper," he whispered. "He's sure a bold one, if he's not supposed to be here. Hell, Deputy, this place isn't so far off the trails he couldn't expect to be found sooner or later."

"Maybe he was figurin' on it being later," muttered Bob, testing the porch planking. It was solid. He stepped up, loosened his six-gun, motioned for Bolley to stand off to one side, then reached for the door latch. The door was unlocked. He and Bolley exchanged a look about that. Bolley shook his head as though he were bewildered by this kind of a housebreaker.

Bob pushed the door gently inward, drew his gun, and stepped over the threshold into the parlor. Bolley shifted position to the far right so that he could also see inside the house. But he remained out in the shielding night with his gun palmed and ready.

The tantalizing aroma of frying steak came from the rear of the house. A man back there somewhere was whistling an off-key ballad of the cattle trails. Bob turned, beckoned for Jack Bolley to come inside, then he went forward toward the door leading over into the next room. They progressed in this fashion, one giving the other one support from behind and to one side.

In this way they passed through the parlor into the dining area, and from there on across to a closed door beyond which was the kitchen—and that cheerfully whistling, uninvited boarder. Lefton reached the obstructing panel, lay a hand lightly against it, and very gently pushed. Over at the wood stove a man's very broad back showed. The shirt was slovenly tucked into a sagging waistband, the old vest was patched in the back, and the greasy old hat was pushed far back.

Bob stepped through into the kitchen and left the door open for Bolley to see through. "Walt," he said sharply, and the big man over at the stove gave a little start, stopped whistling, and turned.

"Well, howdy there, Deputy." Patterson grinned. "By golly you're as quiet as a redskin."

Bolley glided up into the doorway. Patterson eyed him from eyes nearly hidden between rolls of flesh as he kept smiling. He nodded at Bolley but addressed Bob Lefton.

"Figured you'd be along directly, Deputy. Waited you out last night an' the night before, but you never showed up."

Bob holstered his weapon, crossed to the table, and pulled out a chair to sit down. As he did this, he said: "Jack Bolley . . . Walt Patterson."

Walt's little eyes widened slightly. "Bolley . . . ?" he murmured.

"Ralph's brother from down in Colorado," Lefton explained. "Now let's have it, Walt. What're you doing here? Don't tell me Kate gave you permission. I talked to her earlier and she said. . . ."

"I can imagine what she said, Deputy. Didn't no one have any right to be in here."

"That's right."

Patterson turned, stabbed his frying meat with a fork, and said: "You boys et?"

Bob and Jack Bolley exchanged a look. "We haven't," replied Bob, "but that can wait."

"Naw," muttered the big, unkempt cowboy over at the stove. "I'll dish it up in three plates if one of you boys'll pour the java, an' we can talk while we're loadin' up."

Walt turned toward a cupboard where plates were stacked.

Bolley raised his eyebrows in Lefton's direction. Bob got up, shrugged, and went after some cups. When Lefton did this, Bolley assumed correctly that Lefton did not anticipate any serious trouble, and put up his gun as he crossed toward the stove for the coffee pot.

None of them said anything until the plates had been laid out, the cups filled, and they straddled chairs. Then Walt Patterson dropped a bombshell. He fished a crumpled paper from a shirt pocket, smoothed it out, and put it squarely in front of Bob Lefton.

"I figured there had to be something like this here letter somewhere around, Bob," he said, slicing his meat with a clasp knife that had a six-inch, wicked blade. "It ain't signed, but it's addressed to Judge Horace Heber over at the county seat, an', as you can see, it says he better make sure Ralph Bolley wasn't shot from behind before he sets Miss Kate an' her daughter free, because there was plenty of reason to believe that's what happened."

Bob read the letter twice without moving. When he finally raised his eyes, Walt was heartily chewing on a big cud of fried steak, his little eyes straight on Bob's face, his tough smile still softly visible. Jack Bolley bent, got hold of the letter, and leaned back to read it impassively. He put it aside very gently and stared hard at Walt Patterson. He didn't say a word, but Lefton did.

"Where'd you get that letter, Walt?"

Patterson put aside his knife and fork, reached for his coffee cup, and looked from Bolley to Lefton before he said: "Bob, I been nosin' around a little ever since old Heber put them two ladies back into your jailhouse. I even spent a few days over at the county seat." He pointed with his upraised coffee cup at the letter in front of Jack Bolley on the table. "I found that thing in a drawer at Judge Heber's office."

Bolley reached up to scratch the tip of his nose and turn a wry glance upon Lefton. Bob didn't look away from Walt. He said: "You mean, you broke into Heber's office, Walt . . . burglarized the place?"

"Ain't that being a mite hard on me?" said Patterson mildly. "Bob, you 'n' I both know Miss Kate wouldn't shoot a dog in the back, let alone a man, even a man like . . . excuse me, Mister Bolley."

Jack said: "I've known what my brother was a lot longer'n you have, Mister Patterson. You can call a spade a spade, I'm not likely to get mad."

Patterson nodded and returned his attention to Bob Lefton. "Well, we know she'd have shot him head on like she thought she did, Bob. So I went over there to sort of snoop around. I was in that courtroom, remember. I seen how that old cuss looked at a letter just before he handed the ladies back into your custody."

"Wait a minute," broke in Bob. "How did you know Ralph Bolley had been shot in the back, Walt?"

Jack Bolley straightened in his chair. Until this minute he hadn't known this. He stared hard at old Walt. Patterson gulped some coffee, and took up his knife and fork again. He was obviously very hungry.

"Just had to be like that, Bob," he muttered, stuffing meat into his mouth. "Why else would someone write a letter like that to old Heber?" Patterson jabbed toward Lefton with his fork. "Someone don't want the Willard ladies set free. That same someone made damned sure they wouldn't be set free."

Bob leaned over, picked up the crumpled letter, and reread it. He was trying to recognize the wording or the handwriting, but in both cases he failed. For one thing, the letter used no colloquialisms. For another it was very painstakingly written, as though the writer hadn't been used to writing letters. Bob tossed the thing down again. He said: "Walt, I don't like what you did. I don't approve of it at all. In my position, I can't approve of it." He drank some coffee, then said: "But I'm not too concerned with that right now. I'm concerned with who wrote this letter, who shot Ralph Bolley in the back, and why these things were done." He turned. "He was shot in the back, Bolley. I had confirmation about that this afternoon. Walt was right without knowing that he was."

"Why?" asked Jack Bolley. "What's behind all this?"

"Two hundred grassed-out big steers, for one thing," replied Bob. "But that won't be all of it. Anyone as smart and wise as these rustlers are, wouldn't have had to go to all this trouble just to steal a couple hundred head of steers."

"You said on the ride out here they were branded with Given's mark," stated Bolley. "That'd involve Sawyer Given."

Bob shook his head. "Not for a lousy two hundred steers, Jack. Sawyer Given carries that much cash around in his watch pocket. He wouldn't jeopardize everything it's taken him a lifetime to build up, for a lousy two hundred steers."

"He's plumb right," confirmed Walt, eating at a slower pace finally. "An' he wouldn't get involved in no murders, either, Mister Bolley. Y' see, both Bob an' I've worked for Mister Given. We know him. At least we sure know him that well."

Bob took up the letter, folded it carefully, and put it into his shirt pocket. "There's a lot more to this than your brother's killing and those cattle," he said. "That's what we've got to ferret out."

"How?" demanded Bolley.

"Well, to start with we've got to find out who your brother was running with when he got shot."

Walt Patterson leaned back, sucking his teeth. "I can do that," he said. "I know every rider between here 'n' Green River. The fellers'll talk to me, Bob, when they wouldn't talk to you or

Mister Bolley here. You, because o' that badge. Mister Bolley because he's a plumb stranger."

"All right, Walt," said Bob. "Do your ferreting around. But no more housebreaking . . . here at the Willard place or in someone's office, either. I can't help you if someone catches you . . . or shoots you. Remember that."

"Sure enough," drawled the big old range rider, grinning benignly at the deputy. "Don't you fret yourself none about me, Bob."

"I got a question," murmured Bolley, studying big Walt Patterson. "Who shot Judge Heber?"

Walt's grin didn't fade at all. He looked Jack straight in the eye and said: "Well now, Mister Bolley, I reckon that'll come out in time, too. Most murders do get found out. But right now I don't figure we got to concern ourselves too much with that. Do we, Bob?"

Lefton bent forward to start eating. He looked up at Patterson as he said: "Not right now, no. Anyway, it didn't happen in my territory. I'll have enough headaches without borrowing someone else's, too." He sliced into his cooling steak, chewed a moment, then said: "Eat up, Jack. I've tasted worse fried meat in my time."

They ate, the pair of them, while slovenly old Walt Patterson went back to the stove for the coffee pot. He refilled all their cups and sat down, replete and half smiling, watching the pair of lawmen from half hidden, sharp little eyes.

# IX

Walt's hunger, it turned out, was genuine. He'd been on the range and over at the county seat constantly, taking scarcely any time out to get around a decent meal. Not that he couldn't have lived off his paunch for a while; he could have, but even fat men get hungry. Also, he'd cleared up something else that had been bothering Bob Lefton. That story he'd told Bob a week back about trying to see Sawyer Given about a job, and being unable to find Given. It had obviously been a cover-up for what Patterson had really been up to. As it turned out, whether Walt had done things the right or wrong way, there was no denying that he'd accomplished a lot.

On their ride back to Mandan, Jack Bolley chuckled, gave his head a hard wag, and said: "Lefton, that Patterson's a man after my own heart."

Bob looked around. He was riding with his reins looped, making a smoke. "You mean because he broke into Judge Heber's office and stole that letter?"

"That'll do for openers," answered Bolley. "But also for the way he reasons things out. Hell, you'd think a man with his shrewdness'd own half the territory by now."

"He's shiftless," stated Bob. "Walt's a good friend and all that, but he doesn't like to work very much, and he's an accomplished loafer."

"He's still a man after my heart," stated Bolley. "And that's more'n I can say for Sawyer Given right this minute. I realize you don't believe he's mixed up in this, but I tell you it's hittin' too close to home for him not to be involved some way."

Bob didn't argue. He didn't even bother thinking too much about Given. But when they arrived back in town and put up their horses, then parted out front of the livery barn, Bob went down to his jailhouse and stepped inside to find himself face to face with the very man Jack Bolley had been speaking of.

Given was alone this time, and he looked impatient. "Been waitin' long enough for you," he growled. Then he said: "I want a few words with Missus Willard."

"Sure," assented Lefton. He fished around for his cell-door keys. As he did this, Sawyer Given kept watching him. Just before Bob found the right keys, the cowman spoke again.

"How come you to be holding both the Willards, Bob? As I heard it only Kate's suspected of murder."

"Georgia's a material witness," replied Lefton. "That's enough, under territorial law, but that's not why I'm holding her. She volunteered to stay with her mother. She asked to be locked up, too."

Given stood up. "Loyalty," he said softly. "It's an almighty rare trait, Bob."

Lefton opened the cell-block door, called down it to Kate, then stepped back and permitted Sawyer Given to walk down there alone.

He ambled over to his desk, saw some mail lying there, shuffled through it, and selected one long envelope to open. It was from the clerk of the Superior Court over at the county seat; it gave the date set for the trial of Kate Willard as seven days hence.

Bob put the letter down, stood a moment in thought, then turned as Sawyer Given came out of the cell-block, crossed to the door, nodded without saying a word to Lefton, and stamped on out. Bob gazed over at the cell-block door, then strolled over, went down to Kate's cell, and asked a blunt question.

"What did he want?"

The large green eyes were candid when she answered. "He offered to import the best lawyers in the territory and to pay them to defend me."

Bob's eyebrows shot up. "For what in exchange?" he asked.

"No strings attached, he said."

Bob scratched his chin and dubiously gazed over at Georgia. She nodded her head gravely at him in confirmation of what her mother had said. Bob remarked—"Well, good night ladies."—and returned to the office.

It wasn't impossible that Sawyer Given had made that offer from the goodness of his heart, but on the other hand it wasn't usual for him, either. He yawned, looked at his watch, blew out the lamp, and went out into the dark roadway. Up at Oldfield's place there were lights and laughter. They did nothing at all for him, so he started on across toward the rooming house.

It hadn't been a very eventful day, but it certainly had become eventful after sundown. His mind was still full of tangled skeins of thoughts and unanswered questions, the foremost of which had now to do with the deliberate murder of a murderer—Ralph Bolley.

He slept on that, awoke with it still teasing him, had breakfast, and took two trays down to the jailhouse with him, where he told Kate and Georgia when the trial had been scheduled. After that he made a cursory patrol up through town and met Art Flannagan over at Carl's store. When Bob walked in, those two abruptly ceased whatever it was they'd been discussing. He eyed them wryly and said: "Well, you amateur sleuths, what's going on between you this morning?"

Hicks cleared his throat and leaned across the counter to speak in a subdued manner. "Art was just tellin' me there's somethin' fishy goin' on out at the Willard place. Lights in the night an' all."

Bob gazed at the blacksmith, who slightly reddened, then defensively said: "Well, it's a fact an' you know about it, Bob, so what's wrong with talkin' about it?"

"Nothing," replied the deputy. "Nothing at all." He turned as someone walked in, spoke his name, and waited in the doorway for him to turn. It was Jack Bolley. Bob walked away from Art and Carl, followed Bolley up the plank walk a short distance, and would've stopped but Bolley growled under his breath.

"Talk later. Just walk along with me."

They went over into the livery barn, down through and out into the back alleyway, across past three sheds and into the fourth one, a spider-infested, abandoned old milking lean-to.

There, big Walt Patterson was waiting, sitting upon what remained of a badly cribbed old manger, swinging one leg and smoking a cigarette. At sight of Lefton he blew out a bluish cloud and said: "Found him, eh? You're learnin' your way around, Mister Bolley."

Lefton looked around. The shed was empty but for the three of them. He looked back. "You hiding from someone?" he asked Patterson. The old cowboy softly smiled with all his face but those small, bright, alert eyes.

"Sort of," he said. "I'd just as leave no one saw me talkin' to you right after I been out with some of the range riders." Walt sucked down a big inhalation. He was enjoying himself. "You wanted to know who Ralph Bolley was runnin' with. All right, I found out. But you aren't goin' to believe it."

"Try me," said Bob.

"Some Wyoming Cattle Company riders, including Sawyer Given's big herd boss, Buzz Hilton."

Bob's brow slowly furrowed. He stared hard at Patterson. "Where'd you pick that up? Hell, Walt, Hilton wouldn't be mixed up in something like this."

"I didn't say he was, Bob. All I said was that him and some other riders of Given's were close friends with Ralph Bolley, an' not just lately, either, but back for a year 'n' more. It wasn't hard to find that out. Seems most of Given's men didn't approve of it. But still, there it is, Deputy."

Bob went to an old bench and sat down. He didn't know Buzz Hilton well. About all he actually knew of him was that he kept pretty much to himself, was a good stockman, a top hand, and Sawyer Given seemed to have worlds of faith in him.

Jack Bolley, eyeing Bob, said: "What's wrong with this Hilton feller bein' mixed up with Ralph's killing? Who's he that you got to look so solemn?"

Walt Patterson explained that Hilton was Sawyer Given's

right-hand man. All that information did was make Bolley curl a lip at Bob.

"I told you last night," he said, "that Given's got to be mixed in somehow."

But Bob stood up, shaking his head. "Hilton, maybe," he said. "Given . . . never." He then told them what Given had offered to do for the Willards the night before at his jailhouse, and this seemed to cause Bolley some trouble. He said perhaps Given was deliberately doing that for some private reason, or maybe he wanted the Willard ranch. It wasn't even impossible, he said, that Given didn't have an eye on one of the women.

Walt Patterson shook his head over these suggestions, stamped out his smoke, and said: "Mister Bolley, you just don't know Sawyer Given or you'd never say things like that."

Bolley threw out both arms. "Then what?" he demanded. "It's his range boss that's involved, isn't it?"

Lefton agreed but stuck to his original conviction that whether some of Given's men were involved or not, Sawyer Given definitely would not be. "Especially when it's got to do with murder," he said. The second he'd made that statement, though, he recalled the story Carl Hicks had told him of another murder many years back, where Walt Patterson had been involved. He looked over at raffish old Walt. "By the way, when I saw Mister Given a couple days back, he said he'd have a job for you."

Patterson smiled, but somehow Bob got the impression that smile was for show. "That's right decent of him," drawled Walt. "I'll ride out 'n' get signed on." He didn't say when he proposed to do this. In fact, he left Bob with the definite impression he had no intention of doing it at all.

Jack Bolley, turning impatient as the conversation seemed to drift, dragged the other two back with a rough question directed at Bob Lefton. "All right, Deputy, what do we do now?"

Bob lifted his calm gaze to the older man's face. "We take a little ride tonight. This thing's beginning to make a little sense at last."

"Is it?" exclaimed Bolley. "Not to me it isn't. But if ridin' out with you tonight'll help, I'll be at the livery barn right after sunset like last night."

Walt said: "Not me, Bob. I already got my neck out a yard. I don't want Buzz or them cronies of his to see me with the law, the very next night after I took two bottles of rotgut out to the cow camp an' sat up half the night gettin' them to drop a word here an' there."

Bob nodded. "Fair enough," he said. "And thanks, Walt. Keep in touch."

Patterson accepted his dismissal with a droll smile. After he'd walked out of the shed into the morning's golden dazzle, Bolley crossed to the same old rickety manger, eased down, and said: "Out with it, Deputy. What's on your mind?"

"Two hundred head of rustled Rocking W steers . . . and one of the rustlers who got shot because he was too troublesome for the others to risk having loose."

Jack Bolley sat a long moment staring at Lefton, then he lightly slapped one leg. "You were 'way ahead of me on that one," he said. "All right, I knew my brother better'n anyone around here, and I tell you that it fits. He and this Hilton feller, and maybe those others Patterson mentioned, were organized into a rustler ring. Something went sour for Ralph. The others arranged his murder to look like he was tryin' to break into the Willard place, to get shed of him."

"Good theorizing," stated Bob, standing up and beating dust off his britches. "That's about how I've been putting it together, too. Only . . . what do you think of Sawyer Given being involved now?"

Bolley's eyes opened wide. "Hell's bells, Deputy," he said,

making a complete about-face, "am I the first feller you ever knew who made a mistake?"

"No, not by a long sight, Jack. But you're one of the first I've ever known who'd admit he made a mistake. Come on, let's get out of here. I want to talk to the Willards."

Bolley shook his head as Lefton went past. "I don't want to talk to 'em," he said, "so you go alone. See you at the livery barn same time again tonight."

Bob returned to his jailhouse, went directly to Kate's cell, and asked her three questions. "That time Buzz Hilton came down to tell you he'd found some Rocking W steers on Sawyer Given's range, Kate, did he say whether they were branded or not?"

"No, Bob, he didn't say."

"And when Bolley was roaring around out in the yard, did he mention money at all?"

That time Georgia answered. She sprang up and gripped the bars. "Yes! I distinctly heard him say something about a strongbox full of money."

Bob nodded. That solved the riddle of how Hilton and the others had gotten Bolley to attempt breaking in. They'd told him there was a strongbox of hidden cash inside the Willard house, and he'd evidently been given plenty of liquor to make sure he'd try for that mythical hoard.

"One last question," said Bob to Kate Willard. "When you fired at Bolley, where, exactly, was he standing?"

"Facing the front door. He'd already kicked it once. He was getting ready to kick it again when I fired."

"I see. In other words you fired down the front of your house, westward."

"That's correct."

Bob touched the brim of his hat, turned, and marched back out of the cell-block. He locked the door and went over to his desk thoughtfully to roll a smoke, light it, and deeply inhale. Things were falling into place, but what he needed more than anything else now was proof. He had enough theories; he needed substantiating evidence that he was either on the right trail or the wrong one. He proposed to see whether or not that evidence was available when nightfall finally came. One thing he was certain of; if Hilton was involved, Sawyer Given knew absolutely nothing about it.

# X

Jack Bolley was ready and waiting out back, down at the livery barn, when Lefton came along. Together they left town after nightfall exactly as they'd previously done, and, also, Bob led out in the same direction. Bolley didn't say much on the ride out to the Willard place; he never once asked what Bob had in mind, but when they cantered into the yard out at Rocking W, he seemed to have expected this.

Bob stepped down at the hitch rack in front of the house, went up onto the porch, and made a close study of both the upright railings and the front siding, which was soft pine and would therefore have showed where lead pellets had struck.

Bolley joined him. They went back and forth very carefully, but found no evidence at all of buckshot ever having been scattered down the front of the house, westward from the front doorway. When Lefton was satisfied, he strolled over, leaned upon an upright under the porch ceiling, and gazed around the yard.

At Rocking W the bunkhouse was on the west side of the yard not more than two hundred feet from the barn, and about equal distance from the house. Otherwise, there were only two other outbuildings; one seemed to be a hen roost while the other one looked like a combination workshop and shoeing shed. They were on the north side of the yard. As Jack strolled over, manufacturing a smoke for himself, Bob said: "If they'd shot Ralph from over by the shop or chicken house, pellets would still have splattered westerly along the house front."

"Yup," Jack agreed, licking his paper, folding it, crimping both ends, and popping the completed cigarette between thin lips. "So they had to shoot from over yonder by the bunkhouse or the barn." Bolley stepped out, walked eastward down the long front of the house before striking the match for his smoke. He lit the quirly, then paced very slowly along with the match held high. When it flickered out, he turned back.

"From the bunkhouse," he said quietly. "Come over here. You can see 'em if you light a match."

Lefton went over and verified that tiny lead pellets had irregularly peppered the easterly front wall of the Willard house. He didn't make a very thorough examination because he didn't have to. "Let's go," he said, heading out for the hitch rack.

Now they loped almost due northward. Now, too, Jack said: "Deputy, I'm a long-sufferin' man. But I got limits just like anyone else. Tell me. Just what in tarnation are we up to now?"

"We're going over and get Mister Given out of bed, if he's retired, and have a tough talk with him."

Bolley inhaled, exhaled, looked ahead over the starlit range, and for a while was silent. Eventually he said: "I'm all for it, o' course, Deputy, but Stan Oldfield up at the saloon told me Given's got a mighty tough crew of riders, an' a lot of 'em."

"That's right, and it's also why we're going to slip in there after folks are bedded down."

Bolley said no more until they were a long mile and a half from the Willard place. "You better know the place right well, Deputy, because if you don't, we just might get shot for burglars or horse thieves or somethin', and whether a man stops lead by accident or by design, believe me he's just as dead."

Sawyer Given's home place lay atop a long plateau that was

as flat and round as a table top. His buildings were log, like all the buildings in the Mandan country, but there were a lot of them. Aside from a spacious, aloof two-story main house, there were three huge barns that dwarfed the scattered array of shed, shops, and two long bunkhouses. What Bob observed as he came along the lower plain, looking upward, was that no lights were glowing, and that was exactly what he wished to be certain of. He had no intention of letting Buzz Hilton or anyone but Sawyer Given himself know that he'd paid the Given ranch a visit this night.

The road leading up atop that low, flat head land was well maintained and well marked. Bob rode right on past it, turned in where a crooked horse trail lay, and jerked his head at Bolley as he started upward.

Given's plateau actually didn't rise more than sixty or seventy feet from the prairie below, but in the pewter light of this moonless night it seemed higher, and the buildings up there looked for all the world like the conglomerate buildings of some old-time castle and environs.

When they topped out and Bolley saw that they'd come in behind a long, low horse barn, he eased over from the saddle and softly said: "This place is more like a cussed fort than a ranch."

"When he first built it," replied Bob, "that's just about what it was. There are sawed off arrow shafts in most of the buildings." Lefton stepped down and led his horse on up into the low barn. Bolley followed his example. They left their animals tied near the rear of the building in narrow tie stalls, then walked out into the yard. Bob didn't hesitate; he knew this place well enough, having once lived and worked here.

They skirted around to the left, always keeping some dark shed or log wall behind them. When they finally got over to the large main house, where it aloofly sat several hundred feet from the other ranch buildings, Lefton slipped easily along the east wall, cut around behind, and halted near a screened rear doorway.

"No watch dog?" asked Bolley in a low whisper, looking apprehensively around.

"No," said Bob. "He used to keep a couple of peacocks but the cussed coyotes got them. He doesn't like dogs."

Bob didn't make any particular effort to open the screen door; he just tried it once on the off chance someone had forgotten to latch it, found that this was not the case, drew forth his clasp knife, slit the screen, reached through, and lifted the latch without making a sound.

Bolley stepped through last. He turned and gave the latch a hard twist just in case someone might try closing off this avenue of retreat behind them, then tiptoed ahead after Bob.

Lefton knew exactly which rooms to pass through to reach a stuffy, gloomy old hallway. They passed down that Stygian corridor to a large bedroom, and there, as they glided through the opening, a man lying in bed heavily heaved his weight half around and made some bubbly sounds in his throat.

Lefton motioned for Bolley to go around upon the bed's opposite side where a gun belt hung from the headboard. Jack carefully slipped around there, reached, lifted out the six-gun, and stepped back one pace to watch the sleeping man as Bob came up on the other side of the bed, leaned down, and gently touched Sawyer Given's shoulder.

That was all it took to awaken the cowman. But Given hadn't lost all his old-time wariness even now, so many years after there was no longer any need for it. As he opened his eyes and even before they'd fully focused on an intruder in his bedroom, he was swinging his right hand and arm up where the shell belt hung. The pistol was gone. Given rolled his head on the pillow, saw Bolley standing there holding the gun, and he blinked, jerked his head back toward the deputy from Mandan, and slowly got rid of his sleep-induced cobwebs as he eased up very carefully in his bed to squint hard.

"Bob . . . Lefton," he growled. "What in the hell do you mean?"

"Keep your voice down," commanded Lefton. "Sit up, Mister Given, and just listen for a minute."

The grizzled rancher sat up. He threw another belligerent glare over at Jack Bolley, who he did not know, then turned back again. "It better be good," he snarled at Lefton.

"Just listen," repeated Bob. Then he told Sawyer Given everything he and Jack Bolley knew or suspected about what had been happening down at the Willard ranch, and elsewhere. The first indication of astonishment Given showed was when Bob told him who Jack Bolley was. The second flash of astonishment came when Bob told Given who he thought was involved in the killing of Ralph Bolley. Finally, when he made his final statement, Sawyer Given was wide-awake and stiffly sitting there.

"The best way for Buzz and whoever's in this with him to get those stolen Rocking W steers to market, Mister Given, was to trail brand them with your mark. You don't go on the drives. Buzz Hilton is always trail boss. He'd have two tallies. One would be your tally of the number of critters you were selling, and the other tally would be the complete number of beeves on the hoof. Maybe Hilton wouldn't take any drovers but the men who're working with him in this. But whether he did that or not wouldn't make much difference. Even the men who ride for you and who aren't in with Hilton's crew wouldn't see anything unusual about the number of cattle being taken to rail's end as long as they all had your mark on them. When he sold the herd, Hilton would be the only one of your men who'd give a bill of sale and collect the bank draft. Only in this case he'd collect two bank drafts, one for you . . . one for himself and his friends."

Given threw back his covers and reached for his trousers. "I'll damned soon find out who's crazy here," he snarled, but Lefton stepped over in front of the chair where Given's clothes lay.

"You won't do a damned thing," he said curtly.

Given looked at him. "What?" he growled. "What did you say to me, Bob?"

"You heard me, Mister Given. I don't want Hilton scared off. You're not going to say a word to him. You're not going to act one bit different tomorrow toward him than you've ever acted. You're going to go right ahead completing the gather for your drive, and leave the rest of it to me."

Sawyer Given continued to regard Lefton stormily for a moment longer, then he seemed to understand because he gradually lost his irate stiffness. "Who's got some makings?" he muttered.

Jack Bolley stepped around, holding out his papers and sack of tobacco. For as long as it took Sawyer Given to make a cigarette and light it, none of them said anything. Clearly Given didn't need that smoke as much as he needed the time it took to create it, to get his thoughts organized and under control.

As he lit up, he said: "Bob, if you're wrong, there won't be a place in this territory big enough for you to hide in. You've just called my best man a murderer and a thief."

"I thought of that on the way out here, Mister Given, and, if I'm wrong, you won't have to pull any political strings to get my badge. I'll come out here, apologize, and hand it to you myself."

Given smoked, then said: "You're so sure, Bob? Couldn't it be some of the other men? I've got a pretty big crew an', while I know most of 'em by name, I don't really know too much else about them. It wouldn't be the first time in forty years I found out I had an outlaw or two ridin' for me."

"No, Mister Given, I'm not all that sure. I don't have too much in fact to go on right now. But the proof'll show up if you'll just go on giving Hilton all the rope he needs."

Given glanced sideways at Jack Bolley. "And you," he queried. "Are you satisfied about Hilton, too? After all, that dead man was your brother."

Bolley was less direct in answering. "I'm sure my brother was murdered. But beyond that I'm concerned less with your ranch boss than I am with some other things."

Given nodded. If he wondered what those other things were, he didn't say so. He leaned back finally, against the headboard of his bed, and continued grimly and silently to smoke. After a while he said: "All right, Bob. I'll do it your way. But I tell you frankly Buzz Hilton's the best range boss I've ever had. Even if you're plumb right, I still will hate losing him."

Bolley dryly said: "I've never met this foreman of yours, Mister Given, but already I know two things about him. He's a damned smart cowman to know how to rustle cattle so's they'll only have one brand on 'em. An' the other thing I've figured out is that he sure pulled the wool over your eyes."

Given flared: "No one's proved a damned thing against my range boss yet, Mister Bolley. No one's convinced me he's an outlaw yet, either. Until they do, I'll reserve judgment. I'd suggest you do the same."

Bolley didn't bat an eye. "Deputy," he quietly drawled at Lefton, "give Mister Given that there letter to Judge Heber to read. If he didn't write it himself, then maybe he'll be able to figure out who did."

Given looked perplexed. "What letter's he talkin' about?" he asked. Bob fished the thing out of a pocket. Given gently unfolded it and went over by the window in his long nightshirt to read it. He bent closer the second time he read it. Then he turned and stared hard at Lefton. "Is it genuine?" he asked.

"I'm satisfied it is," stated Bob, holding out his hand to get the letter back. "I'm also satisfied that whoever wrote it did so specifically so's he could get rid of the Willard women."

Bolley was eyeing Given coldly. "Maybe to buy their land," he murmured. "Providin', o' course, his own land adjoined theirs."

Sawyer Given was slow picking up that implication, but he got it finally, and gave a low growl as he swung around heading straight for Jack Bolley. Lefton stepped in front of the charging cowman, leaned ahead, and braced for the shock when they met head on. He stopped Given hard and pushed him roughly over toward his bed. The old cowman glared. He said: "Lefton, who's this damned saddle tramp think he is, coming in here and . . . ?"

"He's a lawman just like I am, Mister Given, and he's got his reasons for suspecting what he just said." Bob paused, then said: "And so have I, if it comes right down to that."

"What? What in the hell are you driving at, Bob Lefton? Damn you, anyway, I hired you on when you didn't have a second cent to bless yourself with. I. . . ."

Bob broke in coldly to say: "Mister Given, tell me that you didn't get Walt Patterson out of trouble with the law many years back, when Walt shot and killed a man in the roadway down at Mandan, who didn't even draw his gun when Walt killed him."

Given stared. "Where'd you hear that?" he asked, then licked his lips. "You listen to me, Bob, that was a long time ago. In those days we killed when we had to and no one went around sayin' a horse thief shouldn't be done in any way we wanted to do it. That man Walt killed stole seven horses with my brand on 'em. Walt found 'em. He always was right smart at figuring things out. We waited for the horse thief to come back . . . he worked for me at one of the cow camps . . . then Walt went after him. The reason no one ever said anything was just because that saddle bum was a thief."

Bolley heard Given out with both thumbs hooked in his gun belt. He afterward said quietly: "Mister Given, Hilton also works for you. The fellers he's maybe in cahoots with also are in your cow camps. If it happened twenty, thirty years back, how can you say it isn't happenin' again, right now?"

Given didn't even look up at Jack Bolley. He punched out his cigarette in a bedside ashtray and heaved a mighty sigh. "All right, Bob," he said, sounding suddenly old and tired. "I'll say nothing. We'll go right ahead, get the gather completed, organize the drive south to rail's end, just like always, an', the day it leaves, I'll come into town an' let you know. Satisfied?"

"Right well satisfied, Mister Given," stated Lefton, and turned to leave the room.

# XI

When they left the Given place, riding back down to the lower plain, Jack Bolley said: "I've run across my share of cattle thieves, I think, but this is the first time I ever heard of 'em deliberately putting another man's brand on them. Usually it's the other way around."

Bob agreed, reined off in the general direction of town, then explained why he thought it had been done like that. "First off, those critters were two-year-olds, according to Mister Given, and he'd know if anyone would. So, what Hilton and his friends've had to do was keep those slick-eared Rocking W critters hidden somewhere back in a mountain meadow, or some equally as private place, so's no one else'd see 'em, brand 'em, and claim them. On top of that, Jack, they've had to look after those danged critters since they were six or eight months old, or since they were weanlings, and that means they've had to work at it summer and winter both. Now that takes some doing, let me tell you, working full time for another man and also running a few head on the side by yourself, and not getting caught at it."

"Couldn't do it," stated Bolley, "unless someone's tall in the saddle, like maybe a range boss . . . or an owner . . . was in cahoots with you."

Bob nodded. "Just about have to be something like that. Then, when the critters were ready, they'd drifted 'em down onto Sawyer Given's range."

"Yeah, all that's clear enough, but will you explain to me why this Hilton feller told old Given there were some new-branded two-year-olds on Given's range? That was bound to make the old cuss suspicious."

"He had to tell him," stated Deputy Lefton. "Given inspects all the herds he sends down the trail. He'd have spotted those fresh brands right off, and Hilton knew it. But he could always have said maybe some of the cow camp crew up on the far north range found a few slicks and marked them. Except for us, and what we actually know is happening here, that yarn could very easily be believed."

Bolley ruminated for a moment, then said: "This Buzz Hilton . . . he's got to be a top hand."

"He is," Lefton confirmed. "One of the best cowmen in the country, I'd say."

"And smart," murmured Bolley.

Bob looked around. "What're you getting at?" he asked.

"That if Hilton's this good an organizer of cow thieves, then there's a better'n even chance he's just as good at picking his outlaw crew. And that, my friend, is a heap more important to me than all the rebranded, or misbranded, or unbranded steers in Wyoming Territory, 'cause steers don't go round packing guns, but cow thieves sure as hell do!"

Bob Lefton grinned. It was late, the night was turning cool, and on ahead the little flickering lights of Mandan showed low along in the ebony night.

They got back to the livery barn and put up their stock. Roadway lamps showed, but otherwise Mandan had retired. Even Stan Oldfield's place was dark, but then this was a week night, not a weekend night. Bob invited the Coloradoan down to his jailhouse for a cup of coffee before turning in. He didn't expect Bolley to accept, but he did.

They got down there, stoked up a little fire, put the coffee pot on to boil, then sat down to smoke and rehash what they'd done, what they knew, and what they suspected. When that was all sorted out and gone through, Bob said: "The problem isn't so much getting proof against Hilton. A couple of steer hides'll do that, plus Sawyer Given's testimony."

"Yeah, I know," muttered Bolley. "The problem's tryin' to figure out just how big this renegade crew of Hilton's is before we tackle Hilton or anyone else. I'm right partial against the notion of bein' shot in the back, Bob, but unless we can pretty well pin down an' identify all of Hilton's crew before we move against him, we just darn' well might get that slug in the back."

Lefton nodded. "There's a way," he said. "Walt Patterson."

Bolley slowly nodded as he considered this, then he said: "Maybe I could ride along with Patterson. No one out there knows me, anyway. In Patterson's company I'd be just another two-bit saddle tramp."

Bob liked the idea, but talked against it for an elemental reason. "I didn't tell Stan Oldfield not to say who you were, Jack." Bob reluctantly shook his head in a negative fashion. "Nope, you better not do it. This is a small town and a pretty sparsely populated community all around. Someone will know who you are by now, besides Stan and Walt and me. It could've gotten back to Hilton, too."

"Let it," insisted Bolley stoutly. "Who'd be better qualified to dislike folks hereabouts than a dead outlaw's brother?"

Lefton went over, poured two cups of black java that'd been aromatically brewing, took one cup back to Bolley, took the other cup back to his chair, and sat down to sip it, still turning in his mind this notion of getting Jack Bolley actively engaged.

Finally he said: "It'll be darned risky. Someone out there killed not just your brother, Ralph, but I'll bet a month's pay that same shotgun man also killed Judge Heber."

Bolley turned a tough expression toward Lefton. "I'll run the risk, Deputy," he said. "I've been runnin' risks like that for a long time, an' I'm still above ground."

They drank their coffee. Behind the wall where Jack Bolley was leaning, Lefton's prisoners were sleeping. Elsewhere, the town was quiet, the night ran on in its endlessly hushed manner, and in the far distance coyotes howled at the stars.

Bob finally arose, put aside his empty cup, and said: "Past my bedtime." They left the jailhouse office together, but parted up near the livery barn, one heading for his rooming house, the other one heading for his bedroll in the livery barn loft.

The following morning, Lefton made his initial round of Mandan about 8:00. At the livery barn he strolled down between the opposite stalls, as was his custom, to see what strange animals had been ridden into town during the night. He'd never yet made an arrest based on this inspection, but the possibility always existed that sooner or later he might; horse thieves usually rode branded animals.

But this morning he made a quite different discovery. Jack Bolley's saddle horse was gone. He went up to the harness room to ask the day man about that. All he got was a dumb look. "If that feller pulled out," the hostler said, "he'd have to done it sometime last night. I been here since six an' ain't no one rid out . . . or in either, for that matter."

Bob returned to the golden-lighted roadway and stood for a moment in thought. Bolley didn't believe in wasting time once his mind was made up evidently. He and Lefton had parted company after midnight the night before. Sometime between then and 6:00, Jack had rigged out and ridden off. Bob wasn't too concerned, actually, for Bolley's health. Jack looked to him like a seasoned lawman. He'd be careful. But what he did speculate about was how and where Jack proposed to locate Walt Patterson.

The morning coach rattled in, which was always somewhat of an event around Mandan, and later on Sawyer Given drove in behind a smart team of dark chestnuts, sitting ramrod straight upon the tufted leather seat of his yellow-wheeled runabout. He saw Lefton standing out front of the livery barn, looked him straight in the eye, and never moved a muscle as he spun past, turned in alongside the plank walk down in front of Hicks's general store, and climbed down to stride inside.

Bob smiled to himself. Given was keeping his word about keeping things as they always had been. He stepped out into the roadway bound for Stan's saloon. It was too early even for beer, so when he entered, Oldfield was alone behind his bar, sleeves rolled up, rinsing out glasses from the night before. He nodded at the deputy sheriff, finished polishing a shot glass, held it up critically to examine it, then turned, put it on a backbar shelf, turned back, and said: "Was lookin' for you last night. Couple of drunk idiots started a fight in here."

"Glad I wasn't around, then," murmured Bob. "You jerk the starch out of 'em?"

"Yeah, me 'n' my oak spoke I keep under the bar just for such customers. They were a couple of Mister Given's riders. I think I've see 'em around once or twice before, but wouldn't take my oath about that. Walt Patterson came in late, about when they got to hoorawing the place. After I'd laid 'em out, he gave me a hand carryin' 'em outside and leavin' 'em propped against the wall out there. He said they were Wyoming Cattle Company men from one of Mister Given's cow camps up near the divide." As Oldfield plunged an arm into the oily bucket for another glass to be polished, he said: "I wish those half wild ones he keeps up there in the lousy mountains'd go down the far slopes and visit the towns out yonder."

"Generally," said Bob Lefton, "that's what they do. Did either of them say anything that'd tell you what they were doing in Mandan? This is one hell of a long ride from up on Mister Given's north ranges."

"Naw, they didn't say anything. Even when they first came in and started drinking. In fact, until they got pretty well oiled, they didn't even speak to each other. Then . . . all that changed."

Lefton leaned on the bar, thinking. He'd had time now to reflect on what he'd said earlier about being glad he hadn't been in town. Now he wished he had been around.

"Old Walt did a pretty fair share of drinkin' last night himself," stated Oldfield casually. "But you know Patterson. If he's got the cash, he'll show up." Stan vigorously rubbed the glass in his hand, then said: "How're your prisoners?"

"All right," answered Lefton. "Georgia's a little pale from being locked up these past couple of weeks, but Kate's. . . ."

"Yeah, I know," interjected Stan, and sighed, lowering the glass he was holding. "She'd be somethin' special for a man to look at, even in a jailhouse."

Bob absently nodded. He was wondering where Walt Patterson was right now. If he'd been in town late last night, perhaps that's why Jack Bolley had pulled out. He'd possibly spotted Walt, and, when Patterson had pulled out, Bolley had followed him. If this were so, of course, it simplified something. If it were not so, then Walt was still somewhere around town very likely. Perhaps even at this very minute looking for Lefton.

He strolled out of Stan's saloon, paused a moment upon the plank walk, gazing up and down the roadway, saw nothing that held his attention particularly, and started down toward the jailhouse. Until he entered his office and saw raffish, slovenly Walt Patterson sitting there, he'd felt a little worried. Now, for a reason he didn't even try analyzing, he felt somewhat better.

Patterson smiled, his little deep-set eyes looking shrewd but pleasant. "Been waitin' around for you since last night," he said. "Don't tell me. Let me guess. Last night you went out 'n' talked with Mister Given."

Bob closed the door, went to his desk, and sat down before he said: "Why, Walt? Why were you looking for me?"

"To tell you somethin' sort of interestin'."

"All right. Tell it."

But Patterson kept placidly smiling. "Maybe it'd be better if I showed you, Bob. If I just up an' told you, there's a right good chance you wouldn't believe me."

Lefton gazed with rising exasperation at the larger, older man. Controlling his impatience, he said: "Try me, Walt. Just try me."

"All right. But I'll still have to show you. By the way, where's Jack Bolley?"

"He rode out of town last night. I thought maybe he'd spotted you and had trailed on out behind you."

"I didn't see him," stated Patterson. "What's he doin', ridin' out?"

Bob shrugged. He didn't know; he said he didn't know, then he said: "Come on, Walt. What's this big mystery you're going to show me?"

"Six hundred head of cattle in a mountain meadow, all recent-branded with Sawyer Given's mark," the old cowboy drawled, and broadened his raffish smile at Bob Lefton's slow-growing look of astonishment. "Yep, six hundred head at the very least. Not just two hundred head o' Rockin' W critters like you figured. I reckon we underestimated Ralph Bolley's cow-stealin' friends, didn't we?"

"Are you sure they weren't Given's critters, Walt? Are you absolutely certain of that?"

"I'm sure, Deputy. I worked for Mister Given off an' on too

many years not to know something like that. An' I'll tell you somethin' else, too, before I ride you out there 'n' show you the herd. Buzz Hilton knows all about 'em, too, no matter what he says after you arrest him. I know, because I sat up on a bluff in among some tall trees watchin' that bunch of rustlers in their camp, an' Buzz rode in, ate with 'em, talked a spell, then rode back down to the plain again."

"How many were there of the others?" asked Lefton.

"Seven. Eight, countin' Buzz. They're from one of the north range cow camps. I don't rightly know any of 'em, but I've seen 'em among Mister Given's reg'lar hands." Patterson's grin lingered. "Nice kettle of fish for you, Deputy," he drawled. "You 'n' me 'n' Jack Bolley against seven cow thieves, an' Buzz Hilton. Somethin' else, too. Those seven friends of his up there are readyin' their private herd to move. I'd say, if Mister Given's about ready to commence a drive down to the railhead, why then them fellers are fixin' to drift their stolen beef right along with the reg'lar herd."

"Six hundred," muttered Bob. "Hell, Walt, this's a lot more serious than I thought."

"Two hundred Rocking W critters," stated Walt, "an' I'll lay you a month's pay the other four hundred were stolen right from Mister Given's own herds. That's what comes of lettin' one range boss run the whole cussed ranch."

# XII

Bob said: "Where's your horse? Go get him and meet me out back of the livery barn."

Walt arose, nodding. "But what about Bolley?" he asked.

"Never mind Jack for now. You just take me up where I can verify what you've just told me and we'll start some fireworks around here. Six hundred head!"

Patterson was grinning again when he departed, bubbling

over with amusement at the lawman's reaction to what he'd been told.

Bob went back to see if his prisoners needed or wanted anything. He told Kate and Georgia he'd leave his keys with the café man next door, that the café man would see to it that they were fed and looked out for. As he was walking away, Mrs. Willard called after him. But Lefton neither turned back nor even slowed down. He'd just finished relocking his cell-block door when Sawyer Given walked in from out in the roadway. Given closed the door and said: "I'm organizing my midsummer drive, Bob. I told Buzz this morning we'd head out within a week, whenever he was satisfied we had all the two-year-old steers ready to ship."

"Yeah, I know," muttered the deputy. "I reckon Hilton had it figured out yesterday you'd come around and give him that order today. Last night he passed orders for his private herd to be drifted down into the regular Wyoming Cattle Company herds." Bob paused, gazing straight at Sawyer Given. "Tell me something, Mister Given. How could you be rustled four hundred head worth, and not know it?"

Given's testy eyes dully flashed. "What're you talkin' about?" he growled. "No one steals twenty head without my knowing it."

"Well, maybe not," replied Lefton. "But for your sake I sure hope you're wrong." He went to his wall rack of guns, filled a pocket with carbine ammunition, turned back, opened the roadway door, and held it open. "After you," he said to Given. "I'm locking the place up for a while."

Given walked out, turned, and put a perplexed stare upon Lefton. "What's wrong with you?" he demanded. "What'd you mean . . . four hundred head of my cattle being stolen?"

"Come back tonight," said Bob, turning away. "By then I'll know a lot more . . . one way or another."

"Hey!" called Given, indignantly. "Hey, Bob . . . !"

But Lefton kept right on walking. He entered the café, flung down his keys, and gave the café man instructions to feed his prisoners, then hastened on up to the livery barn. Walt Patterson was already out back, waiting. But Walt was not an impatient individual. He leaned in the shade, smoking and holding the reins to his big jugheaded, gimlet-eyed saddle animal until the deputy joined him. Then Walt heaved himself up across leather, hauled around, and headed out of Mandan, riding northward in an easy lope.

The mountains were northward. Actually they curved around from east to west, but their actual location in any case was northward from Mandan. They were a good distance off, too. Where some little rolling foothills lifted off the plain, far out, was where the mountains really began. Those foothills were several miles deep; a man—or two men—could work their way back and forth through them for several hours before striking up into the forested slopes with the good fragrance of pine oil all around them.

When it was hot out on the plain, it was invariably cool in the hills. The farther in a rider might go, the more pleasant it became, too. There were innumerable small, brawling creeks, and carpets of needles so dense horses sank almost to their fetlocks as they silently walked along. There were a good many trails, some old, some newer, made by Sawyer Given's cattle as they worked their way back and forth up the side hills, bound for the large grassy parks up in the higher, broader expanses of forest.

Walt Patterson would've known this land anyway, because off and on he'd been a Wyoming Cattle Company rider. But today he followed the obvious trails only until he'd led Deputy Lefton beyond the common places lower down. Where he left the known, marked trails was at the base of a gigantic basalt upthrust that was streaked and stained from centuries of wintertime run-off. There, he skirted the cliff, rode up through a concealed draw full of thorny thickets, then reached the head land with a minimum of work for his saddle horse. After that, he cut through a dense patch of old forest where tracks wouldn't have shown even if a large herd had been driven through, and cut sharply back to the east where they came upon the first park.

Sawyer Given's cattle were up here, fat and sleek and dark red. They had six-month-old calves by their sides, some of them so large they had to get down on both front knees to drain the old wet cows. It was a good sight to a pair of range men like Lefton and Patterson, but Walt didn't pause to admire the sight like he probably would've done under other circumstances. He went right on past, heading even higher and deeper into the mountains.

Bob Lefton knew these hills, but only in a general way. When he'd worked for Mister Given, he'd only once or twice been sent to work the highland meadows. Ordinarily, unless he was critically short-handed, Sawyer Given kept his distant mountain ranges manned by altogether separate crews from the men who rode for him out of the home ranch. But Walt knew the mountains. That was patently evident the way he wove back and forth, never hesitating in a gloomy world of tall pines where even an experienced mountaineer would have usually had to have taken a bearing now and then. Once he looked back and grinned. But that was all he did until, with the sun past its zenith, he finally pushed down out of a dark stretch of forest straight into a huge meadow, perhaps five or six hundred acres in size, where more greasy fat Herefords grazed in grass reaching past their knees.

"This here is what we used to call Middle Meadow," he told Bob Lefton. "When I first hired out to Mister Given a long time back, this is where I camped for six months one spring an' summer, watching out for first-calf heifers. Pardner, I'm here t' tell you that was the busiest, toughest summer I ever worked . . . anywhere. Them heifers'd all been bred to one of Mister Given's three-quarter-ton New Mexico horned bulls, an' those dog-goned calves was half growed before they was born, and I rode m'self to a frazzle with my lass rope draped over one shoulder, pullin' calves from heifers too small to deliver 'em." Patterson chuckled. "I'll never forget that summer if I live to be a hundred."

"Yeah," grunted Lefton, not the least bit interested. "Where are we now, and how much farther do we have to go?"

"Midway to the high country," replied Patterson, squinting as he carefully scanned the meadow all around them. "It'll take us another three, four hours o' steady ridin' to get where we're going."

"Three hours," protested Lefton, and Walt turned on him irritably.

"Well, consarn it, what'd you expect, Bob? There ain't no way to hide six hundred head of cattle without you got a heap of ground around between them an' other critters. Now let's go."

They didn't stop until they were across Middle Meadow. Then Patterson wouldn't even dismount. He watered his horse at a shallow creek crossing and kept on riding.

From Middle Meadow onward, though, the mountains seemed to flatten out for a goodly distance, with rich, grassy meadows of varying size, interspersed between long runs of gigantic, virgin trees, most of them being over a hundred feet tall. When Patterson eventually did halt and dismount, they were in a fold of the purple hills where no one, even by accident, could've stumbled onto them. Here, Walt made a smoke and offered his makings to Bob. Lefton had his own papers and tobacco. He also got down and created a cigarette. As Patterson leaned, close to grinning, to hold the match for Lefton to light up, he said quietly: "I had to bring you this way, Bob. There are better trails, but that badge you got pinned on the front of your shirt gives me the willies. Like I said, there are seven of 'em up here, an' seein' me ridin' with you, them boys'd just naturally salivate me right along with you."

Bob inhaled, exhaled, looked all around, speculated on the time of day from the position of the lowering sun, and said: "Walt, by the time we get back down out of here it's goin' to be damned late in the night."

"All the better," chirped Patterson.

"Yeah. If we don't get lost and spend all night riding around in circles."

"No chance, Deputy. I know this place like I know the inside of my hat."

Lefton gazed at Patterson. "How much farther?"

Walt turned, ran a thoughtful gaze along some rims on ahead and slightly westerly, then said with a low grunt: "See them rimrocks? Well, that's where we'll fade into forest shadows, walk out an' look down. That's where the big meadow is."

"Why stop here then?" asked Lefton. "The horses could've pulled that last half mile with no sweat."

"I wasn't much thinkin' of the horses, Deputy," Walt dryly replied. "I was thinkin' of us. Of you 'n' me, an' someone up yonder who just might be up there havin' a go at sentry duty."

They didn't leave that spot until Patterson was satisfied no one was up ahead, watching the intervening country. But even then, he took the long way out and around in a circuitous, stealthy manner, so that when they eventually dismounted for the last time and hid their horses, then moved out on foot carrying their carbines, they were actually in among the rough and ragged old stone spires that formed the southernmost rim of an enormous valley.

Walt led over through some spindly trees where deeper soil nourished a more formidable stand of firs and pines. There, as he knelt and made an intent study all around, Bob Lefton got his first good view of the park below. It had to be at least six miles across and even wider at its longest east-west boundaries. There was a creek that nourished creek alders, several gigantic old cottonwood trees, and acres of short, wiry, very dark green grass. And there were cattle down there, hundreds of them like small bugs ponderously waddling along as they grazed. From the heights, Deputy Lefton estimated their numbers at about what Walt Patterson had said—six hundred head. He sat back, put his shoulders to a rough-barked old tree, and tipped up his hat. Walt watched, and chuckled as he, also, eased down and settled himself comfortably.

"Quite a sight, ain't it?" he murmured. "They got a real good set-up, providin' Sawyer Given don't take a notion to ride up through here. When he was twenty years younger, I recollect the fellers used to say you never could tell when or where he might pop up. 'Course, a man slows down with age."

"That," surmised Lefton, "would be Buzz Hilton's job. Keeping Mister Given from coming up through here, and also keeping the hired hands who aren't in his crew from having any reason for being on this part of the Given range."

"Wouldn't be hard to do," stated Patterson, turning sober as he gazed far down where those sleek cattle contentedly grazed. "Hilton's range boss. He could keep riders out of here except his cronies without no trouble at all."

"Unless," murmured Lefton, "they happened to stray in here."

"Then," suggested Walt, "they'd likely spend all eternity buried up here."

Bob shook his head about that. "Naw, Walt. That's the beauty of it. They're all marked with Sawyer Given's brand. Even stray riders in here wouldn't think much of it. You take an outfit that runs as many thousands of head as Given's Wyoming Cattle Company does, and five or six hundred head more or less wouldn't cause even a ripple of interest . . . providing they had Given's mark on 'em."

Walt nodded, picked up a pine needle, chewed it for a while, then tossed it aside and canted his head for a look at the reddening sun. "Seen enough, Deputy?" he inquired, and, when Bob nodded, they both arose.

"I think I got it figured out finally, why Hilton had Bolley killed over at the Willard place."

"Sure," muttered Walt as they walked slowly back where they'd left their mounts. "So's he could take over the Willard place. That ain't no mystery."

"But more than that, Walt. So he could take it over because it adjoins Given's range."

Patterson thought on that for a moment, then waggled his head back and forth. "Hilton ought to know Mister Given better'n to try anything like that. He'd have Buzz killed sure as I'm a foot high, when he found out. I know that for a fact."

# XIII

Getting back down out of the mountains didn't prove as difficult as Bob Lefton had feared it might. Patterson hadn't been exaggerating in the least; he knew just about every cow and deer trail heading down through the increasing gloom, and delivered Lefton back into the lowland foothills before the new moon started its high left-to-right crossing.

Bob breathed easy only when they had those dark uplands at their backs. He had feared all along that they might be intercepted, and, when they were not, he made a remark about Hilton's rustlers being careless.

"Not careless," corrected Patterson. "Careful about who they let ride up into the mountains. Hell, they've had it all their way for a couple of years, an' I reckon you'd figure the same as they do, if, in that length o' time, no one ever got in your sights. Naw, Bob, Buzz Hilton's smart. He's had this scheme of his organized so well for so long he don't have to worry too much. I been thinkin' about somethin' you said back up there about cattle branded with Mister Given's mark bein' Buzz's cleverest move. Y' know what I come up with? Well, suppose you was to get up a big posse an' go back up there an' arrest every blessed one of 'em. Tell me how you'd prove Buzz rustled them critters, if he swore up an' down he didn't rustle 'em?"

Lefton said: "Sawyer Given could show by the number of cows he's got that he couldn't have had that many more calves out of the cows over the past couple of years."

"You're wrong," explained old Walt. "The best year Mister Given's ever had, he didn't get no more'n sixty-five percent calf crop. Spread that over two years an' it amounts to a lot more cattle than six hundred head . . . providin' Hilton says the losses for those years weren't sixty-five percent, but were only maybe seventy or seventy-five percent."

Lefton gazed at raffish Walt Patterson, wondering at his shrewdness. Walt was perfectly correct. Given could've had another six hundred calves from his cows in the length of time under question. Not only that, but if Hilton couldn't be shaken from such a statement, the law would have a hard time—a very hard time—making any case against him. "All," grumbled Lefton in a low voice, "because he was too smart to use a brand of his own."

They didn't arrive back in Mandan until well past midnight, and, when they'd put up their animals at the livery barn, Walt strolled as far as the front roadway before he said he thought he'd bed down. "It's been a right long ride today," he explained, "an' for the past couple of days I been pretty much on the move."

Bob nodded. "One last thing, Walt. Keep an eye peeled for Jack Bolley. If you run across him, fetch him down to the jailhouse. We've got to hold ourselves a war council."

Walt agreed, then turned and sauntered back into the barn.

There were the usual doorway lights burning here and there as Deputy Lefton headed wearily down toward the jailhouse, but otherwise, the same as it had been the night before, Mandan was hushed and slumbering.

His footfalls sounded loud upon the plank walk. A dog heard him passing and drowsily barked. Somewhere out back of town, westward, a mule brayed, its see-sawing, hoarse croak rising and falling, rising and falling.

There was a light at the jailhouse. He saw that and speculated that the café man had probably left it burning. But when he opened the door, he saw at once that he'd made a mistake about that. Sawyer Given was sitting on a tipped-back chair over against the east wall, smoking a little black cigar. He had his hat brim tilted down to shield his eyes from the overhead light, and swung them boldly to scrutinize Lefton when the deputy walked in. Given didn't look very amiable; he'd evidently been keeping this vigil a long time, but when he first spoke, at least he didn't sound unpleasant, although as usual he was brusque.

"Well, if you'd waited just a little longer before comin' back to town," he said, "we could've had breakfast together."

Bob went over to help himself to the coffee that was perking over where Sawyer Given had lit the stove. "And if I'd come back any sooner, I wouldn't be able to tell you that Hilton's got six hundred head, not two hundred, all neatly marked with your brand, ready to be drifted down a few at a time . . . at least this is my guess . . . and filtered into the big herd that'll be heading south for rail's end directly."

He took the cup back to his desk, dropped down, and put both hands around it to savor the pleasant heat. Given kept eyeing him without speaking, evidently awaiting an explanation. When it was slow in coming, he eventually said: "This morning when you walked off you said for me to see you tonight. All right, I'm here. I've been here since nightfall. My horse is tied in a shed out back of your jailhouse, so no one'll know I'm here. Now then, what's it all about?"

Bob told him bluntly and without wasting words. He explained where he'd seen the cattle, how many of them there were, how many men Walt Patterson had said there were with the herd, and finally he sketched out the difficulties involved in riding up there and making a wholesale arrest. "Because those animals carry your brand, all Hilton's got to do is swear up and down they are your critters. Then he loses a small fortune, but at least he comes out with a whole hide. While I look like a fool for even trying to make him look like a rustler."

Given said: "That's no particular problem, Bob. I told Buzz this afternoon I want the trail herd on the road no later'n three days from now."

Lefton waited for further explanation. When none was immediately offered, he said: "Can he complete the gather by then?"

"Sure. He's already completed most of it. Now then, you 'n' I'll ride on down to Bellflower and be around down there when the cattle arrive. We'll get the law lined up, plus the buyers. When someone hands Buzz two bank drafts, one made out in my name, the other one made out in his name, we step in and make the arrest." Given chewed his cigar savagely a moment, then added: "What's wrong with that?"

"Nothing," conceded Lefton, and drank some coffee. "In fact, I like it, Mister Given. As far as I can see now, that's about the only way we're going to catch him."

Given removed the cigar, glared at it for a moment, then raised his face. "There's just one thing. Suppose Hilton is only given one bank draft, the one with my name on it?"

Bob pushed aside his cup and sighed as he returned the crusty old cowman's stare. "Then, like I told you before, I'll ride out, hand you my badge, and apologize to Hilton."

"Remember that," growled Given, and brought his chair down off the wall with a loud report. "There are two kinds of folks I never could abide, Bob. Thieves and fools. Buzz has to be one, or you have to be the other."

Given departed after making that final, tough judgment, leaving Lefton to sit with his empty coffee cup thinking past to all he'd seen this day, and also dwelling soberly on Given's last statement: *Buzz has to be one, or you have to be the other.* It was very true. If Hilton didn't turn out to be the leader of an enterprising band of cow thieves, then Bob Lefton had to be a fool for trying to make him one.

He strolled over, refilled his coffee cup, and thought about going in for a talk with Kate Willard. But it was very late now, past 1:00 A.M., so he stood by the stove until his office door open around, wondering who'd be up and abroad this time of night.

It was Walt Patterson, wearing his crooked little grin, and right behind Walt was Jack Bolley. They both looked as though they hadn't even brushed trail dust off their clothing as they barged on in, gently closed the door, and headed for some of Lefton's coffee.

"I found him all right," said Patterson, reaching for the tin cup Bob held out to each of them as he lifted the coffee pot. "He come along an' bedded down in the livery barn loft about ten minutes after I shucked my boots to get some sleep."

Bolley gravely watched his cup fill up, lifted it, and sipped. The coffee was black as death and hot. He made a bitter face, lowering the cup. "Went out huntin' Patterson," he said. "Never found him. He told me why on our way down here. Then we saw Given leavin', so we stood back in a dogtrot out of sight until he was plumb gone, an' came on down here."

"Where'd you go?" asked Lefton.

"Out an' around," stated the Coloradoan. "Back to that Willard place in daylight to study how an' where my brother was killed."

"And?"

Bolley lifted his shoulders and dropped them. "We had it figured right last night. After that I just poked around on the range, tryin' to imagine what Ralph and this here Hilton had in mind."

"Find anything?"

"Well, to start off with, I was a long way westerly from the Willard place before I saw anyone, then it was a cowboy headin' across Given's range toward the mountains. I followed him. It took a little doin', him actin' kind of skittery all the while, and me not havin' much concealment, but I got up into the forest after a while, an' from then on it wasn't so hard."

"What'd you see up there?" Lefton asked.

"This feller, Buzz Hilton. I knew it was him, because when that cowboy seen him and they came together, I heard him call the newcomer Buzz. I snuck around through the trees until I was close enough to loosen 'em both in their saddle with a couple of rocks, if I'd wanted to."

"Never mind that," urged Bob. "What did they talk about?"

"Cattle, Deputy. They talked about driftin' their hidden herd southward startin' tomorrow before sunup."

Bob looked perplexed. "Southward?" he said. "You mean they don't aim to drift them into Given's trail herd?"

"No, sir. They figure to push them about twenty miles southward below Mandan, and let 'em graze along down there with only one or two men to sort of ride guard over 'em, until the regular Given trail herd comes along, then incorporate them into the bigger herd, and keep right on goin' down to rail's end."

Lefton put aside his half empty coffee cup. This, of course, wasn't going to upset Given's plan at all, but it definitely wasn't how Lefton had thought Hilton would work his scheme, either. He told Bolley and Patterson what Given had said about trapping Hilton down at rail's end. The two older men thought on this for a spell, sipping coffee and turning solemn. Finally Walt said he didn't see where there'd be any trouble.

"He'll still cut 'em out and sell 'em separately at rail's end, Bob. He's got to do it like that."

Jack Bolley agreed with Walt. He also said he liked Given's plan. "It'll be handier that way," he stated. "Let Hilton get the drafts in his hands, then yank the carpet out from under him."

"Except for one thing," mused Lefton. "Suppose he's already contracted his rustled herd? The minute his private buyer is warned by Mister Given and the law down at rail's end, what's to prevent him from also warning Hilton?"

That kept the pair of older men quiet for a long while. Meanwhile, Bob returned to his desk, sank down there, and turned to making a smoke. The more he thought about it, the less sure he became that Given's plan would work after all.

"One slip," he said, lighting up, "and they'll scatter like quail." He swung his chair around, eyeing Walt Patterson narrowly. "Walt," he softly said, "ride out to the Given place in the morning and tell Mister Given I'm not going down to rail's end with him after all. Tell him to hire you on as a trail hand to go with the herd. Also, tell him what Jack overheard about how Hilton figures to drift in his stolen bunch. Then tell him I said for him to go on down and set the trap for Hilton at rail's end. Jack Bolley and I will trail the herd, just in case there are any more last minute switches that might upset our cart of apples."

"All right," Patterson agreed. "But listen here, you two. If there's any trouble down the trail, just don't you fellers get to shootin' too free down there. I'm a big man. I make a big target. An' danged if I cherish the notion of gettin' killed by the law while I been to such pains to help it, lately. You boys hear me now?"

Jack Bolley laughed and Bob Lefton almost did. Walt's seamed, weather-checked ugly old features were screwed up with deadly serious anxiety. Bob said: "We'll take care, Walt. If it comes to a fight, we'll only shoot thin fellers. How's that sound?"

"Not very funny to me," growled Walt, and went over to the door. "An' suppose Mister Given wants to see you, Bob? What'll I tell him?"

"You tell him not to try and see me from now on, unless it's damned important, and then to only make the effort after nightfall. Jack and I'll be somewhere behind the herd. If he needs something more definite than that, tell him to wait for us down at rail's end." Bob got up. "Good luck, Walt. You've sure been more'n just ordinary help in this mess."

Patterson, somewhat mollified, rolled his eyes around and said to Bolley: "Jack, mind you're nowhere around when he gets to shootin'. They tell me he shuts both eyes."

Jack smiled at Walt. "I'll watch him," he said quietly. "You watch those rustlers." After Patterson had gone out into the late night and closed the door, Jack also said: "He's my kind of man, that one."

Bob yawned and rubbed both eyes. "I hope Buzz Hilton doesn't try to set any records getting down to rail's end. I've missed so much sleep the past couple of days that I'd like to get in about eight hours sougan time tomorrow night or the night after."

Jack had a hard observation to make about that. "If you get real tired," he said, setting down his cup and heading for the door, "you just might make a slip-up, Deputy. An' if you do that, I got a feelin' you just might get all the sleep you'll ever want . . . in a grave." He opened the door and stepped through. "See you in the mornin'. Good night." He closed the door and was gone from Bob Lefton's sight.

# XIV

Deputy Lefton didn't get his rest. Jack Bolley found him eating breakfast at the café next to his jailhouse the following morning at 6:00 and said Given's range riders were pushing a large herd southward from Wyoming Cattle Company's headquarters ranch. Bolley called for a cup of coffee and some fried beans, then leaned closer on the counter bench and said in a tone so low even Lefton had to strain to hear: "The rustled herd left the mountains about three o'clock this morning. I was out there. I saw it snake out an' around Given's home place, moving southward. Four riders drivin' it."

Lefton pushed aside his plate, pulled in his coffee cup, leaned both elbows on the counter, and sadly shook his head. He wasn't going to get that sleep after all.

"Given told me yesterday Hilton wouldn't start his drive until tomorrow or the day after," he mumbled.

"I don't care what anyone else told you," retorted Jack Bolley, leaning back so the counterman could put down his plate of fried beans. "I'm tellin' you, Deputy, both bunches are on the move."

Bob nodded, drank his coffee down, shoved the cup back, and groped for his tobacco. "Don't you ever sleep?" he plaintively asked.

"Yeah," Bolley replied from the corner of his mouth as he wolfed down his food, "when there's nothing else to do. I learned that trick from the Shoshones when I was a kid. Sleep an' loaf for weeks at a time when you get the chance. When you've got work to do . . . do it an' don't worry about rest."

"Very good theory," said Lefton, lighting his smoke and casting a rueful look around at Jack Bolley. "But I've known my share of Shoshone diggers, too, and one thing I noticed about them. They can spout more adages an' give more sound advice, without ever botherin' to follow any of it themselves, than any other people I've ever known."

Jack looked up, reached for his coffee, and grinned around a mouthful of fried beans. "Odd you should have 'em figured that way," he murmured. "So did I." He gulped the coffee and got up to dig for some coins.

They walked out of the café together. Jack had left his horse over at the livery barn with instructions for his outfit to be peeled off it and put on another animal. As he told Bob Lefton, his private animal'd had about all the abuse one horse ought to have to take over the past twenty-four hours.

They got astride, eventually, and jogged casually out of Mandan southward. Stan Oldfield was down at Carl Hicks's store getting a can of bicarbonate of soda. Both Stan and Carl saw those two go past on their way out of town.

"Right rough pair," observed Stan, craning around. "That Bolley feller's mean like his brother was. I'll give you big odds on that, Carl."

Hicks shrugged. "He better not be too mean, or Bob Lefton'll have him for supper. One thing a man's got to hand old Sawyer Given . . . when he turns 'em back in the mainstream, they're tough as a boiled owl. I've seen Bob Lefton riled up a time or two."

"Amen," breathed Stan. "Well, how much for this damned soda? If I'd get married an' quit cookin' for myself, I wouldn't have to use the stuff."

"A dime," stated old Carl, and puckered up his little eyes. "An' if you did get married, it'd cost you a heap more'n a dime a week, too. So take your pick. Indigestion and freedom, or no indigestion an' no freedom."

It was always chilly so early in the morning, but it would warm up; it always had in Wyoming's cow country in mid-summer. Sometimes it even got downright hot. The air was as clear as polished glass all the way up to the high azure sky that had not one blemish in it all the way across its curved vastness. The rearward mountains were starkly standing against green plains, brooding, old beyond reckoning, aloof, spiked with pines and firs, alternately beckoning and forbidding.

Southward, the land was nearly level for as far as a man could see. There was a town down there, below the sweep and curve of the horizon, called Bellflower. The name was a variation of the name columbine, which was the state flower of Colorado, but columbines didn't just grow in Colorado, and, besides, when the emigrants had first arrived in the Sioux country, they hadn't known the little blue flower was named columbine and had ignorantly called it a bellflower.

The village of Bellflower had just one reason for its existence, the end of the railroad tracks. But that was usually ample reason for a village to grow into a town anyway, since freight depots sprang up, shipping pens were erected to collect and hold enormous numbers of cattle to be shipped East, and, whether terrain favored it or not, prosperity arrived hand in hand with the steel ribbons. But between Mandan and Bellflower was a huge blank space. There were infrequent shacks, forlorn and deserted, where homesteaders full of high hopes had wrestled Nature and had lost. Otherwise, all the land between Mandan and Bellflower was open range—free-graze country for any cow-man who wished to use it.

The main problem for drovers steering a trail herd, once they cleared the mountains and hit the plain, was open range cattle. Once a herd got into unfamiliar country, there was practically no danger at all from cut-backs—those homesick critters that sometimes turned tail and bolted for their home range, or slipped off stealthily and hid among trees or in underbrush until the herd passed, then went back. The nature of driven cattle, once they were beyond their home ranges, was to hang close. A good man on a top horse couldn't drive one or two critters away from their companions, which was fine because it minimized the amount of labor for both two-legged and four-legged herders. But when passing across other ranges, invariably, if strange cattle spotted a herd, they'd hasten down to sniff or fight, or just fall in with the strangers and drift along. That was what the riders had to watch out for. They had to spot these curious beasts and turn them back before they joined the trail herd; otherwise, it was nearly impossible to cut them out and chase them off once they mingled in.

For Bob Lefton and Jack Bolley, there was the obvious risk that someone from the rustled herd might see them. They knew those four renegade Wyoming Cattle Company horsemen would be more vigilant even than the legitimate herders coming along farther back with Sawyer Given's herd. For that reason they didn't try to do any more than keep the dust cloud in sight.

It was one of those totally clear, unobstructed days, when a wary man sitting atop a horse could see as far as the curve of the earth in all directions. Could detect movement before he could even make out what might be making it. The riders with the misbranded herd of six hundred steers would be extremely careful, not just of open range critters trying to join their herd, but also of any strange horsemen. Equally as alert, but perhaps with less intent interest in riders, would be the men coming along with Sawyer Given's regular drive. But in either case, it amounted to the same thing—discovery—and neither Lefton nor Bolley wanted that. At least not just yet.

It was near noon before the Given herd passed southward around Mandan. By then the pair of lawmen were between both drives, but well to the east of both to minimize inadvertent discovery. It wasn't hard to gauge the pace, the distance, even the direction of both herds, from their dust banners. Jack said he thought Hilton didn't intend for the two herds to meet until his legitimate herd was a good long distance below Mandan. That's how it looked to Bob, also.

Along toward sunset they noticed that the rustled herd was moving out faster. They speculated about the reason for this, arrived at no definite judgment, and began a slow, careful ride far out eastward, then on downcountry in the direction the rustled herd was hiking along. Lefton, who knew this end of his territory well enough, said he thought the renegade riders meant to bed their six hundred head near an old dry lakebed where a spring of good, cold water gushed.

They were within scenting distance of the stolen cattle before the sun finally sank behind the rearward curve of peaks and plateaus. Bolley grumbled about getting any closer. As it turned out, he was quite correct. They spotted a cowboy loping toward them with the last dying blaze of red light in his face, before he saw them. The man loped past less than a hundred yards west of where they crouched, holding the nostrils of their horses. Bolley asked if Lefton knew the man. Bob shook his head. "But all that means is that I haven't gotten to know all Sawyer Given's riders this summer. Come on, let's get away from here."

"You want to follow him?" Bolley asked, as he swung up and settled across his saddle.

"No. What for? We know where he's going. He's on his way back to meet Buzz Hilton and get instructions. My guess is that they'll merge the herds tomorrow. They've got to do it pretty soon. Otherwise the cattle'll do it for 'em, when they catch each other's scent."

Bolley had nothing more to say until, with full darkness down and that little thin scimitar of a moon hanging above the ragged peaks, his stomach reminded him that all he'd had to eat all day was one plate of fried beans and one cup of coffee.

They halted out where a patch of green denoted subsurface water, loosened their *cinchas,* slipped off their bridles, and hobbled their horses. Bolley then said: "Say, you didn't happen to fetch along anything to eat, did you?"

Bob rummaged in his saddle pocket, tossed over a flat can of sardines, and watched Jack's face. "What's the matter? Don't you like sardines?"

"Oh, sure," replied the Coloradoan, eyeing the little tin. "I like 'em, sort of. It depends on how hungry I am just how well I like 'em." He raised his battered, bronzed face and looked Lefton squarely in the eye. "Tonight, I'd say they'll taste about like rattlesnake. But now then, you take sardines tomorrow morning . . . pure chicken. And by tomorrow night. . . ."

"Yeah, I know, roast turkey with all the fixings."

They ate, drank the oil, wiped their fingers, and went for their tobacco sacks and papers. Behind them, both horses greedily cropped the succulent greenery around that underground water hole. Wyoming's sickle moon got higher, the daytime heat faded, and very gradually a hushed lull stole over the range country world.

Lefton leaned back, tipped down his hat, crossed both hands upon his chest, and drowsily said: "Sleep's the same way. I'm used to a bed with genuine rope springs, but tonight I'll rest like a baby on the ground. It all depends on how bone weary a man is."

Bolley nodded and smoked and gazed moodily out at the horses. A little twig snapped and he stiffened, then very slowly turned his head to peer to the rear. He was looking straight into the solitary eye of a blue-black, cocked six-shooter held in the brawny hand of a lithe, slit-eyed range rider he'd never seen before in his life. He didn't move. He barely even breathed.

The crouching cowboy put one finger over his lips commanding Bolley to be silent. He then held out his free hand, pointing at Jack's holstered six-gun. With towering disgust and nearly fatal hesitation, the Coloradoan finally reached around, lifted out his six-gun, and dropped it. The man with the gun nodded approvingly, then motioned over toward Deputy Lefton. This time he whispered.

"His, too, mister. One bad move'll be your last one."

Jack hunkered there, glaring from the six-gun to the face of its owner. He tried his best to find something, anything at all, in the armed man's stance that could be interpreted to mean uncertainty, fear, lack of confidence, doubt, but with no luck at all. The armed man's trigger finger was gently curled. His shadowy face was flinty with determination. Jack turned, got onto all fours, and silently crawled over to pick Lefton's gun out very gingerly—he had no idea how sound a sleeper the lawman from Mandan was—and finally he dropped the gun. Not until then did Bob reach up, drowsily push back his hat, cock one eye at Bolley, and solemnly regard him. Bolley rocked back on his haunches and jerked a thumb over his shoulder. At the same time the armed stranger straightened up and boldly walked right on up.

Bob's other eye jumped wide open. He stared first at the gun, then at the face above it. He looked over where Jack had dropped his gun, then straightened up into an erect sitting posture. "Just what the hell do you think you're doing?" he demanded of the armed man who was eyeing them both from a distance of no more than thirty feet.

The gunman drawled: "I could tell you boys I'm takin' a census out here. Only I don't reckon you'd much believe me, would you?" He dropped his bantering manner and abruptly gestured with his cocked six-gun. "On your feet, both of you."

As Bob got up, he said: "Mister, I'm the deputy sheriff up at Mandan."

The cowboy nodded. "Yeah. I saw that badge before I saw anything else, Deputy. But right now that don't cut no ice. Now you fellers just relax. We're goin' to take a little walk an' see a man. If he don't care about you boys skulkin' around out here in the night, why then neither will I." The gun barrel flicked up and down. "Deputy, you take the lead. Walk along slow 'n' easy through that cussed brush. Walk due west, an' don't get no silly ideas, 'cause I'd as soon leave you lyin' out here for coyote bait as look at you. Now let's get to walkin'."

Bolley and Bob exchanged a look. "How do you like that?" growled the Coloradoan. "Snuck up on by a slope-shouldered punk wearin' his pappy's pistol." He turned with a hard curse and began hiking westerly through the pale-lighted cool night. Behind them the cowboy said: "Hey, you up front. In case you're wonderin', my pappy's pistol shoots real straight."

# XV

The tough-faced little cowboy drove them over where two men squatted by a tiny little fire. The minute Lefton stepped into the reflection he recognized the nearer of those two. That one slowly unwound up off the ground, staring straight at Mandan's deputy sheriff.

Lefton said: "Hello, Buzz."

Hilton was an even six feet tall and weighed in the neighborhood of a hundred and sixty or sixty-five pounds, none of it surplus and none of it fat. He was a cold-faced, hard-eyed individual, taciturn and calculating. "Hello, Lefton," he said, and looked past. "Put up the gun, Nick," he ordered. "Where were they?"

" 'ittle ways east in a dry camp. Feller'd sure never think they was lawmen the way they let me slip right up on 'em."

Both Lefton and Bolley were surprised. That Hilton and his men might know Bolley was their former friend's brother wouldn't have particularly surprised either of them, but that he knew Jack was also a peace officer very definitely did surprise them. In fact, Lefton began getting a bad feeling about this. It was beginning to appear that Hilton wouldn't continue his charade and turn them loose after all.

Hilton considered Jack for a moment, then said: "Bolley, you shouldn't have come up into this country. Y' see, Ralph told us all about you one night." Bob had his answer as to how Hilton knew who Jack was. When Hilton went on speaking, he also had his answer to something else. Hilton dropped his cold gaze upon Lefton. "You, too, Deputy. We know all about you, too. Put your minds at rest, boys. You're not goin' anywhere. Squat down and we'll have a cup of java . . . and talk. I'll talk, you'll listen."

The pair of wary-eyed men there with Hilton moved back a little from the fire. One of them had put a battered coffee pot on that little fire. Those two moved off, smoking and murmuring back and forth, but they went out only as far as the darkness, and stood hip-shot out there, watching and smoking and listening.

Lefton said—"What's going on here?"—trying to be boldly indignant as though he knew nothing. It didn't work. Buzz Hilton, in the act of pouring three tin cups full, raised a hard look at Lefton.

"When a man takes long chances," he said softly, "he figures all the angles, Lefton. He figures what can happen and what might happen. He also figures what he thinks had better happen. You two, for instance. I had a man in town last night. In fact, I've had a couple of men hangin' around Mandan for the past four, five days. Night before last the pair I had down there made a mess of it, got drunk at Stan's place, and came almighty close to upsettin' my pot of beans."

Bob recalled Oldfield telling him of two cowboys raising Ned in the Texas Belle, but he was too intrigued by what Hilton was now implying to pass over that.

"Last night," said Hilton, "Sawyer Given hid his horse out back of your jailhouse and waited until past midnight for you to come back into town." Hilton held out two cups of hot coffee. Bolley accepted his cup and so did Lefton, but neither of them drank. They were watching the range boss. "Before that, Lefton, you went out to the Willard place and looked around. So did Mister Bolley here. Now a feller in my position, like I just said, has got to know what's goin' on. He can't take any chances at all when he's waited as long as me an' my friends have waited to make our big killing. So. . . ." Hilton shrugged, lifted his own cup, and tasted the coffee. "A little bitter," he admitted. "But it's hot. Drink it down."

Still, neither Hilton nor Bolley drank. Bob said: "All right, Buzz. You know that we know, so let's end the charade. What's next?"

Hilton lowered his cup. "Two bullets," he murmured. "I don't know any other way, Deputy. But first, tell me something. How much does Sawyer Given know?"

"Why don't you ask him?" Bolley growled.

Hilton flicked a cold look at the Coloradoan. "Maybe I will, when I'm damned good an' ready." He made a cold smile. "But there's no hurry about that. I sent a man to the ranch before sunup this morning to catch Mister Given in bed."

Bob raised his coffee cup, finally, and sipped as he studied Buzz Hilton. He'd never underestimated Hilton, right from the beginning, but now he wondered if perhaps Hilton hadn't caught them all flat-footed. If he had Sawyer Given prisoner, too, there was no chance of anyone down at Bellflower intervening when the integrated Wyoming Cattle Company herd got down there. He lowered his cup. "Buzz, it won't work," he said.

Hilton looked interested. "Why not, Deputy?"

"For one thing the riders who aren't in this with you are going to wonder when you run the two herds together."

Hilton smiled. "They won't know," he said. "Besides, doing this at night when only my own men are riding herd, the regular hands have been sent ahead to scout the land and make certain no open range cattle are close by. I took care of that this afternoon, Deputy. You got some other notion?"

Bob didn't have, so he said: "What happened between you and Ralph Bolley?"

Now Hilton's cold eyes lost their smile. He jumped his glance over at Jack Bolley while he considered his answer. Eventually he said: "You two were smarter than I figured. Everyone else believes Kate Willard shot him."

"No," interrupted Jack Bolley. "Not after you sent that unsigned letter to Judge Heber, they didn't, Hilton. That was a mistake, that letter."

"You think so?" said Hilton. "I don't. The only mistake was when old Heber decided to come down and see Mister Given."

Lefton said: "You, Buzz . . . you killed Heber?"

Hilton inclined his head. "Sure, I had to. The old fool would've told Given about that unsigned letter. Heber was no fool."

Bob set his coffee cup down on the ground. "Buzz," he said very quietly, "that shotgun killed Bolley, too."

Again Hilton inclined his head. "Had to do that, too," he said. "Ralph was a good man right up until we got to figurin' how much cash those cattle were goin' to fetch when we sold 'em. Then he started schemin'. He tried to wean a couple of my men away from me. He planned on gettin' rid of me and takin' over. I had to get rid of him first."

Jack said: "You did it right well, Hilton. You were clever the way you engineered Ralph into dying. How much whiskey did it take to get him drunk enough to go down where you'd hinted the Willards had a cash box?"

"About a quart," answered Hilton candidly, eyeing Bolley with that merciless cold glare of his. "I'm glad you think it was a smart move. Anyway, so far it's workin'. The Willard women'll have to hire lawyers to keep from goin' to prison. That'll take more money than Justice left them. I'll loan it to 'em . . . on the ranch."

"What about their cattle?" Lefton asked, surmising what Hilton's reply would be.

"What cattle, Deputy?" asked the range boss. "They won't have any after we get back from this drive."

Lefton sighed and reached for his makings. "I'll hand you one thing," he said. "You sure figured it right down to the last grunt, Buzz."

"Not quite," Hilton said. "I didn't figure on you sneakin' down here tonight. Not that it makes much difference. You 'n' Bolley will just disappear. I reckon yours won't be the only two unmarked graves out here, Deputy. Of course, folks'll wonder back in Mandan, but then folks soon forget things like strange disappearances, don't they?"

One of the cowboys standing back behind Hilton called over: "Buzz, Patterson's comin' back!"

Hilton nodded, kept eyeing Lefton and Bolley a moment longer, and then stood up. "The man I sent back to take care of Mister Given is coming," he said, then turned and beckoned the two cowboys behind him on up. "Watch 'em," he ordered, and walked off into the darkness.

Lefton's heart was pounding. He fixed a frozen expression upon his face and lifted the coffee cup. He didn't trust himself to glance over at Jack Bolley. In every chain there is one weak link. If Buzz Hilton had put his faith in raffish old Walt Patterson, that was his weak link.

Bolley said to the pair of bronzed, lean range men guarding them: "I don't reckon you fellers'd be interested in five hundred dollars to be split two ways, while Lefton and I just walk off?"

One of the cowboys said scornfully: "Five hundred's only a fraction of our share from the cattle, lawman. Try again."

Somewhere out in the night a rider walked his horse in out of the gloom and dismounted where Hilton waited. Lefton and Bolley heard those two talking, their voices a low rumble of indistinguishable words out where they couldn't be seen from the little cooking fire.

There were cattle farther out, too, that occasionally lowed or stamped, or clicked horns, but mainly it was their smell that let the prisoners know about where they were bedded down. It wasn't very late, not more than 8:00 or 9:00, but it was dark enough to be past midnight. The night this far from the hills was cool, too, and Bob Lefton buttoned his jumper and turned up its collar.

He eyed their guards. The lithe, youthful one was the man who'd captured them. To this one he said: "How did you find us, out there?"

"No problem about that," said the cowboy. "I was headin' back to see Buzz with the other herd, and caught a flash of reflected light off metal where you two were skulkin' down in the brush. I rode on like I hadn't noticed anything, told Buzz, an' he sent me back to get you."

Bolley said, looking up at the pair of armed riders: "A thousand?"

Now that lithe cowboy turned on Bolley with a sharp answer. "Try it one more time, lawman, an' I won't wait for Buzz to give the word. I'll shoot you right here an' now."

Bolley sighed, reached for his tin cup, and looked straight at Bob Lefton over the rim. "Well, Deputy, looks like we rode right into a cyclone this time, don't it?"

Two men came strolling toward the little fire, their spurs musically jingling. One was Buzz Hilton; the other man was slovenly, small-eyed Walt Patterson. It was old Walt who halted first and gazed from one captive to the other, grinning.

"Wouldn't have believed it," he drawled to Hilton. "I always figured Lefton was smarter'n this, Buzz. About that other one. Hell, he couldn't have been very smart or he'd never have come nosin' around."

Hilton looked straight at Bob and said: "In case you're interested, Deputy, Mister Given is . . . dead."

Bob looked from Hilton to Patterson. He kept his pokerfaced expression. "Congratulations," he said. "It takes a real tough man to shoot a friend, Patterson."

Old Walt's smile faded a little; his small, sunk-set eyes turned dull and lusterless. "No friend to me," he said. "I done Sawyer Given's dirty work before you was born, Deputy. All I ever got for it was a job now an' then at rider's wages. A feller broods about things like that." He dropped his right hand to the butt of his holstered .45. "For the same price, Buzz, I'll walk these two out a ways on the range and salt them down, too."

"Not just yet," replied Hilton. "Go take care of your horse, Walt, then check around and make sure everything's ready to let the herds drift together. There's always the chance one of the regular riders might be comin' back. We'll put these two down when the herds are mingling." Patterson and the other two riders gazed at Hilton, not comprehending. The range boss explained: "Wait until the cattle are making their own noises, bellering and pawing and sniffing each other up. No one'll hear a couple of gunshots then."

Bob studied Hilton and wagged his head slightly. Hilton was

a shrewd and clever man. He'd never doubted it, but being around the crooked range boss like this gave him a closer insight into how the man's mind worked. Hilton had trained himself to think ahead, to consider options and contingencies. That kind of a man, when he went bad, made the most dangerous kind of an outlaw.

Walt Patterson and one of the other riders went pacing off through the gloom. One man—the same one who'd captured Lefton and Bolley—remained with Hilton. As Buzz hunkered down to fill one of the empty tin cups with coffee at the little fire, that lithe, bronzed cowboy hooked both thumbs in his shell belt, saying: "They offered me a bribe, Buzz. A thousand dollars to let 'em walk away."

Hilton wasn't angered. All he said was: "You got to admire men who never quit tryin'. In their boots you 'n' I'd try the same thing. Go get my horse. I want to ride out an' watch the herds come together."

The cowboy walked off and Hilton reached down, slipped the little tie down off the hammer of his six-gun, which made the weapon available for instant use, and was careful to lift his cup of coffee with his left hand.

Lefton was playing for time when he said: "Buzz, you worked it pretty neat. I don't mean about taking more than a year to make your gather, but the way you hoodwinked Mister Given, using men he was paying to do your riding and spying."

"When a feller has the time, and the authority, he can figure out how things ought to be done, Lefton," Hilton replied. "As Given's range boss I had it all my way. There was danger. Not from you . . . hell, you never even suspected right up until you 'n' old Given got to rubbin' horns . . . but from those damned fringe ranchers like Justice Willard. Old Given quit even ridin' his own range a year or so back. Rich men get complacent, hungry men never do, Lefton."

A jarring thought came to Bob. "What about Justice Willard?" he asked, breathing shallowly while awaiting the answer.

Hilton's cold eyes faintly brightened in the fire glow. "You attended his funeral, Deputy," he quietly explained. "You believed, just like everyone else also did, that he broke his neck when a horse fell with him."

"Didn't he, Buzz?"

Hilton shook his head. "His neck was broken by a rope. He found the big meadow and recognized some of his steers down there. We caught him tryin' to sneak back down out of the hills. He cussed me out and accused me of being a rustler." Hilton sipped coffee, lowered the cup, and said: "Shooting'd be too dangerous, so we worked it out to look like it happened differently than it really did. The same way we worked it out for Ralph Bolley."

Bob's forehead creased with a puzzled frown. "Then why," he asked, "did you write the letter about Bolley? You surely figured out folks would hear about that and begin to wonder?"

"Of course, Lefton, an' that's exactly what happened. Folks wondered. But they thought Kate lied, that she shot him from behind with that shotgun."

Now Jack Bolley asked a question: "She did shoot, didn't she, Hilton?"

"Sure she shot. But I had a man watching. When Kate and Georgia left to go down to Denver, I went in there, took all the buckshot out of the shotgun shells, left the wadding and powder in, and, when she pulled the trigger, it sounded and felt just like she'd shot your brother. Only she didn't. I did . . . from behind him."

# XVI

Patterson came plodding back, looking thoughtful. He didn't look at the prisoners at all, but he said: "Buzz, they got your horse out there. The critters are driftin' along. They smell each other now."

Hilton nodded and got upright. "Stay an' watch these two," he said. "I'll send Nick back to join you."

Walt squatted, drew himself a cup of coffee, and still avoided the glances of both Lefton and Bolley. Not until Hilton was gone and even the sound of his horse had died away did Patterson so much as raise his eyes. He shot Bolley a close look, and turned a little to face Lefton. As he lifted the tin cup, he said in a low whisper: "I'll get you out of this. I got no idea how, just yet, but if he sends me out there to knock you two off, that'll be fine. Otherwise, don't stir up anything until I give you the signal."

Bolley said, speaking swiftly: "Where's Given?"

"I told him not to waste time gettin' down to Bellflower. I said for him to head straight for Mandan and get up a posse. Now I'm glad I did that, because otherwise you boys're up to your ears in hot water."

The bronzed, lithe man named Nick came strolling in out of the gloom. He eyed the prisoners, dropped down near Patterson, and fell to work making a smoke. When no one spoke, he lit up, snapped his match, and cheerily said: "You boys care to make a cigarette?"

Lefton shook his head. So did Jack Bolley, but the latter also said: "The only thing I'd like right now is for you to shed that gun and stand up."

Walt growled. "Cut out that kind of talk, mister. Ain't no one goin' to oblige you, so just rope in that kind of talk."

Nick stared thoughtfully at Bolley. Finally he said: "Y' know, mister, for a feller one breath away from meetin' his Maker, you got a lot of grit in your craw. But I reckon I could take you, with a gun or without one."

Now Patterson turned on Nick and darkly scowled. "You,

too," he said. "Can it. We don't need any arguin' an' fightin' right now."

Nick was unperturbed by Walt's black look. He turned, looked off where the sound of moving cattle sounded, and quietly went on smoking.

Lefton was weighing their chances. If Hilton sent Walt out to kill them, everything would be fine. If, however, he decided to send Nick, or perhaps one of the others like Nick, their chances of surviving were very slight. Evidently Bolley was coming to this same conclusion because he eased back upon the ground, pushed back his hat, and said: "Nick, without our guns we're helpless against just one of you fellers, let alone the pair of you."

Nick went on smoking as though he hadn't heard, but when he'd listened to the sounds of the cattle long enough, he swung forward and said: "Sure, Deputy, you'd like me to take a walk so's maybe you two could jump Patterson. But I'd like it better if you tried it when we're both here." He made a leer at Jack, as though pleased that he'd outsmarted the Coloradoan.

Lefton looked off northward where a man sang out in a hooting call toward some cattle he was driving. Evidently the two herds were going to meet somewhere over to the west of the little fire. Evidently, too, Hilton was short-handed after having sent the regular riders southward so that he could merge his two herds; otherwise that cowboy who'd yelled wouldn't have sounded so exasperated.

A noticeable skiff of invisible trail dust filtered down to the area of the little fire. Somewhere a steer bawled a challenge when he caught the scent of other cattle in the darkness. Bob reared back to gaze at the little scimitar moon. It was slightly thicker tonight than it had been last night, but it still cast a very weak variety of light; the stars were brighter.

That stench got stronger and more than one critter bawled as the two herds came steadily closer. There was a solid reverberation in the earth that the squatting men picked up through boot soles or pants pockets. Nick said to Walt Patterson that it looked like everything was going according to Hilton's plan. Walt grunted and didn't answer. He kept taking his coffee down a gulp at a time, gazing with his little eyes narrowed, straight off into the shadowy night, his thoughts evidently cinched tightly around his particular dilemma. Once he shot Bob Lefton an annoyed glance, as though he were piqued that the pair of lawmen had allowed themselves to be taken. But as soon as his expression mirrored this, the thought evidently passed, because his expression smoothed out blankly again. However Walt might feel about Bolley and Lefton being captured, just one thing really mattered now. They had been captured. It was up to him to rectify that if he could.

"Hey," said Nick, nudging Walt. "You daydreamin' or something?"

Patterson turned, looking irritable. "Why? What's it to you?"

"I just said I heard a rider comin'. Must be Buzz comin' back. Now we'll get rid of these two."

Walt heaved himself up to his feet and smoothly said: "Go get his horse for him, Nick."

Bob held his breath. Whether Nick went or not was going to mean the difference between life and death for Lefton and Bolley. He waited the couple of seconds it took Nick to make up his mind whether to obey or not. Then the lithe cowboy stood up and, without a word, walked away out into the darkness.

Walt hissed quickly: "Stay calm. This is it for you two . . . one way or another."

Hilton came striding toward the fire. He looked at the prisoners, then at Patterson. He didn't say a word. He hunkered by the fire, extended both hands, and turned them over and over. It was getting increasingly chilly now. Bob guessed that it was close to midnight.

"Squat down, all of you," ordered Hilton. When everyone was down on his level, he said—"Cold night for this time o' year."—as though nothing more important was on his mind. Farther out, perhaps a quarter or a half mile away, the herds were getting within a few hundred yards of one another. Cattle began to bawl, to snort and stomp the hard earth.

Lefton and Bolley kept watching Buzz Hilton; he seemed to know this without once raising his eyes to their faces as he kept on warming his hands over the fire. He was obviously waiting for the noise out there to reach its lusty peak. Eventually he withdrew his hands, tossed a couple of little twigs on the fire, and looked around at Patterson, who was impassively hunkering beside him, smoking and waiting.

"Walk 'em out to the west," Hilton said as calmly as though he were discussing cattle. "Wait until the noise is loudest. Then take care of 'em. Go on now, Walt."

Patterson didn't move at once, but he drew back one final deep-down inhalation from his cigarette, tossed it in the fire, and coldly said: "Buzz, same price?"

Hilton nodded. "Two hundred each. Same price as for Given, Walt. Then get on back here. I'll need you to keep the cattle from driftin'."

Walt stood up, hitched at his sagging shell belt, made a curt gesture toward Bolley and Lefton, and growled at them: "On your feet and commence walkin'. Don't run or try nothin' cute. Otherwise you'll get it right here. All right now, stay ahead of me, and walk!"

Bolley stood up, gazing down at Hilton. "Thanks for nothin'," he said, turned, and started away. Hilton looked after him, his face a fire-lighted bronze mask. When Lefton turned also to walk away, Hilton spoke to him.

"Tough, Lefton. Nothin' personal."

Bob neither looked back nor answered; he kept on walking.

The underbrush was sparse; star shine limned all three of them. There were no trees this far out on the plain, so if they'd thought of trying to dodge clear, they couldn't have done it before they were shot from behind. Fortunately Buzz Hilton's one serious mistake had just been made; neither of them would have to risk running for their lives. But Patterson kept his gun on them just the same, and, when Lefton glanced back once, hesitating, Walt growled at him: "Keep walkin' an' don't turn around."

They heard the cattle coming together out there. Dust rose thick enough to chew. The noise was loud and tumultuous as strange steers butted heads or made wicked swipes with their horns at one another. It wouldn't really amount to much; steers had their fighting instincts all but eradicated when they were altered from being bull calves, but still there was some vague, hazy instinct in the remembering blood that urged them to go through at least some preliminary fighting moves when they came up against other, strange steers.

Bolley finally halted, turned, and looked back where Walt had stopped to twist from the waist, looking back. They were almost back out where they'd originally had their dry camp. Walt squared around, saw Bolley looking at him, and hastened over to them. Bolley pointed. "Our horses and guns are over yonder where we were makin' a dry camp," he said.

Patterson waved his pistol barrel. "Go on," he said breathlessly. "Run, don't walk. They'll be listenin' for the shots."

Jack and Bob lit out in a twisting, turning rush through the brush as far as their camp. The two horses were still there in lush grass, hobbled. Bolley dived for his six-gun where Nick had made him drop it. As he came up, he held forth Lefton's gun toward the deputy. Bob said: "Walt, you better fire off two rounds, then get on back."

Bolley threw up a hand. "Wait a minute! Hilton said we'd be put in unmarked graves. Sure as hell he'll come out here to plant us. Walt, you better come with us. If you go back an' they don't find our bodies, they'll kill you sure."

Patterson glanced at Lefton. "I kind of had in mind ridin' off with you fellers," he said, "bodies or no bodies. I hid my horse up north a ways."

Lefton nodded. "Shoot," he said. "Let go a couple of rounds, then we got to get away from here." He expelled a long breath as Patterson raised his six-gun and cocked it. "Man, I don't mind admitting that until you got rid of Nick, I thought we might just get it anyway."

Patterson fired, hesitated a second, then fired again. After that he put up his gun and started legging it northward through the night. The sounds of those herds mingling was at its height now. Bob and Jack Bolley got astride after bitting up and yanking loose their hobbles, and started off behind big Walt Patterson.

The noise and dust cast a harsh pall over the otherwise serene night. Dust obscured the stars somewhat, making the night even darker. For these things, Bob was thankful. Walt began to gasp after he'd covered a half mile, but he never slackened his stride. He carried a good deal of surplus weight, and it eventually dragged him down. Bob spurred ahead, coursing from left to right in search of Patterson's mount. He didn't find it, but eventually, when he got up another quarter mile, Walt ducked into a particularly heavy stand of sage, heaved his hulk around with lots of anxious profanity, then came popping out the far side of the brush, leading a saddled horse. Bob glanced at Bolley and the Coloradoan said: "You'd never have found it."

Patterson leaned with both arms up over the seat of his saddle for a long minute, greedily sucking down big drafts of cold night air. When he finally stepped back and reached for the stirrup, he said: "Hell, why is it I always got to fetch up doin' the hard work?"

They sat in their saddles for a moment, listening. Down where the big herd was fanning out restlessly now, wide-awake and bawling, men's catcalls back and forth sounded faintly.

"He'll figure it out," stated Walt. Then he looked at his companions. "Why'n hell did you two let that tinhorn take you, anyway?"

"We didn't have a whole lot of alternatives," muttered Jack Bolley. "He pulled it real slick."

"Slick," grumbled big Walt, still panting. "Why, good Lord, Deputy, he's not even a good horse wrangler." Walt gave his unkempt big head a hard wag and hauled around on his reins. "We better head straight north an' hope Mister Given had luck raisin' that posse, 'cause Buzz'll sure as the devil have someone on our trail within fifteen minutes o' now."

They turned and loped ahead where the underbrush got thicker, forcing them to ride single file and also to slow now and then while they felt their way around and through. Walt was out ahead. His horse suddenly gave a violent sideward leap, shying in sudden panic that came within an ace of dumping the rider. A big old moldy wolf jumped out of his bed, even more startled at this abrupt appearance of men in his normally manless world than Patterson's horse had been at sight of the predator. He was confused, probably still dulled by sleep, and ran straight toward Bob Lefton's horse. Bolley flashed for his six-gun but could not fire as the wolf swept in too close and Bob had to swerve hard to keep his mount from seeing or scenting the wolf.

"Don't shoot!" he yelled at Bolley. "They'll hear it back there!"

The wolf ran off through the underbrush, a gray, moth-eaten old hide with the bones showing through. Walt Patterson had to dismount, right his saddle, and cinch it up again. He swore at the top of his lungs all throughout this, and just before he remounted he cuffed his fidgeting horse and commanded it to stop jigging around.

They went ahead once more, badly shaken but otherwise none the worse for their encounter. Later, when they dared slow to a walk so that their animals might catch their breath, Jack said: "That damned animal must've been old and deaf not to have picked up the sounds of us coming onto him."

"That ain't all he was," announced Walt Patterson fiercely, and launched into another vivid, articulate, and profane description of the old frightened wolf.

Bob Lefton laughed. That soothed all their raw nerves.

# XVII

They'd covered at least two miles when Patterson hauled up, got down, and put his ear to the ground. He looked up, rolled his eyes, and tried again. Finally he stood up, shoved his shirt tail carelessly into his waistband, and reached for the saddle horn as he said: "Too much other noise back there to tell whether they're trailin' us yet or not." He gave a big grunt, dropped down across his saddle, and gigged his horse over into a loose lope. "But you can cussed well bet they are," he called back, "by now!"

They changed course a little, at Lefton's suggestion, then changed it again when Bolley pushed up beside Walt to say he thought he'd caught the quick, bright little flare of a lighted match somewhere up ahead. Maybe he'd seen something like that, but after a half hour of general searching and finding nothing, they booted their beasts over into a lope again, and reverted to their straight northward course. If that had actually been a horseman out there somewhere lighting a smoke, he'd heard them coming and had rapidly and prudently withdrawn from in front of them. They never saw him or his little light again.

Finally, when they'd put enough country behind them so that even the bawling noise of the big herd was no longer audible, the night turned somber again, cold and dark and gloomy with twisted shadows here and there where they passed clumps of brush or low dips in the land. Bob was making a smoke, his reins looped, and Jack Bolley was saying it was too bad they hadn't been able to stay with Sawyer Given's original plan of nailing the rustlers down at Bellflower, when Walt suddenly shot an arm into the air and twisted to hiss backward at the other two for silence. Bob dropped his half finished smoke, grabbed his reins, and veered sharply off to the left. Bolley followed Lefton's example, but old wily Walt Patterson dismounted, flung his reins to the other two, and, as his horse turned, he snatched out his carbine.

"Go on," he called softly. "I hear 'em out there, but maybe they'll come down here farther to the west. You fellers keep watch over yonder. I'll cover us from here."

The sounds that Patterson had heard were clearly audible now. Bob jerked his head at Bolley. The pair of them cut away from where unkempt Walt sank down in a dusty patch of sage, his carbine wetly shining in the ghostly night. They walked their horses twenty yards away, got down, unshipped their Winchesters, left the horses, and paced on ahead where the muted roll of men's voices could be heard, along with the soft jingle of rein chains, spur rowels, and carbine rings striking saddle forks.

Bob leaned and said: "It's got to be Mister Given."

Bolley answered tartly: "You mean . . . it better be Mister Given."

It was. But the first man Lefton picked out and recognized as the dark mob of horsemen came in close was Stan Oldfield from the Texas Belle Saloon. Riding beside Stan was old Carl Hicks, packing a rifle instead of a carbine, the barrel sticking out from across old Carl's lap nearly a yard and a half.

Art Flannagan was there, and so were a dozen other men from Mandan that Lefton recognized. He didn't catch sight of Sawyer Given until the cowman pushed away from the side of Frank Eberly, the stage company's local ramrod, and started forward toward Stan and Carl Hicks. Then, as Bolley cocked his carbine, Lefton said: "Easy Jack. It's Given and his posse."

But because he knew those men riding toward him, Bob didn't stand up right away. Instead, he sang out in a loud call and kept down where some excited posse man would probably miss if he fired in Lefton's general direction.

"Art! Carl! Stan! It's Bob Lefton. Hold your fire and hold up!"

At once the horsemen piled up in a quick halt. Guns bristled. Men's hat-shadowed faces turned hard and flinty. Sawyer Given said: "Bob, if that's you, stand up."

Lefton obeyed. Then Jack Bolley also arose and stood in plain sight. Oldfield called out, sounding enormously relieved: "Damned if it isn't!"

Given reined forward, leading the others on up. Bob sent Bolley for their horses. He also told him to call out for Patterson to join them.

Given gazed flintily at the deputy sheriff. "Where are they?" he asked. "Where are the cattle?"

"Southward a ways, and right now you're going to see some of the renegades, too." Lefton explained how he and Bolley had been captured, and how Walt Patterson had extricated them from Hilton's hands, and how they'd been heading northward hoping to intercept the Mandan posse. He wound up by saying to Given: "I'm sorry. Your way would've been better . . . catching them down at rail's end. But when they caught Jack and me, it upset that plan. There's just one thing left to do now. Nail Hilton and his renegade cowboys before they get away."

Given looked up as Jack and Walt came trudging back, leading horses. He said: "Walt, what're our chances?"

Patterson's drawl came right back briskly: "Right good, I'd say, Mister Given, providin' we head on back down there an' trim their wicks before they get set up to bushwhack us."

Given growled at the lawmen. "Get astride. We're goin' on."

They mounted up and milled around briefly, then got lined out. Bolley rode up on one side of Given, Bob Lefton appeared on the other side. Bob reached over and tapped the cowman on the arm. "You just gave your last order," he said. "From here on, Mister Given, you take 'em, you don't give 'em."

Given bristled. On his far side Jack Bolley leaned down and said: "Given, sometimes folks get so damned puffed up with their own importance they lose sight of the real facts. Lefton's been tryin' to save your herd, an' even your life, at the risk of his own neck. So don't go get all huffy because just now he told you a plumb fact."

Bolley straightened in his saddle and looked straight ahead. Around him the men from Mandan were watching Sawyer Given for his angry reaction. But there was none. Given sat up straight and rode right along like all the rest of them—until someone up ahead let off a big yell—then Given ducked just like everyone else did, including Bolley and Lefton.

Right after that high howl, a gun flashed and thundered. Another gun, farther off to the east, also exploded with blinding light and a deafening racket. The men around Lefton cried out in surprise and dived out of their saddles. Bolley was crying out to them to stay in close, not to scatter.

Lefton and Sawyer Given were almost side-by-side when they hit the ground, tugging at carbines. Over the tumult and gun thunder Given said: "Where are they?" Lefton pointed with his gun barrel southward and eastward. He'd scarcely ceased pointing when a ripple of answering gunfire flamed and snarled up and down the line of posse men. Walt Patterson was yelling in his deep-down voice for the men to get flat, to get down, and move after each shot.

Lefton wasn't worried. If Hilton had sent only two men to hunt down the pair of escaped lawmen and Patterson, the posse men would very shortly now either silence them or rout them. The odds were just too great.

A horse went down without a sound not ten feet away. Lefton held his fire to study the manner in which those unseen ambushers were shooting. When he was certain, he called out over the crash and roll of gunfire. "Take the horses back! Get them away from here. They're trying to cripple us by killing the horses!"

Patterson turned and began bellowing out names. He roared for these men to take charge of the horses. Someone flashed by, grabbed the reins from Given and Lefton and Bolley, and hastened away. Before this had been accomplished, however, three dead animals lay with the posse men. The loss would not seriously cripple them, but it certainly would slow them down.

Given sang out: "Form a line, men! Scatter out and head for them over there!"

Lefton started onward with the rest of them. He saw a gun flash in his general direction and shot from the hip with his carbine as he walked on. Everyone on his left and right also fired. Muzzle blasts winked redly, the men's ears rang from rolling blasts of gunfire. Those onward guns suddenly winked out. The posse men kept on advancing and firing. From far out one ambusher turned in his flight and threw three desperate shots backward. Ten carbines swung to zero in on his muzzle blast.

The second ambusher began to yell out that he'd had enough, that he'd thrown his weapon away and was surrendering. "Too late!" bawled Walt Patterson, and halted to fire deliberately into the brush patch where that man had cried out. The outlaw range rider's voice was stilled as other guns swung also to probe that patch of undergrowth. The last shot was fired by Jack Bolley.

A hundred yards eastward from where the fight had started the remaining bushwhacker made his stand. He'd evidently tried to reach his horse, and, since the animal was not afterward found, it was correctly assumed that he'd broken free in panic and had raced away. The cowboy was on foot, alone, pinned down by a powerfully advancing number of grim posse men, and had the vivid killing of his companion to gauge his own chances by. He decided to fight it out.

The posse men kept coming, but now they were fanning out left and right, firing and moving clear, and firing again. It was only a matter of time at best. At worst, he could jump up and try hard to take at least one posse man with him. He made the mistake of springing up a hundred feet in front of Jack Bolley, who proved himself anything but a novice. The second that shadowy silhouette appeared above the brush, Jack whipped half around sideways making of himself the slimmest of dark targets, and fired from the hip with his six-gun. The outlaw also fired. His slug sang past, missing by twelve inches. Jack stepped sideways and fired his second bullet. The outlaw gasped, his carbine drooped, he made a fluttery little sad gesture with one hand, then dropped his gun. Bolley squared up and raised his six-gun. Lefton called over to him.

"Hold it, Jack. Hold it! He dropped his gun."

For three seconds Bolley's cocked six-gun didn't waver, but in the end it did. Jack lowered his arm reluctantly and cast a bleak look over where the others were starting forward where the wounded outlaw was slowly going down on his knees.

Sawyer Given passed Jack without a glance. "You had the right," he snarled. "In your boots I'd have finished him."

They reached the hard-hit man. He was hatless, rumpled,

obviously not going to ride away from this spot. Both Jack's slugs had hit him, one high, one low.

Now, there was silence nearly as loud as the gun thunder had been. Several of the posse men walked back, looking for the one Walt had killed. They found him lying, face down, half in and half out of a spidery big chaparral bush.

Lefton and Stan Oldfield eased the wounded one down and shoved their hats under his head. Art Flannagan bent to swipe bloody froth from the cowboy's lips. Old Given stood above the man as grim as death, as unrelenting as his kind usually were. He and the cowboy exchanged a long glance, neither one willing to address the other.

Lefton leaned down close. "You won't ride away from this one," he told the dying man. "Anything you want to say?"

"Not much," muttered the cowboy. "Anybody got a drink?" No one had. The cowboy sucked in a shallow breath and weakly coughed. "A man takes his chances," he said softly to Lefton. "Sometimes he wins. More often, I reckon, he loses. I don't feel bad. If I'd hit the jackpot, I'd have won big. I just didn't hit it. Sure, we stole Given's cattle, and Willard's, too. I got no remorse, Deputy." He rolled his eyes. "Where's Patterson?"

Walt stepped up, sniffled, and looked down. "Right here," he said.

The cowboy looked upward and called Walt a bad name. Patterson gently shook his head, not angered. "Every man does what he figures he should do. That's what I been doin' these past few days, buckaroo. That's all there is to it."

The cowboy died quietly; the breath just leaked out of him; he flattened, and that was his ending.

Bolley, who'd stood there, listening and watching, now turned away to say: "Let's get goin'. Hilton's sure to have heard all the darned gunfire."

Their horses were back a short distance, waiting. Only Sawyer

Given had much to say about the pair of dead men. "They worked for me all summer," he told the others as they were getting astride again, reloading their guns and glumly awaiting someone's order to move out. "Good boys, both of 'em. And young." He lifted his reins. "Just not very smart, or they'd never have listened to Buzz. Let's go."

Bolley left the others, riding on ahead. Walt Patterson went after him, but first Walt had to take the time to reload completely; he'd shot both his .45 and his .30-30 empty. The others asked around to see who was hurt. No one had been injured, but three of them had to ride double with their friends because their horses had been killed.

It was a different crew that went downcountry after that furious little fight with Hilton's bushwhackers. Most of them had nothing to say; all of them were alert and watchful and solemn. It was one thing to see dead men. It was something quite different to stand over a man and see him die. Particularly when he died defiantly like that young cowboy had died. Defiantly and unrepentant.

Jack and Walt came back holding their carbines high as though to call upon the others to halt. They did; they bunched up around Lefton and Given to hear better. Bolley said: "Cattle . . . we can hear 'em down there, runnin'. If Hilton's got wind of what happened up here, he'd be a fool not to turn that herd straight toward us. They'd either grind us to red dust or push us so far back Hilton and his remainin' men could get one hell of a good head start toward escaping."

It made sense the hard way Bolley said it. Bob Lefton gestured toward the west and reined off in that direction. "Cut around 'em," he said sharply, meaning the oncoming cattle. "Get clear around 'em, and forget the cattle. It's Hilton we're after."

They kicked their animals over into a lope and went careening along behind Bob. They'd covered nearly a mile when the earth underfoot began to shake and rumble. Back where they'd come from, the vanguard of a stampeding huge herd of red-backs were scuffing up an enormous cloud of black dust. They saw some stragglers far out on the wing of the main herd, but had no difficulty at avoiding these animals. Sawyer Given complimented Jack Bolley on his shrewdness when Lefton swung southward again, having led them clear of the rolling stampede north and eastward. All Jack said in reply was that he valued his neck, and he kept on riding.

It was late now, and quite cold, although the posse men didn't especially feel the chill. Their mounts had to set a pace that wouldn't overtax the three horses carrying double, but eventually Lefton called Bolley and Patterson to him, said they'd ride ahead, and told Sawyer Given to bring on the rest of the riders as best he could.

Those three cut loose and spurred hotly down the cold, faint-lighted plain in the general direction of that camp where they'd been previously in contact with Hilton. Around them was the dust and din of a stampede they couldn't see.

# XVIII

Buzz Hilton was smart, but he'd made a bad mistake when he'd assumed raffish old Walt Patterson would be on his side. He made his next mistake when he assumed that fight up there hadn't involved as many men as it actually did involve. Later, the survivors of the last fight with Hilton's renegades, were to speculate endlessly on why Hilton didn't run. Bob Lefton always felt that Hilton, with so much confidence in himself, just couldn't face defeat, and had therefore turned back to rid himself of the posse men so he could still arrive down at Bellflower with the herd. Whatever the reason, the fact remained that when Jack and Walt and Bob Lefton were almost past the place where the renegade range riders'd had their little fire, someone let fly at them with a carbine, shooting by sound because it was too dark and uncertain at that distance for any other kind of shooting.

Bob thought it was another two- or perhaps three-man ambush. He left his horse in a low dive as Walt replied with a handgun shot. Bolley took all their animals and went back through the brush with them. Then, with only Walt beside him, Bob Lefton was brought face to face with a hard fact: Hilton and all the rest of his men were out there, had evidently been out there all the time, waiting to end this chase with one big, blasting ambush. It didn't work out that way because the posse men weren't with Lefton, but at first, anyway, Hilton didn't know this. He rapped out a hard command for his men to close in and polish off the lawmen and Walt Patterson.

Now, the situation was reversed. Exactly as had happened in that earlier fight, a large body of men began inexorably to close in around a much smaller band of desperately battling men. Jack got back to join the fight. Almost at once a bullet creased over the top of his shoulder, knocking him down, tearing his shirt badly, and searing the flesh, but otherwise not seriously injuring the Coloradoan. For a bad moment, though, Patterson and Lefton thought Jack had been hard hit. When he got back up onto one knee and swore loudly as he resumed fighting, the others were relieved.

They hadn't been too far ahead of the posse men when they'd loped into this ambush, perhaps a mile or a mile and a half. Still, it could be the same as a hundred miles if Hilton's advancing men got completely around them before the others heard the fight and came racing up. Patterson's greasy old hat sailed away like a startled bird. Walt clapped a hand to his head and dropped lower down. Lefton saw him from the edge of one eye begin to reload.

Hilton cried out once more, urging his men to get this over with in a hurry. Lefton whipsawed four rapid carbine slugs into the area Hilton had yelled from. After that the renegade range boss did not cry out again. At least one of those bullets must have come perilously close.

Over to the north a rattle of fresh gunfire suddenly erupted and Walt let off a loud hurrah. "Get 'em, boys," he howled at the posse men. "Cut 'em to mincemeat!"

Hilton's men turned, under this fresh attack from a new direction, and that permitted Bolley, Lefton, and Patterson to catch their breath. Help had arrived in the nick of time. Hilton's men were rapidly closing the surround; within minutes they'd have saturated the place where those two lawmen and old Walt crouched. Now, though, the surround began to break up as the rustlers turned, facing northward where an increasing rolling thunder was scathing the underbrush all around with lead. The outlaws had to keep moving, had to start fighting as individuals rather than as a group now, because each man was under personal attack.

Walt kept up his excited howling. He'd fire, look out to see what he might have hit, let off a howl, and fire again.

Westward a man gave a sharp howl that died away in a low moan. Someone out there had stopped a bullet. The posse men were doing down here what they'd also done up at that earlier battleground; they were spreading out and inexorably advancing. Gun flames flashed blindingly sharp, red stabbing lances of deadly light that winked on and off in a fraction of a second. The scent of burned powder was strong and acrid. Overhead, above this deadly place, serene moonlight softly fell, and the myriad rash of silvery stars was aloofly detached.

A silhouette appeared off where Bob could make it out, ducking and twisting as someone tried to get away. It was decidedly unsafe for anyone to raise up now; even the posse men advancing from the north were firing at any kind of movement. Still, Lefton heaved himself around and looked over, and down beyond his immediate protective scrub brush. That man was desperately seeking to get clear. He was whipping back and forth with a cocked six-gun in his right fist, but made no attempt to fire it. Clearly whoever he was, he did not mean to give his position away by shooting.

Elsewhere, men were fighting for their lives without giving a foot willingly. Bolley and Patterson were engaging a pair of rustlers to the west, beyond the scope of the oncoming posse men. They were so absorbed, they didn't even see Bob Lefton slip out of his place of concealment on the trail of that escaping renegade.

Several men besides Walt were howling now, but it was impossible to determine whether they were rustlers or posse men. The gunfire dwindled slightly, not because there had been that many kills in the darkness, but because both sides were beginning to maneuver and counter-maneuver. This took a little time during which the battlers did not fire.

But that was temporary; everyone got back to full firing again eventually, and meanwhile Lefton got clear of the brush, got in behind that fleeing man, tried to anticipate his course, failed because he didn't know why anyone would be zigzagging like the fugitive was doing, and settled down simply to pacing the man. One thing he was certain of; he was trailing one of the rustlers. The posse men were still too far northward, while Walt and Jack Bolley were about where they'd initially been battling. That only left the outlaws—and one particular outlaw was trying to sneak away while his friends fought for their lives, giving him this chance.

Twice, Bob got a good look at the hastening man's crouched form. Twice he raised his six-gun to shoot the man. Each time, though, the vague shadow faded out in underbrush and kept rushing along, spoiling Lefton's aim and making him take up the chase again.

Where it finally ended was out where four saddled horses were tied to a stout old sagebrush. Out there was where Bob finally understood why the man he'd been chasing had consistently, despite innumerable little detours, always bore to the southwest. He knew where the horses were; those horses were his last chance to get away alive.

Lefton glided over into a clearing, gauged the distance, and recklessly jumped up to run at the horses from an angling approach, seeking to reach them ahead of the rustler. He almost made it, but not quite. The renegade sensed that he was in danger. He whipped around, his six-gun raking back and forth, up and ready to fire. Bob dropped and rolled and took a long shot with his six-gun. The outlaw fired straight back, but he'd been badly shaken when he'd fired. The bullet slashed through sage but was far too high.

Lefton got to one knee and fired straighter that time. The outlaw jumped, whirled, and raced for the horses. Bob stood up, took long aim, tracked the zigzagging, dim shadow, anticipated a move, and squeezed his trigger. The renegade gave a tremendous bound into the air and fell, rolled off a wiry bush, and dragged himself around it where he thumbed off two rapid shots, then became still and motionless.

Bob dropped low and scuttled off to the right again, still intending to prevent the outlaw from getting to those four saddled animals down there in the sooty night. He got as close as he dared, then stopped to catch his breath. There was a solid-cadenced thunder in his ears; his heart was pounding in its dark cage.

The rustler shot twice, low through the underbrush, but he wasn't even close. Bob shot back where he knew the man still was, then jumped up, ran forward fifty feet, and threw himself belly down again. In this fashion he got to within a hundred feet of the bush where the outlaw had gone down. Until he raised his head, listening, he wasn't aware that all the westward firing had stopped. He turned slowly to look over there. Walt Patterson's rumbling voice called out in tired protest.

"Cut it out, Bolley. Them two give up. Put that danged gun down or I'll make you eat it."

Evidently Jack lowered his gun because there was no more said over there as the posse men closed in around the surviving rustlers, who evidently had surrendered.

Bob hardly raised his voice as he now said, speaking to that unseen man over behind the chaparral clump: "Toss out your guns, cowboy. It's all over."

A bullet sliced neatly through the limbs beside Bob's left shoulder. He ducked down. Another bullet broke branches where his head had been. He got flat down, inched ahead, and, when he eventually saw something dark and bulky, he fired at it. A man gasped, the underbrush quivered violently, then gradually grew still again.

"You win, Lefton," said a fading voice. A six-gun came sailing over into the brush near Bob. "No more. You win, Lefton."

Bob gingerly got up and peered over the top of his brush clump. He hadn't known until this moment that the man seeking to abandon his companions and escape was Buzz Hilton himself. He stood up and looked around. Over to the west men were distantly visible, herding other men. Someone over there saw him standing up from the waist in his patch of brush and called down to him.

"That you, Lefton?"

The voice belonged to Sawyer Given. Bob answered back, and Given started working his way through the brush toward him. Bob stepped out, crossed to where Hilton was loosely propped in the sage, knelt down, and looked closely. Hilton had two holes in him. One had broken his right leg up near the hip. That was probably the shot that had dumped him down where he'd been lying. The second bullet had cut through from front to back. Buzz Hilton was dying exactly as that first wounded man had also died, slowly from internal bleeding. He wasn't in any great pain; in fact, the shock of being hard hit prevented him from actually feeling anything at all, right then. He'd lost his hat when he'd first fallen. Hair hung almost to his eyes. He crooked his lips into a mirthless little ragged grin as Lefton knelt at his side.

"I should've run," he huskily said. "The boys wanted to."

"Why didn't you?" asked Lefton.

"Why? Well, I reckon because I just didn't believe you 'n' Bolley 'n' Patterson could cut me down like this. Not after outsmarting even old Given all this time."

"Old Given," growled Sawyer Given from fifteen feet away, his voice low and dour, "wasn't as much outsmarted as he was disappointed, Buzz."

Hilton rolled his eyes up, gazed at his employer a long moment, then looked down. "Sure," he murmured. "You're disappointed. You had someone to do all your rough stuff for you, while you raked in the money. No man'd go on like that all his life, Mister Given. Every man deserves one good chance.

Given nodded. He knelt and said, his voice as soft as Bob Lefton had ever heard it: "Buzz, you'd have got that chance. You'd have been richer than all the rustled cattle in the Mandan country could ever have made you. If you'd just waited."

Both Lefton and Hilton looked at Given. The older man gravely inclined his head. Several more men drifted on up. Walt Patterson was among them, more slovenly and unkempt-looking than ever.

"You were the sole heir in my will, Buzz," said old Given. "It'd've all have been yours directly. All you had to do was hang an' rattle until I died. All of it, even the cattle and the ranch." Given settled back on his heels, trading long looks with Buzz Hilton.

No one said a word until Hilton looked up at Lefton. "How many are left?" he asked.

Patterson had the answer to that. "Two alive and wounded. That's all, Buzz."

Hilton lifted his eyes; they were getting cloudy. "And you," he murmured to Patterson.

Walt shook his head. "Never was with you, Buzz. Never would've been. I got my faults, plenty of 'em, but stealin' from the hand that feeds me ain't one of 'em."

Hilton eased his head around, gazing straight at Bob Lefton. "Turn the Willards loose," he whispered. "You know who killed Ralph Bolley and Judge Heber. It's all over now, Lefton. . . ."

Sawyer Given stood up as brisk as ever, but with a noticeable drag to his voice when he said: "Walt, you take over as range boss where Buzz left off, from here on. All right?"

"Sure, all right, Mister Given."

"Let's get the horses and tie the dead ones across 'em. Let's get back to Mandan." Given drew in a big breath and let it out raggedly. "I need a drink. I don't recollect when I needed a drink as bad as I do right now. All right with you, Lefton?"

Bob nodded and turned away. "The horses," he said to Jack Bolley and the others. "It's all over."

# ABOUT THE AUTHOR

**Lauran Paine** who, under his own name and various pseudonyms has written over a thousand books was born in Duluth, Minnesota. His family moved to California when he was at a young age and his apprenticeship as a Western writer came about through the years he spent in the livestock trade, rodeos, and even motion pictures where he served as an extra because of his expert horsemanship in several films starring movie cowboy Johnny Mack Brown. In the late 1930s, Paine trapped wild horses in northern Arizona and even, for a time, worked as a professional farrier. Paine came to know the Old West through the eyes of many who had been born in the previous century, and he learned that Western life had been very different from the way it was portrayed on the screen. "I knew men who had killed other men," he later recalled. "But they were the exceptions. Prior to and during the Depression, people were just too busy eking out an existence to indulge in Saturday-night brawls." He served in the U.S. Navy in the Second World War and began writing for Western pulp magazines following his discharge. It is interesting to note that all of his earliest novels (written under his own name and the pseudonym Mark Carrel) were published in the British market and he soon had as strong a following in that country as in the United States. Paine's Western fiction is characterized by strong plots, authenticity, an apparently effortless ability to construct situation and character, and a preference for building his stories upon a solid foundation of historical fact. *Adobe Empire* (1956), one of his best novels, is a fictionalized account of the last twenty years in the life of trader William Bent and, in an off-trail way, has a melancholy, bittersweet texture that is not easily forgotten. In later novels like *The White Bird* (Five Star Westerns, 1997) and *Cache Cañon* (Five Star Westerns, 1998), he showed that the special magic and power of his stories and characters had only matured along with his basic themes of changing times, changing attitudes, learning from experience, respecting Nature, and the yearning for a simpler, more moderate way of life. His next Five Star Western will be *Promise of Revenge*.